Nia felt the sexual energy emanating from Damon's every pore. She knew what he was about to do as he pulled her near and anchored her to his body. As mad as she was, she still wanted to feel his lips against hers.

Nia turned her head, but Damon wouldn't have it. With both hands, he grasped her face. She saw his lips descending and when they finally gently touched hers, she thought she was going to melt. Slowly, he stroked her lips and increased the pressure, teasing them until they parted and she opened to him.

Damon softly growled as his tongue darted inside and began to explore her mouth's soft recesses. He plunged deeper, stroking her velvety tongue with his own. She leaned in farther to feel his hard, lean body, and when Damon released her, they both took a deep breath.

"Good night, sweetheart," he whispered and bounded down the stairs, leaving Nia totally off balance with shaking knees. Minutes later, she was still standing in the same spot he left her, could still smell his aftershave on her clothes. Shaken, Nia gathered her senses and closed the door behind her.

# ONE MAGIC Moment

YAHRAH ST. JOHN

**BET Publications, LLC**
**http://www.bet.com**
**http://www.arabesquebooks.com**

ARABESQUE BOOKS are published by

BET Publications, LLC
c/o BET BOOKS
One BET Plaza
1900 W Place NE
Washington, DC 20018-1211



All Kensington Titles, Imprints, and Distributed Lines are available at special quantity discounts for bulk purchases for sales promotions, premiums, fund-raising, and educational or institutional use. Special book excerpts or customized printings can also be created to fit specific needs. For details, write or phone the office of the Kensington special sales manager: Kensington Publishing Corp., 850 Third Avenue, New York, NY 10022, attn: Special Sales Department, Phone: 1-800-221-2647.



First Printing: December 2004
10 9 8 7 6 5 4 3 2 1

Printed in the United States of America

*To my mother, Naariah Yisrael,*
*my cheerleader and biggest fan.*

## ACKNOWLEDGMENTS

I would never have written this book without the enthusiasm, support and unwavering faith of my mother, Naariah Yisrael; my best friends and counselors, Dimitra Astwood, Dawn Zucco, Beatrice Astwood; and the 3Ts: Therolyn Rodgers, Tiffany Harris and Tonya Mitchell; my cousin Gita Bishop; and finally my uncle Marvin Smith. Sometimes, when I'd almost lost faith, you stayed positive and optimistic. Thank you so much for believing and encouraging me to pursue my dream.

Shout-outs to my writing crew for offering invaluable critiques and suggestions: Deatri King Bey and Michelle Shell. To my editor, Demetria Lucas, thanks for all your help, and to my publisher, BET Books, thank you for believing this book could be a success.

# Chapter 1

He was absolutely stunning. Looking like a black Adonis molded from clay by Zeus himself. With strong African features, a proud nose, chiseled cheekbones and sensuously thick lips, the man exuded a powerful dose of sexuality that could send any woman into overdrive. His dark blue, three-piece Italian suit with navy-and-white-striped silk tie suited his massive chest and shoulders to perfection.

He was by far the most attractive man in the room, and, apparently, Nia Taylor wasn't the only one doing the admiring. She caught the handsome stranger with the sexy bedroom eyes checking her out, too. And while she wanted to look away, his gaze held her steadfast. Nia could practically hear her heart thumping loudly in her chest, could feel the hairs on the back of her neck stand straight up. Taking a deep breath, she willed herself to calm down.

Finally, she looked away, embarrassed at the attention he bestowed upon her. This was all Lexie's fault, she thought. Nia had made the big mistake of allowing her best friend to talk her into wearing a cocktail dress Nia'd bought during one of their infamous shopping sprees earlier that season. "If you got it, flaunt it," Lexie had said.

Although the deep burgundy color of Nia's dress

was perfect for a Christmas party, the velvet material of the low V-neck garment overly emphasized her already large breasts, and the short skirt accentuated her wide and curvaceous hips. Nia felt like she was on display for men to ogle. *And this one is definitely ogling,* she thought, sneaking another glance at her handsome admirer.

At twenty-seven, she knew the look he was giving her. It was the one most men gave when they were imagining a woman without any clothes on. Trying to ignore him, Nia turned her focus back to her best friend, who was standing right beside her. "Thanks for coming with me, Lexie. I really didn't want to come to this party alone."

"Not a problem, that's what girlfriends are for," Lexie quipped, "to be your date, when you can't find a man."

"Thanks," Nia replied sarcastically, laughing at her silly friend. She'd practically begged Lexie to accompany her to the Dean, Martin & Whitmore Christmas party after Chloe, her boss, had told her it would be a great opportunity to break bread with the higher-ups. Nia had agreed to go to the celebration only after Lexie promised to accompany her.

The weather for early December had been mild, until earlier that night when light snow began to fall after rush hour, causing traffic to move sluggishly as Nia and Lexie drove to the Whitemores' home. The roads were slick and Nia had had to brake suddenly several times, causing her tires to grind in protest. After they reached the exclusive neighborhood, finding her boss's estate through the mist of the snow had been easy, due to the multitude of cars lining the driveway.

The butler immediately greeted them and relieved them of their coats at the door. He ushered them into the living room where a large, overly decorated Christmas tree stood center stage. It was clear the Whitmores had spared no expense for the party; the place was lavishly decorated with holiday cheer, and the family's finest crystal and china were on display.

Nia's colleagues and various higher-ups were decked in their holiday best. The women wore the latest in cocktail fashion and the men sported tuxes. Nia immediately wished she was at home curled under a blanket with a good book and a hot cup of cocoa, instead of being forced to compete for her boss's attention with all the other hopefuls.

"Ya know," Lexie continued, "you could find one if you wanted to." Nia raised a brow in confusion. "A man," she clarified. "That is, if you wanted one. It's what I've been telling you for years. You just have to loosen up some."

"Does Spencer Morgan ring a bell?" Nia asked, referencing an old boyfriend.

"Of course, but all men aren't dogs like Spencer. Some are faithful. Take my new beau Michael; I've got that man's nose wide open."

"You are a trip, girl," Nia said, laughing. "Hey, do I look all right in this dress? I feel like my chest is hanging out for the entire world to see."

"It is." Lexie smacked Nia's hand away from adjusting her bosom. "And you want them to see some of it. Matter of fact, it looks like you have a secret admirer." She nodded her head at the handsome stranger who was walking toward them. "In fact, I'll make myself scarce. I'm going to grab us some champagne and a few more of those delicious shrimp puffs the waiter is circulating," she said, walking away to catch him.

"Lexie, wait!" Nia hissed.

It was too late. She tried to think of a fast getaway before the sexy stranger reached her. Nia caught sight of Chloe out of the corner of her eye and figured now was as good a time as any to start schmoozing. She began her escape, but wasn't fast enough. Mr. Tall, Dark, and Handsome had blocked her path.

Damon had been listening to his father and Mr. Whitmore discuss their favorite topic—who was the better golfer—when he spotted Nia. She appeared to be very young, twenty-five, perhaps twenty-six. She was about five-five, maybe shorter, with bright eyes, a gorgeous smile and one of the most voluptuous bodies he'd seen in a long while. Damon usually fancied his women more on the slender side, but he very much liked the way her form-fitting dress hugged every delicious curve. Her full and inviting breasts complemented her round derriere, and all screamed to be touched—by him, he thought. He could just picture that luscious body writhing underneath him.

Damon felt his heart race with anticipation and his manhood harden with longing. It was strange—he'd never had such an instant attraction to a woman he hadn't even met. Yet he knew he was going to meet her tonight.

He excused himself and moved quickly across the room.

* * *

*Wow, is he tall.* Nia looked up at the mysterious six-foot stranger standing before her. Even in three-inch heels, her head barely reached his shoulders. She drank him in, from his tiger eyes with thick ebony lashes to his glistening bald head. The man oozed masculinity and sexuality.

"Hello, there," he said, smiling down at her.

His naturally deep voice swirled around her like a tornado. Nia stared blankly for several seconds; she couldn't believe he was speaking to her. He was just so yummy! Guys like this seldom looked her way.

"Do you like what you see?" Damon queried. He'd been appreciating Nia as well and was happy to have a closer look at this siren. Her short layered mane of auburn curls surrounded her pixie face, complementing her big brown eyes. She had skin the color of honey and her light makeup covered skin he was sure was as smooth as a baby's bottom. Everything about her was beautiful, but it was her lips that beckoned him. Damon wanted to feast on them until his craving for her was completely satisfied.

"Do you always look at ladies like you're ready to eat them up with a spoon?" Nia asked, interrupting his thoughts.

Damon grinned, showing off an amazing set of perfect white teeth. Nia's heart thumped wildly and her pulse raced. "Not usually, but then again—"

"Then again, what?" Nia asked, flirting playfully.

"I apologize," Damon said, extending his hand. "Allow me to introduce myself." He clasped Nia's palm in a firm handshake. "I'm Damon Bradley, and you are?" Her satiny skin felt soft to his touch, just as he'd imagined.

"Nia Taylor," she replied, removing her hand from his solid grasp. In spite of herself, she couldn't stop her body from reacting to his appreciative male gaze.

"Champagne?" asked a nearby waiter, bringing Nia out of her daydream. Caught in Damon's spell, Nia had forgotten where she was.

"Yes, please," she replied, taking a crystal flute of chilled champagne from his tray and drinking a long gulp. It was quite dry and went straight to her head, causing her to cough slightly. Nia preferred the more fruity sorts of wines on the market.

"Good, huh?" Damon smiled as he watched Nia lick a remaining drop of champagne from her upper lip. She couldn't possibly know how erotic that tiny action was to him. He swallowed and took a deep breath.

"Mmm-hmm," Nia lied, placing the remainder of her drink on a cocktail table next to her.

"So, Nia," Damon began. "Might I be so bold as to ask for your number so that you might accompany me to dinner one evening?"

Nia's body wanted to accept the offer, but her mind had other plans. From the way Damon was looking at her, she knew what his intentions were and she wanted no part of his mischief. "Sorry, Mr. Bradley, but I'm not interested in *GQ* smooth guys such as yourself," she replied firmly. "But thanks anyway."

She turned on her heel to walk away, but Damon reached out, grabbing her hand and pulling her toward him. The hungry look in his eyes caused her to give in and she let herself be drawn back to him.

Damon sensed several inquisitive eyes, including his father's, burning a hole in his back. He disregarded them and focused on the feisty woman standing in front of him. "Are you always this blunt?" he asked.

Nia looked at the hand Damon still had on her arm. He removed it and looked into her brown eyes, thinking *tough cookie.*

"I am. I find that honesty is always the best policy in these kinds of situations, Mr. Bradley," she said with assurance.

"Your candor is refreshing. And please, call me Damon."

"No need, as we will have no further acquaintance, but have a good evening." With that, Nia turned again and marched into the crowd before Damon could stop her.

Visibly shaken, Nia looked around the room for Lexie and spotted her chatting it up with one of her male coworkers. *Probably weaving her magic spell around the dumb schmuck,* she thought, heading toward the ladies' restroom to compose herself.

She was so glad Damon hadn't tried to stop her a second time. Had he felt her pulse quicken at his touch? It was like an electrical charge had shot through her. Her arm still tingled. Did he feel it, too?

Nia found a line forming outside the small powder room. Instead of waiting, she walked through the myriad of people streaming down the hallway and found herself outside on the terrace. It was elaborately decorated with muted red and green lighting; holly and garlands gently covered in snowflakes were placed throughout. Nia could still hear the soft holiday tunes from the party and smelled the scents of pine and eucalyptus. The scene was downright romantic and it reminded her of another evening not so long ago when she'd reluctantly agreed to accompany Lexie to one of the endless fraternity parties being held on campus at Northwestern University.

Nia had grown bored of all the sloshed frat brothers trying to hit on her that night. She knew they all had one idea in mind and that was which freshman girl they could get to drop her panties the quickest. She'd gone outside on the terrace to get away from the noise and drunkenness and it was there that she'd met Spencer.

Spencer Morgan. He was a brother so fine, he could make a girl melt just by looking at her. Towering over her at six feet three inches, he was bald with dark chocolate skin and a slightly crooked smile. As president of Alpha Phi Alpha fraternity, star player for NU's basketball team and head of the African-American Cultural Society, everyone on campus knew him and every woman on campus wanted to sleep with him. Nia was thrilled when he showed so much attention to her that evening, and at the time he hadn't seemed at all interested in getting in her pants. Seemingly a gentleman, when Spencer saw her shivering outside, he'd offered her his fraternity jacket.

He'd been the first man who had shown her genuine interest and Nia really thought he just wanted to get to know her better. What a fool she'd been. Spencer was a true ladies' man and knew how to work his game. He'd been very attentive: calling her every day, walking her to class, studying with her. He spent so much time in her dorm room that Lexie, then her roommate, started joking that he should start paying rent.

Nia floated like she was on cloud nine the whole time they were dating. To have Spencer Morgan as her man was giddy stuff. Until he'd shown his true colors, people on campus had even treated her differently, with respect, as if he were a prince and she his princess.

After several months of hand-holding and intense passionate kissing, Spencer was ready to move their relationship forward sexually. Although Nia's sheltered upbringing offered her little opportunity to socialize with men, she wanted it, too. Spencer made her feel special and he'd told her he loved her and she believed him.

Her first time wasn't everything she had dreamed it would be. She remembered the tiny dorm room. She could still see the small twin bed with a blanket thrown over it, the dirty clothes, jock straps and filthy socks strewn across the floor. Intuitively, Nia had known that the evening would turn out differently than the other frustrated nights they'd spent together.

Spencer had quickly dispensed with their clothing before climbing on top of her without any preamble, foreplay or gentleness. There had been no candlelight, no soft touches, no feather kisses. He hadn't cared that it was Nia's first time, hadn't cared about her pain or awkwardness. Spencer Morgan only cared about his own pleasure and release. When he was finished, he had collapsed on top of Nia and she recalled his weight suffocating her so much that she could barely breathe.

"Get off me!" she had finally been able to murmur when she got over her humiliation. He'd rolled off and started to put on his shorts.

Afterward, Nia was so ashamed. Her aunt raised her to wait for marriage and to give her virginity to her husband as a special gift. She'd been willing to forget those teachings because Spencer told her he loved her, but he'd screwed her—literally and figuratively. She couldn't help the tears that fell as she'd started to dress or the way her hands shook when she tried unsuccessfully to button her blouse. It was then that Spencer Morgan had delivered the final blow.

"Why are *you* crying?" he'd asked, pulling on his jeans. "You weren't that good anyway."

"I don't understand why you're treating me this way," she said, the hurt in her heart evident in her voice. "Why are you being so cruel to me?"

"Don't you get it?" he'd sneered. "Most women I sleep with know how to please a man. They give and respond to a man's touch. They don't lay there expecting me to do all the work."

"I—" Nia was horrified as a fresh set of tears spilled down her cheeks. Could this be the same man she had fallen in love with? How could she have been so wrong?

"I guess all the guys were right," he added. "You *are* an ice queen."

Devastated, Nia ran out of his room with her shirt flying open. The next day at lunch in the cafeteria, Spencer sat with his fraternity brothers and completely ignored her when she walked by. She hadn't known what to expect, but for him to act like she didn't even exist, to act like he hadn't just had sex with her, that was the final nail in the coffin. Nia vowed she would never give her heart—or her body—to another man. And she hadn't.

Nia felt goose bumps already starting to form on her arms. As much as she wanted to stay in the beautiful moonlight with a million stars overhead, it was time to go in. She rubbed her arms, shivering as a gust of cold Chicago wind off Lake Michigan swept over the terrace. There was no point in getting lost in the past, she thought, turning to head back inside. Especially in painful memories that were best left forgotten.

Still standing in the living room where Nia had left him, Damon couldn't remember the last time his advances were rebuffed. Not many women would turn down his invitation to dinner, he thought. She was a pretty gutsy lady, but he would not be deterred. His instincts told him that having Nia's acquaintance was well worth the effort. Not only had she proven to be intelligent and quick-witted, but she also had a lush figure that called out to everything male in him. He grinned roguishly. He would find out more about Ms. Nia Taylor this evening. Nothing would stop him, not even the lady herself.

Instead of rejoining his father, who continued to glare at him from across the room, Damon decided to get a bit of fresh air out on the terrace before facing his father's questions. He already knew what his father was thinking. Marcus Bradley hated public displays of affection and never showed them. Yet in private he could be the most loving and affectionate father anyone had ever seen. It amazed Damon how his father showed two totally different faces: one to the world and one to his family.

Damon shook several colleagues' hands as he made his way down the hallway in what he thought was the direction of the terrace. The Whitmores' home was a grand maze of intricate hallways and opulent rooms and it had been a while since he had last visited.

When Nia swung open the French doors, a pair of very masculine shoulders greeted her. She shivered again, taking a step back. Something told her that standing too close to this man could be lethal. Maybe downright dangerous.

"Are you following me?" Nia asked, watching Damon step outside into the cool night air.

"Not at all." He removed his jacket and wrapped it around her shoulders. "Better now?" he asked huskily.

"Hmm. Thank you," Nia said. "You didn't have to do this." She inhaled the heady masculine scent that emanated from his jacket, his cologne filling her senses. It was absolutely invigorating, she noted, thinking that the smell suited him well.

"I know you think very little of us *GQ* types, but some of us are still chivalrous," he quipped.

Nia smiled. The brother was smooth, but she mustn't let herself get carried away. Dating Spencer taught her to be cautious of men like Damon.

"I'm sorry about earlier." Damon shrugged. "I didn't mean to use strong-arm tactics. That's not usually how I get women to go out with me."

"No?" she queried. "I half expected you to club me over the head and take me back to your cave."

Damon smiled. "Oh, and the lady has a sense of humor, too."

"I try," Nia said between laughs. "You know, it's really quite chilly out here. What do you say we go back inside and try acting like civilized adults?"

He opened the door. When they were both inside, they stood in the hallway, letting the warmth soak their chilled bones. Neither was too eager to walk away. Maybe it was the time of year or the soft lights and low music, but for some reason Nia couldn't put her finger on, she was drawn to this incredibly attractive and charming man whose voice was as smooth as silk. He stirred a physical reaction she hadn't had in years, feelings that had lain dormant for so long, she'd forgotten they existed.

Reluctantly, Nia took off Damon's suit jacket and handed it back. "Thanks for the loan."

He held on to the jacket while steadily drawing her closer to him. She'd tried pulling away, as standing so close to him was making her body go haywire, but something inside Nia just wouldn't let her.

"Nia." He crooned her name. "Do you think you might be able to forgive my caveman tactics and go out to dinner with me?"

"I don't think so," she said, lost in his eyes.

"And why not? What could it possibly hurt to enjoy a meal with an attractive, professional man such as myself?"

Nia was amused at his arrogance. "Well, if they're as conceited as you, the answer would still be an emphatic no."

The funny thing was Damon was right. It couldn't hurt. She'd certainly dated her share of losers, countless men of all shades and backgrounds from thugs to players to choirboys. Yet all she had found were toads. None of them had remotely piqued her interest like Damon did, but she couldn't let him know that.

"I like you, Nia, you've got fire." He leaned in close so they were cheek to cheek.

"If you stand too close to this fire, you might get burned," Nia shot back.

"Hmm, you think you're going to get rid of me that easy, do you? I have fate on my side." He pointed to the mistletoe above their heads and before Nia had a chance to recover, Damon bent down toward her. She saw his lips about to descend on hers and felt the pressure of his chiseled masculine chest leaning into her. She tried to push him away, needing some breathing room, but all she could feel was his rock-hard chest. Despite herself, she licked her lips in anticipation.

"Damon, darling, I've been looking everywhere for you," shrieked a tall, gorgeous beauty from down the hall.

The spell was broken and Nia immediately stepped away from Damon. She was stunned by her wanton reaction to him. To think, she had been ready to accept the kiss of a man she hardly knew. What was she thinking? Even if Nia had accepted Damon's invitation, the idea of dinner would have been squashed just then.

The woman, whoever she was, sauntered toward them and linked her arm with Damon's, letting Nia know quite clearly that he was taken. Almost equaling Damon in height, the woman was striking with her slender frame. She wore a short, thin slip of a black dress that flowed loosely down her lithe body and accented her killer legs; she looked like one of those fashion models that glided down the Paris runways. Her long hair flowed in loose curls down her back and set off her flawless, fair complexion and oval-shaped eyes. Equal parts sophistication and confidence, she was the kind of woman who knew what she wanted and knew how to flaunt her body to get it. She was everything Nia was not.

"Kendall, I was getting a bit of fresh air," Damon replied testily. He tried unsuccessfully to extract himself from Kendall's clinging arm. No such luck. She had his limb in a vice and wasn't letting go.

"Darling, we're under the mistletoe," she rasped, looking up at the fresh holly. She threw her arms around Damon and planted a wet kiss on his lips, then faced Nia, narrowing her eyes as if to say "Take that."

Nia felt like an intruder in the midst of their display and quickly walked away from the couple. She was rather perturbed by Damon's intention to talk to her even though he had a girlfriend. The guy sure had nerve, to flirt with her while his woman was in the next room.

*More power to her,* thought Nia. She definitely wouldn't want a guy she couldn't trust and it was clear she could trust Damon Bradley about as far as she could throw him. One woman obviously was not enough for him. And she had almost fallen prey! Had Kendall not walked up when she did, Nia not only would have locked lips with him, but also would have allowed his charm to influence her to agree to dinner.

Feeling like a complete idiot, Nia headed to the living room to salvage what she could of the evening.

"Nia, wait!" Damon yelled in vain to her retreating back. With a little effort he removed Kendall's arm from around his waist.

He was furious. He had just made a small inroad with Nia, and from her reaction and the truncated kiss, he could tell he'd blown it. He'd wanted to taste Nia's lips, to outline them with his tongue and dip slowly inside her mouth. Now he'd lost the momentum that had slowly started to build between them.

"Did you enjoy pulling that stunt, Kendall?" Damon asked, his irritation clear. "We are over. There is nothing left between us."

Sometimes he couldn't remember what he saw in Kendall besides her good looks and the fact that she knew how to please him sexually. But those days were over. He'd long since seen her true colors and wished he'd seen them before they became lovers.

A couple of years ago, dating Kendall had seemed like the sensible thing to do. They had known each other for years and their mothers served together on one local charity event after another. Their families were pleased when they began seeing each other and everyone thought they were a perfect couple.

Hell, he'd even begun to believe they were a perfect fit. Kendall had all qualities he was looking for in a prospective spouse: brains, beauty and great sex. A year ago, he even fancied himself in love with her and, so eager to please his father, had proposed marriage to the delight of their parents, who dreamed of merging the two family businesses. Damon had thought everything was perfect, but nothing could douse hot water on a delusion of grandeur like finding your fiancée in bed with another man.

"Oh, darling, it was all in good fun." Kendall chuckled, running her fingers down his chest. Damon flinched, recoiling from her touch. "And if your little friend can't take the likes of me, then she definitely is not in your league. Plus, I didn't think you went for the healthy girls," she scoffed.

"How would you know what type of women I go for, since you're obviously not one of them anymore?" Damon retorted.

He stormed away, leaving Kendall glaring after him. Marching into the living room, he scanned the crowd, looking for Nia. He finally found her in a corner with the woman she had been talking to earlier when he'd first approached her. Not wanting to cause another scene, he decided it was not the best time to approach her. Instead, he rejoined his father and Mr. Whitmore by the fireplace in the center of the room.

"Son, we were wondering what happened to you. It appeared that some pretty young thing caught your eye. You should be focusing on our upcoming ad campaign with Mr. Whitmore, instead," Marcus Bradley said, slapping his back.

Damon knew the fatherly gesture was a reprimand. His father wanted his head on business, not women.

"Well, you know how it is with the young fellas these days," Mr. Whitmore interjected. "They see a pretty face and they're like a fox in a henhouse."

Both men chuckled, but Damon was less than amused. He didn't appreciate being the butt of the older men's jokes. He forced a smile, refusing to let his father see that anything could get to him. To the elder Bradley, that would be a sign of weakness.

"Of course I'm focused on the upcoming campaign," Damon offered, rejoining the conversation. "And I have a couple of ideas."

Damon laughed inwardly as the two men huddled in closer for a listen. He'd allowed his father to turn the conversation his way, but Damon was still determined to find out more about Nia Taylor.

Nia had sensed Damon the minute he reentered the living room. She could feel his eyes on her, but she stubbornly refused to look the scoundrel's way. Finally, her natural curiosity got the best of her. When she turned around she found that the statuesque female with him before was no longer at his side. How had he ditched his girlfriend so fast?

"So, I saw you talking to that gorgeous hunk earlier," Lexie whispered in her ear.

"What hunk?"

"Don't play dumb, Nia," Lexie admonished, popping another appetizer into her mouth. "I saw the way that man was looking at you before you disappeared. Did he ask you out?"

Nia ran her fingers through her hair. Why couldn't she be more like Lexie—slim and sexy, flirtatious and carefree. Lexie had already picked up two phone numbers and was happily munching on appetizers without any thought for her narrow waistline. "Are there any more of those crab cakes?"

"Oh, c'mon, Nia. Don't be coy," Lexie chided. "Give up the goods, I'm dying to know. I saw the way he was devouring you with his eyes. Matter of fact, he still is."

"Are you serious?" Nia asked, fighting the urge to look over her shoulder.

"Yes, girl. But don't turn around." Lexie held on to Nia's arm. "Let him stew a little."

"Well, he can stew all he wants with his *girlfriend.*"

"What girlfriend?" Lexie questioned. "I don't see anyone. Anyway, it doesn't matter. As long as he doesn't have a ring on his finger, he's fair game."

Nia considered her last statement for a moment before replying, "I don't think so. Anyway, I turned him down." She ignored Lexie's shocked expression. "Listen, I need to go over to say hello to Chloe and then we can blow this popsicle stand."

She walked with Lexie over to join Chloe, who was bantering with some other ad executives. After introducing Lexie to the group, Nia twirled her fingers through her hair, pretending that her colleagues' jokes were funny and that she hadn't just heard them the day before.

# Chapter 2

"Nia, you have a delivery up front," Susan, the receptionist, spoke from the intercom.

A delivery? From whom? Nia got up from her desk and strolled down the hallway to the reception desk where a huge bouquet of pink and yellow roses awaited her.

"Those are for you." Susan smiled knowingly, pushing the flowers toward her.

"What?" Nia was stunned. She had no idea who could have sent the flowers in the gorgeous crystal vase. "These are beautiful and they smell wonderful," she said, inhaling deeply.

"You're telling me," Susan squeaked. "Well, are you going to read the card?"

"Don't rush me." Nia pulled out a white envelope from the center of the roses. The card inside read *Have lunch with me, Damon.* She dropped it to the floor.

"Who are they from?"

"No one special," Nia replied nonchalantly. She bent to grab the card and then picked up the flowers before she headed back to her cubicle.

She put the vase on her desk and sat down, flabbergasted. It didn't take a rocket scientist to put two and two together. Damon probably figured that she worked for Dean, Martin & Whitmore since she was at their Christmas party.

Nia was amazed that he had given her a second thought. Last Friday he hadn't bothered her again for the rest of the evening. She caught him once or twice giving her the once-over, but then he'd quickly looked away. She'd thought that was the end of it. Why would he pursue her, when he had Kendall waiting in the wings? she wondered.

As much as she had tried to avoid thinking about Damon, the memory of his sexy smile and bedroom eyes had haunted her all week. She even dreamed about him and wondered what it would have been like to kiss him had they not been interrupted while standing under the mistletoe. How would his large, masculine hands have felt caressing every inch of her body?

For heaven's sake! She fanned herself with her hands. Her thoughts were headed for an X rating, but what difference did it make? She would never get the chance to find out what magic spells those his big hands could weave. He had a girlfriend, one that had her claws buried in him so deep, it would take a crowbar to remove them. Nia decided to banish him from her mind, but her treacherous thoughts were working against her.

Until now, the thought of a physical relationship with any man had repelled her. It was why she kept most men at arm's length and was adept at discouraging their advances. Eventually, most would give up and write her off as some ice queen, to use Spencer's wording, or just plain frigid. Damon certainly wasn't the first man to try to break through the wall she had created.

Susan buzzed again from the intercom. "Nia, you have a call on line one."

"Who is it?" she asked, holding her breath. Could it possibly be Damon?

"He didn't give a name."

"Thank you." Nia exhaled. *One, two, three.* "I'll take it," she said, lifting the receiver. "Good morning, this is Miss Taylor."

"Good morning, Nia," Damon replied smoothly. His voice sounded rich and melodic to her ears. "Did you like the flowers?"

"Yes, Damon, they're lovely. But I can't accept them."

"Why not? You do realize that there's no escaping me this time."

"Escaping you?"

"Yes, you ran away so quickly on Friday. You didn't give me a chance to explain."

"I think it was more like I was pushed away." Nia tapped her nails against her desk. "But it's a moot point. You have a girlfriend. And I don't date cheats."

Unfazed, Damon replied calmly, "Listen, Nia. Kendall is not my girlfriend. We haven't been dating for well over a year."

"You might want to remind her of that."

Damon laughed. "You are something, Miss Nia, which is why I am very eager to learn more about you."

"Honestly, Damon, I just don't think you're my type," she said, attempting to discourage him.

He wouldn't be put off that easily. "How would you know that? Maybe you shouldn't be so quick to judge a book by its cover."

Did he just challenge *her* to look beyond the

physical? Nia sighed. If Damon thought she was shallow, he was dirt wrong.

"All right, Damon." She acquiesced against her better judgment. "I'll go out with you, but only for lunch."

"Lunch is a start."

Nia imagined him grinning like a Cheshire cat. He had won this round. But the question remained, could she trust him?

"How about I pick you up at noon?"

"Today?" Nia asked. "Oh, I don't know."

"Why not?"

Why? Because she was by no means ready for face-to-face combat with him. She needed time to prepare, to think about what she would say. She stood and gave herself the once-over in the mirror on her wall. Luckily, she'd put on one of her good suits that morning, completing the professional picture by adding black pumps. All she needed was a quick touch-up of her hair and makeup.

"Hmm, no reason," she answered smoothly. "Noon would be fine." *Am I out of my ever-loving mind?*

"Great, I'll see you then," Damon replied. He hung up before she had a chance to change her mind.

Damon was thrilled when he put the receiver back in the cradle. He couldn't believe how easily she accepted his invitation. He'd thought she would put up a bigger struggle. Things were going his way. Now all he had to do was convince her that one meal with him would not be nearly enough.

He leaned back in his favorite black, high-backed chair and stared down at the file in front of him. His large maple desk was filled with corporate loan requests and memos that needed addressing, but work was the last thing on his mind.

Looking after the family portfolio was often a draining task, leaving him little time outside of the office. That was why his mother redecorated the office, incorporating a private shower and a built-in minibar. Damon walked over to the ceiling-to-floor window he'd had installed at Bradley Savings & Loan Bank so he could peer out at customers three floors below.

His thoughts strayed to Nia, the beautiful and feisty woman who had captured his eye. He'd done some investigating and discovered Nia Marie Taylor was twenty-seven years old and a rising star at Dean, Martin & Whitmore. Unmarried with no children, she was on the fast track to becoming an advertising account executive. Now, whether she was seeing someone was another matter entirely. There was no doubt in his mind that men were falling all over themselves to be with her. He considered himself lucky that she had agreed to lunch.

What was it about her that he found so appealing? It wasn't just her looks, although he immensely enjoyed the sight of her. He had seen his share of beautiful women, but it was her intelligence and spirit that combined into one fascinating package. Most of all, Nia was a woman who spoke her mind. There were no hidden games or agendas and Damon appreciated that. He wanted to get to know her, and maybe over lunch Nia would let her guard down.

Nia tapped her nails against the desk, watching the clock. It was almost noon. She hadn't been able to concentrate on her presentation for Aloha Air. Men of Damon's caliber were never interested in her. Most found her too short, or thought her hair wasn't long enough. The only thing they noticed was her generous figure. The men she encountered couldn't get past the physical and only saw her big breasts and ample buttocks. How many times had she wondered if her figure screamed "easy lay."

When her phone finally rang, signaling Damon's arrival, she nearly jumped out of her skin. "Mr. Bradley is here to see you, Nia," Susan announced over the phone intercom.

"Thank you, I'll be right out." She retrieved her compact and fluffed her hair in the wall mirror. She'd already given her lips a fresh coat of lipstick and added a touch of eye shadow for good measure. Nia smoothed her skirt, grabbed her coat and scarf and headed toward the reception desk.

When she saw Damon, she stopped dead in her tracks, completely mesmerized. He was leaning over the counter talking to Susan—more like charming the pants off her. Damon looked striking in a gray suit and pristine white shirt. Everyone who came in contact with him could feel the sheer masculine magnetism emanating from him. He exuded a powerful sexuality that any woman could sense or smell a million miles away.

Willing her feet to move, she walked toward him. "Hello, Damon."

"Hello, beautiful." He took in her freshly applied makeup and the power suit that in no way hid her voluptuous figure from his roaming eyes.

Brushing his lips against her right hand, he helped her into her coat. Nia wasn't the only one intoxicated. Damon could smell the sweet scent of her fragrant perfume wafting through the air. He wanted her, but that would have to wait for another time and place. Instead, he took her scarf, wrapped it around her neck and pulled her closer to him.

Nia felt short of breath. Just being near him was playing havoc with her senses.

"Ready?" Damon asked, holding out his hand.

She'd kept her eyes downward and when she lifted them to meet his gaze, she was scared by what she saw there: pure, naked desire. She quickly looked away.

"Uh, yes," she replied. Nia took his outstretched hand and together they walked toward the elevator, leaving an openmouthed Susan staring after them.

Damon took Nia to a popular soul-food restaurant in downtown Chicago several blocks away from her job. Maddie's was known for its down-home cooking, but not its decor. The floor was slightly stained and some of the booths were ripped and torn, but the food was the best in Chi-Town. The waiter seated them in a corner booth and left them to peruse the menus stuck in the napkin holder.

Damon helped Nia remove her coat, resting it against the back of the booth.

"Well, Nia," Damon spoke after a short silence. "I'm very happy that you finally agreed to go out with me."

Acutely aware of his dark scrutiny, she waited before answering. "I had a feeling you wouldn't take no for an answer."

"You're probably right. So, what are you in the mood for?" Damon asked, taking the initiative. He could tell Nia was nervous; she'd avoided meeting his eyes since they'd entered the restaurant. He wanted her to feel comfortable with him. He wasn't about to gobble her up just yet. "I hear their smothered chicken and macaroni cheese is excellent. Not to mention the peach cobbler for dessert." Nia bit her lip in angst. *Does she even realize how tempting that is?*

Damon watched her as she studied the menu. Nia possessed a certain innocence and naïveté that Damon found very appealing. He certainly wasn't used to it. Most women approached him, making it clear that they were available.

Maybe it was the thrill of the chase. Or the fact that he'd been celibate for several months. His only post-Kendall "relationship" had been with Shelby, a public relations executive who had been adequate and satisfied his hunger at the moment. But he was a healthy, mature man who had needs and desires that were not being met. Maybe he just needed a romp in the hay? No, that wouldn't work either. If he wanted meaningless sex, all he had to do was look in his little black book and find any number of females willing to oblige him. He was looking for something else.

Weary of the single life, he longed for someone he could share his world with. He was ready to settle down and have a family with that special someone.

"Damon?" Nia said, interrupting his thoughts. "The waiter wants to know your selection."

"Did you order already?"

"Yes, I took your advice." Nia wasn't very hungry at all.

"Good, you'll enjoy it. I'll have the fried pork chops with beans and rice and candied yams." He handed the waiter his menu.

"Wow, you have a big appetite."

"I'm a growing boy." He grinned.

"Boy?" Nia chuckled. "I don't think so. You're

most definitely a man." She'd gotten a good look at his body at the Christmas party. He had broad shoulders, a massive chest and a behind that would make you want to spank Jehovah. He was no boy, that was for sure.

"Do you think you might be able to give this man a chance to prove he's not like all the other *GQ* smooth guys you've met?"

"I don't think so," Nia hedged. "Though I am sure you will have no problem finding someone more suitable."

"Nia, the only person I'm interested in seeing is you." He let her digest that information. "But the more important question is why you aren't involved with anyone. You're a gorgeous, talented woman. What gives?"

Instantly, Nia went on the defensive. "I do date," she replied haughtily. She had the occasional date or two, though none had generated any sparks. She had far better things to do in life than worry about how to find or keep a man, though she was sure that didn't apply to all women. "But what I'd like to know is why you're interested in me? We're from completely different worlds. And if you hadn't noticed, I'm no supermodel like Kendall."

"Not to toot my own horn, but I have impeccable taste in women and a good eye for beauty. And I happen to find you extremely attractive, Nia," he answered confidently.

Nia couldn't resist smiling. Damon knew exactly the right words to say to put her head in the clouds.

"And as far as us being from different worlds, that's a ridiculous notion. I'm sure you and I have a lot in common." He seized Nia's hands and entwined her fingers with his. Nia's breath caught in her throat, the touch of his hands causing butterflies to form in the pit of her stomach.

"How you can say that? You hardly know me." She tried to release her hands from his, but Damon held on tighter. His eyes were fixed on her, and if she allowed herself, she could easily lose herself in them. Nia wasn't sure she could let that happen. As much as she might be intrigued, a man like Damon could really hurt her.

"Well, I intend to rectify that right now." He squeezed her hands. "How about you tell me more about yourself. For starters, what do you like to do for fun?"

"I enjoy the usual stuff—movies, dinner, dancing."

"Hmm. What else?" Damon inquired, listening intently to her every word.

While they waited for their food, Nia found out that they really did have a lot in common. They both enjoyed cooking—Damon professed to be quite the chef in the kitchen—they'd both done a little bit of traveling when they could spare the time away from work and they shared a love of the arts.

"I absolutely love the theater," Nia gushed. "I just saw *Chicago* and *Show Boat*, both of which were excellent."

"Theater, huh? I happen to love the theater as well," Damon admitted. "Don't you see? We're two of a kind. *Rent* is coming to the Chicago Theatre in a couple of weeks. How about I pick up a couple of tickets?"

The waiter picked that exact moment to come to their table with steaming hot plates piled high with soul food. Nia inhaled. It smelled delicious.

"Is that your sly way of asking me out again?" Nia

asked. She took a generous forkful of macaroni and cheese. She had ordered a huge lunch when most women would have ordered a salad, but Damon didn't seem to mind her healthy appetite.

"Absolutely. Are you accepting?" Damon dug into his large platter of smothered pork chops.

"I don't know, Damon," She said thoughtfully. Everything in Nia was telling her to run for the hills, to resist him. She couldn't let herself get carried away in the moment.

"Why are you hesitating, Nia? I know that you like me." Damon moved from opposite her to scoot next to her in the booth.

"What are you doing?" Nia moved over as far as she could until there was no more room. She was literally stuck between a rock and hard place. Every time she moved, Damon just moved closer to her. Nia enjoyed smelling the aroma of his cologne wafting into her nose.

When Damon reached out and touched her face, Nia was struck at the shape of his hands. They were large and firm and felt so good.

"Why are you trying so hard to resist me?" Damon turned her around to face him. He stroked her face while his light brown eyes pierced hers, searching for an answer. "What are you so afraid of? Don't you know that I'd never hurt you?"

"You say that now," Nia said, removing his hands from her face, "but you don't know that for certain. I am not ready to take that chance." Nia remembered what it felt like when Spencer had treated her so abominably and she had no intention of letting herself be taken advantage of again. If she did decide to date Damon, she would do so cautiously, once she'd had time to think things out.

"All right," Damon said. "I won't push. Because I think in time you'll see that we could be really good together. But will you at least *think* about going out with me?"

"Okay, okay." Nia could see that Damon wasn't giving up easily. "I'll agree to think about going out with you again."

"Whew!" He wiped his brow. "That's a relief. Now we can finish our lunch." Pulling his plate over to his new seat, he sunk his spoon into the red beans and rice.

Nia had a sneaky suspicion that her time with Damon was far from over. He had given in way too easy. Damon was a man on a mission. She was certain he had a trick up his sleeve, but she let it ride over lunch. And she was pleasantly surprised at the turn the meal took.

The conversation progressed easily as they discussed a wide variety of topics, ranging from politics to music to both of their careers. Nia learned that Damon was more than just a pretty face and hard body. He obtained his masters degree in business and finance from Harvard University, then started off at the bottom, working for his father. Now he was his father's right-hand man and senior vice president of Bradley Savings & Loan. One day, Damon would run the place.

She also discovered that he was an avid sports man and played basketball, tennis and racquetball. Damon loved adventure and went windsurfing, parasailing and rock climbing whenever he could get away from the office. Nia wasn't surprised at his athletic prowess. *It's no wonder he has the body of god.* And right then, she realized she was in way over her head.

* * *

Damon proved he was not a man to be taken lightly or who would give up easily, evidenced best when, several days after their lunch date, Chloe stopped Nia in the hallway as she was returning from lunch.

"We've got a sales meeting with Mr. Whitmore," Chloe murmured in her ear.

"OK, when is it?"

"Right now. It's very impromptu."

"All right, let me put down my coat and I'll meet you in the conference room."

Nia dropped her coat and scarf on her chair, grabbed her pen and notebook and rushed to the conference room. Luckily, she wasn't the last person to make it. She found a seat next to Chloe's.

"Welcome, everyone," Mr. Whitmore said, entering the room and wasting no time getting down to business. His assistant put several images on the projector and Nia was shocked by what she saw. A picture of the Bradley Savings & Loan Bank was front and center. It appeared that things with Damon were about to get very complicated.

"I want to get right to the point and say that right now is a very exciting time for the company," Mr. Whitmore continued. "We have two prospective deals on the table, one with Bradley Savings & Loan." He paused, waiting as his assistant clicked to the next photograph. "And another with Montgomery Supermarkets."

Nia's mouth dropped open. She heard Mr. Whitmore speaking but all the air had gone out of her lungs.

"Both of these deals would give Dean, Martin &

Whitmore great exposure in the black community. Marcie, could you please hand out the packets?"

Nia accepted a folder and flipped through it. It was filled with information, facts and financials on both Bradley Savings & Loan and Montgomery Supermarkets.

"I want everyone to come up with some inventive ideas on how we could best approach advertising to the urban market. Let's come back to the table in a week or so and brainstorm on the strategies you've put together. That's all, folks," Mr. Whitmore concluded, walking out of the conference room just as quickly as he'd come in.

She should have seen this coming. The Bradleys were at the Whitmores' home for Christmas. How could she have been so stupid? Now she would not only have to contend with Damon personally, but professionally as well.

"Wow," Chloe whispered. "What a great opportunity!" Chloe nudged her in the shoulder. "And it looks like you just might have the inside track."

"What?" Nia asked, dumbfounded.

"Don't be coy, Nia. Susan told me that Damon Bradley took you to lunch the other day. You must have really made some impression." Chloe smacked her on the back and walked away.

Nia shook her head in despair. She understood Damon's motives for giving Dean, Martin & Whitmore a shot at his account, but why Montgomery Supermarkets?

# Chapter 3

Banging around dishes in her sink, Nia fumed. Her efforts to contact Damon were unsuccessful. She'd been unable to reach him since she found out her company would handle his campaign. Suddenly he was unable or too busy. Could he be avoiding her?

The man was driving her crazy. Somehow, someway, he had taken up a permanent space in her head. Nothing she did banished him from her thoughts. And she'd tried everything on Saturday night to forget about him.

Television didn't help, so she listened to music. When that was a wash, she surfed the Internet, which proved equally futile. By ten o'clock, she gave up hope and had even started exercising, working on her abs that were never as rock solid as she wanted them to be. But somehow, she still couldn't shake him.

She seethed. The arrogance of the man. For him to even think that she needed his help in getting ahead . . . She could and would get a promotion on her own merit and without any help from Mr. Smooth. Though he'd try to deny it, Nia knew Damon was responsible for her company getting his account. But she would show him she was more than a pretty face and quite capable of handling anything he put out.

Nia phoned her best friend to go out for lunch. It was a bright, sunny Sunday afternoon and she could use Lexie as her sounding board.

Two hours later, they were seated at a crowded Maggiano's waiting for their entrees while they shared an oversize Caesar salad. Nia couldn't taste a bit of it, though. Her mind was on a certain handsome but infuriating man. She picked at her meal while Lexie ferociously attacked the salad like it was about to run away from her. She might be used to eating rabbit food to keep her size-six figure, but Nia wasn't. She needed real food with parents.

"It's strange, Lex. I don't know why I like him. He's the exact opposite of everything I thought I wanted. He's arrogant and conceited."

"Which is exactly why you like him," Lexie said with a smirk.

"Come again?"

"Nia, you don't need the shy, predictable type, a man who'll keep you in your shell. Darling, you need a man that will get your fires burning. Someone who'll make your mouth water."

"Hmm, and boy does mine water when he's around," Nia said, fanning herself with her hands.

"See, that's what I'm talking about. When was the last time you wanted to rip a man's clothes off? Girl, I'm telling you, you need to jump on him."

"So you're advising me to have a fling?" Nia inquired. "Because that's all I'll be to Damon. Once the thrill of the chase is over, he'll hightail his butt out of town so quick, there'll be tire marks on my back."

The waitress, who had come with the entrees,

blushed. She quickly placed their orders in front of them and walked away.

"Nia, girlfriend, that's what I love about you. You're as dramatic as I am." Lexie laughed as she reached for her fork and took a bite of her cheese ravioli. "All I'm saying is, you need to get your groove on and have a little fun. Because it's long overdue."

"I don't know, Lexie. Damon doesn't strike me as the type to stay around for long."

"Why do you have to be so negative? Why can't you just enjoy the man? From the looks of him, Damon seems like he could fulfill any woman's wildest fantasies." Nia gasped while Lexie took a sip of soda. "Oh, c'mon Nia. Don't be shy. Just take what you want and move on."

"You're always so cynical, Lexie." Nia tasted a piece of her chicken Vesuvio and went straight to heaven. It was delicious and Nia savored every morsel.

"Listen, men have been doing this since the beginning of time. Why shouldn't women join in?" Lexie reached for a piece of Parmesan garlic bread. "I make no apologies for going after what I want. You would do well to do the same."

"Touché." Nia clinked her glass with Lexie.

Nia remembered Lexie's words the next day at her office. Was her anger at Damon a veiled way for her to hide her growing attraction? Her thoughts were interrupted when Chloe poked her head inside her cubicle.

"C'mon, Nia. We've got a big powwow in the conference room."

"What's going on, Chloe?"

"Our brainstorming time is over. Mr. Bradley is here to hear our ideas."

Nia's heart sunk to the floor. Which one? Was it Damon or his father? Reluctantly, Nia followed Chloe into the conference room and found her answer. Damon was seated at the head of the conference table with Mr. Whitmore. Calmly, Nia took a seat opposite him.

Even though he was deep in discussion with Mr. Whitmore, Damon was aware of Nia the moment she walked in the room. She looked amazing as usual in a sexy two-piece peach knit ensemble. He felt her intent glare from across the table and did his best to treat her like any other staff member as her boss made the introductions. Nia showed poise and grace when he politely shook her hand, but her bright eyes remained hooded.

Damon knew Nia was eager to talk to him about his choice of advertising company, but he would let her stew for a little bit. It would serve her right for making him chase after her—not that he didn't love a good challenge. He hoped to get a moment alone with Nia after the meeting to discuss his train of thought and to assure her that although she was part of the reason he'd chosen Dean, Martin & Whitmore, he had absolute faith in their ability to do the job. Otherwise, his father would kill him.

Thirty minutes later, he was impressed by the ideas the staff had come up with to reacquaint the black neighborhood with Bradley Savings & Loan, one of the cornerstones of their community. Chloe's team, of which Nia was a part, had several promising ideas.

"You've put together an excellent presentation,

Mr. Whitmore," Damon said to Nia's boss. "I really liked the ideas from Chloe's team. I think Ms. Taylor has an ear for the pulse of the community."

"Thank you, Mr. Bradley," Chloe said, beaming with pride. Underneath the table, she gave Nia a pat on the knee.

"Have your art department mock up some of your proposals. In the meantime, I'd like to meet with Ms. Taylor and discuss her ideas at length."

"Certainly, Mr. Bradley," Chloe responded. "Nia has time this afternoon. Don't you, Nia?" Chloe's brow furrowed together.

"Of course," Nia said, forcing a smile. Now she had no choice but to go along with Damon's agenda.

"Well, on that note," Mr. Whitmore began, "this meeting is adjourned. Damon, we'll touch base in a few days."

Damon stood, shaking hands with Mr. Whitmore before he left. The rest of the staff slowly filtered out. Damon closed the door behind Chloe, who gave Nia a knowing wink as she left the room.

Now that they were alone, Nia fiddled with her pen. She watched Damon lean against the door, watching her. She had been ready to take him to task for his duplicity, but suddenly that didn't appear to be the right thing to do.

He had given her career a shot in the arm, even if his intentions were not altogether altruistic. If her ideas were successful, she would be heading up her own team sooner rather than later.

"All right, Damon, you went to a lot of trouble to get my attention. What gives?" Nia asked with her arms crossed and brows raised.

"Yes, I did," Damon replied, smiling. "And I know

you might not believe this, but Mr. Whitmore and I were in negotiations on this campaign long before you and I ever met."

"You seriously expect me to believe that my presence here had nothing to do with you giving Dean, Martin & Whitmore your account?"

"Well, I didn't say that," Damon started, "but I take it you don't approve of my methods?"

"No, I don't. So what is it going to take for me to get rid of you?"

Damon laughed heartily as he walked back over to the table and packed up his briefcase. "Agree to go out with me."

Nia shook her head in amazement. The man had a thick skull and "no" was obviously not in his vocabulary. "I don't appreciate being browbeaten, Damon."

Damon held up his hands in defense. "No browbeating going on, just a friendly meal between two people who find each other attractive."

"Fine." Nia gave in. "I'll go out with you."

"I knew you'd see things my way." He smiled that dazzling smile that captivated her from the moment she laid eyes on him. "I'll pick up those *Rent* tickets and give you a call," he said from the doorway.

"Girl, I can't believe you actually agreed to go out with him again. We both know how hard you can be on people." Lexie pushed her way through the throng of women, finding a spot near the sale rack.

"The man's relentless," Nia replied, searching through the dresses for an outfit that would jump at her and say "buy me." They were at their favorite store, The Rack on North Rush Street, shopping for a new outfit for Nia's date with Damon. The Rack housed fabulous bargain designer clothing, lingerie and Lexie's favorite: shoes. Despite her modest salary, Nia could occasionally afford a new outfit.

"Mmm-hmm," murmured Lexie. "Here, try this one on." She held up a sleeveless red sheath with spaghetti straps made out of sheer fabric. Lexie's knowledge of clothes was superior, as her job as a fashion buyer kept her locked into all the latest fashions. "This would look great on you. It would hug all the places you want."

"And then some." Nia laughed, pushing the dress away. "You know I like to downplay my hips."

Sometimes Lexie couldn't resist pushing her best friend. She wanted Nia to be more like her: open, carefree and adventurous. Unfortunately, they were complete opposites. Lexie Thompson was an extrovert. She loved being the life of the party and usually dressed to show it. Her svelte five-foot, eight-inch figure allowed her to pull off the most daring ensembles and Lexie loved it—the more formfitting, the better. She enjoyed watching people's reactions, but her daredevil spirit had never rubbed off on her more introverted friend. Fortunately for them, Lexie learned to accept Nia for who she was, but that didn't stop her from trying to expand her parameters every once in a while.

"Hey, you know my philosophy: if you've got it, flaunt it," Lexie said.

"Yes, I know, but how about this one?" Nia asked, clutching a more demure blue dress with a high collar.

"Unh-unh. Darling, that color doesn't work for

you." Lexie grabbed Nia's hand. "C'mon, you're going to try on my dress."

"Lexie . . ."

"Stop your whining." She led Nia into a nearby dressing room and pushed her inside. "Try it on. I'll be waiting out here to see how it looks." Lexie stepped out of the dressing room and closed the door behind her.

Reluctantly, Nia stayed inside and began to undress.

"So," Lexie asked from the door, "are you still going over to your aunt's tomorrow?"

"Yes, I told her I'd come by and help her hang some drapes since her arthritis is flaring up."

"Girl, you're a saint."

"Oh, stop." Nia chuckled. Lexie and Aunt Olivia rarely saw eye to eye. Nia's aunt thought Lexie was the devil incarnate and a little "too fast" for her taste. To this day, she still thought Lexie was responsible for convincing Nia to stay at school instead of come home during her college vacations.

"Why do you bother to go there if she makes you feel so bad?" asked Lexie. "Why don't you come over to my parents' house for Sunday dinner? You know the folks would love to see you, and of course my brother Sebastian will be there to drool over you."

Nia laughed. She often wished she could be a part of the close-knit Thompson family. Lexie and her younger brother were bosom buddies. They were always spending time together or just lending the other a helping hand. And Nia loved going over to the Thompsons' family home during the holidays. The house was always warm and full of love and affection.

"Sorry, girl, I have to go. I promised." Nia emerged from the dressing room in the dress and twirled around. "So, how do I look?"

"Absolutely fabulous," answered Lexie. "That dress is definitely the one."

Nia pulled her Honda into a space outside her aunt's two-story home in the Chatham area of Chicago's south side. She wished she had taken up Lexie on her offer for Sunday dinner at the Thompsons, but she'd promised her aunt she'd come by after church. Nia tried to visit both her grandparents and aunt Olivia at least once a month.

She heard voices from inside as she dug through her purse for her keys. Hadn't her aunt told her that afternoon services weren't over until two pm? Cautiously she inserted her key into the lock and opened the door. Apparently she was wrong. Her aunt was center stage in the living room with her women's Bible study group.

*God, I am not in the mood for this,* she thought, walking into the room to join them. Nia had purposely avoided making an entrance and had sat in the back of church during the morning service, ready to make a quick exit. She had hoped to avoid all the gossipers.

"Hi, everyone," she greeted, putting on her happy face. She gave her aunt a hug. "Aunt Livvie."

Her aunt was a petite woman with dark brown eyes. Her black hair was graying at the temples and she refused to dye it because gray was supposed to be a sign of wisdom. She was wearing her Sunday best, a fuchsia suit and matching print scarf that went out in the eighties. Why did her aunt wear such dowdy clothes? Nia offered to help her go shopping for more up-to-date clothing but her aunt was content with the status quo.

"Oh, hello, dear, I forgot you were coming," her aunt replied, quickly patting her on the back. As always, her aunt's hugs were short and sweet. She never held her too tight and was always the first to pull away, while Nia liked to linger. "You remember my women's group, don't you?"

*How could I forget,* Nia thought, remembering the countless times she'd sat in the living room and quietly endured their preaching and church gossip. If she was lucky, her aunt would give her a reprieve and she could escape to her old room.

"Of course I do. Hello, Miss Mabel, Miss Doris, Miss Evelyn," she said, inclining her head toward each of them.

"And how are you, dear?" Evelyn asked, the first one to speak up. "Have you managed to find yourself a beau yet?"

"Yes, darling." Doris chuckled. "You aren't getting any younger. And if you don't hurry, before you know it you'll be like one of us."

Nia cringed at the thought. She didn't want to end up like these old biddies, sitting around thinking about what could have been. She was determined to make things happen. Who knows? Maybe Damon would be that man.

"Well, I just haven't found the right person yet, Miss Evelyn," Nia replied evenly. "But I am sure he is out there."

"That's my little Nia," remarked her aunt. "Always

having her head in the clouds. I know what you need to do."

"And what's that, Auntie?" *Dear heavens!*

"You need to come to church. I'm sure we have some suitable young men for you, and if not, you could always pray to the Lord to send someone your way."

Nia had already been to church and she surely hadn't seen any available men. Then again, she had been sitting in the back row.

"Amen, sista," the women chorused in unison. Did they know how much they grated her nerves?

"Thanks. I'll keep that mind. Now, where are those drapes you wanted help hanging, Aunt Livvie?" she asked, changing the subject. Nia would not be an object for their amusement and definitely not their matchmaking.

"They're upstairs in the linen closet," her aunt responded.

"I'll get started, then."

Nia left her aunt and friends sitting where she had found them in the living room. Climbing the stairs, she walked past her old room. She paused to open the door and saw that her aunt still hadn't changed a thing. It looked the same as it had the day she moved out to go to college. Her pink lace eyelet still covered the bed and her stuffed animals were neatly arranged by her pillows.

Her childhood mementos and Barbie collectibles sat atop her oak bureau. Nia walked in and sat down on the padded window seat and wondered what her life would have been like if her mother had lived. She reached over to the bureau and fingered a worn photograph of her mother.

*My mom was so beautiful.* Five feet ten inches with

a slender figure, rich café-au-lait-colored skin, long thick black hair and sparkling brown eyes, Lily Taylor looked like a movie star. Many people in their small, tight-knit black community thought Lily would become a model, due to her height, gorgeous hair and high cheekbones. But Lily had wanted to become an actress. She loved the spotlight, being onstage, able to transform herself into whoever she wanted to be. Her mother had even defied Nia's grandfather, Reverend Samuel Taylor, by moving downtown to pursue her career in the local theaters. He hadn't been happy and had tried to talk her out of it many times. Her grandpa was definitely someone to reckon with. He had been a very strong presence throughout Nia's life, but he hadn't been able to stop her mother from following her dream.

While working at the Shubert Theatre, Lily met and instantly fell in love with Nathan Alexander, a wannabe theater producer. Nathan was known among the theater circuit as being quite the ladies' man. Many tried to warn Lily to stay away from him, but whatever Lily wanted, she often got. There was a short whirlwind romance, and before Lily knew it she was pregnant. She believed Nathan would stand by her and do the honorable thing by marrying her, but she was wrong. Apparently Nia's no-good father had high-tailed his butt out of town the moment her mother confessed her condition to him. Nia hadn't ever seen or heard from him in all her twenty-seven years.

Nia's grandfather was devastated to learn of his only child's pregnancy and had refused to let her come back home. Her mother moved in with her older sister Olivia, a fifth-grade teacher for the

Chicago public school system. Olivia had her own apartment, and although she and her younger sister weren't close, she'd taken her in. Raised to be a good Christian, Olivia felt that everyone deserved a helping hand.

When a complicated labor claimed Lily's life, Aunt Livvie had taken Nia in as a baby. Olivia Taylor was an excellent provider and role model, albeit a very strict one; it had hurt Nia to know she was being punished for her mother's actions. Her aunt had never married and forbade Nia to socialize with any of her teenage peers or to date throughout high school. She felt that dating would be a temptation for Nia to sin and end up like her mother.

High school was awful. Nia was treated like an outcast because she didn't date, go to football games or have the latest clothes. She remembered a few young men asking her out but she'd been forced to decline. Eventually they stopped asking.

"Nia, darling, where are you?" her aunt called, breaking through her reverie. Had her aunt's friends left? Nia hadn't even heard the door close.

"I'm in my room!" Nia yelled. She heard her aunt climbing the stairs.

"There you are," her aunt said, stopping in front of Nia's door. "You know, those stairs are not getting any easier with age." Almost out of breath, she clutched her chest. "Well, are you gonna help me with these drapes?"

"Yes, ma'am."

"Follow me," her aunt replied, heading to the linen closet down the hall.

While chatting, they removed the old drapes in the kitchen and living room and ironed, then hung the new crisp green drapes. Afterward, they sat at the kitchen table for a cup of tea.

"Tell me what's new with you. How's your job going?" her aunt asked, slicing a piece of homemade pound cake and placing it on a plate before Nia.

"Work is going great," she replied, taking a mouthful of the deliciously moist dessert. She knew she shouldn't be eating it, but it tasted so good. "I think I might be getting a promotion soon. Since I helped with the last campaign, I've been on the fast track at work."

"That's great, dear. You deserve it. You've been working very long hours. Lord knows, your family sure doesn't see enough of you."

"I'm sorry I haven't visited more often, Aunt Livvie," Nia murmured, putting down her fork. "But I've been really busy."

"I understand. Are you going to your grandfather's for Christmas service? You know he is expecting you."

"Of course. I wouldn't and haven't missed a service since I was born. Plus, Grandpa would kill me if I did." It would be another sermon she'd have to endure.

"You're probably right," her aunt said, sipping on tea with a splash of lemon. "He'd just love to see more of you. He's very proud of your accomplishments. He and Mom aren't getting any younger."

"I know, I know. How are classes going?"

"Oh, my kids are wonderful. It amazes me how they can still manage to surprise an old lady like me." She chuckled. "I could tell you some stories, but that's actually not why I asked you over today."

Nia poured more water into her teacup and

added a dollop of sugar. "Are you suggesting you had an ulterior motive, Auntie?"

"Honey, there is something I wanted to discuss with you and it is of a sensitive nature. I thought it best to do it in person rather than over the phone." Her aunt paused and Nia wondered what could be of great importance to cause her aunt to fib.

"Well?" she pushed.

Her aunt gently laid her hand over Nia's. "Nia, darling, how much do you remember about your father?"

"What?" Nia asked, snatching her hand away. Did the woman have ESP? She was shocked that her aunt broached that subject; it had always been taboo in their family. When Nia was younger, her grandfather would get enraged if Nia inquired about her father. Often, she wondered about him, that mysterious stranger who had disappeared from her mother's life never to be seen again, even after her death. Nia used to wish he would materialize like a knight in shining armor and whisk her away to a better place, to the safety of his arms. "Why would you mention him?" she continued.

"Well . . ." Her aunt Olivia was never at a loss for words. Nia watched her twist the napkin in her hand. "I wanted to know your feelings on the subject."

"Feelings!" Nia abruptly stood, causing her chair to crash to the floor with a loud thud. "How can I have feelings for someone I've never met? Someone who walked out on my mother when she was pregnant?"

"Nia, please calm down," her aunt said. "I didn't realize how touchy this subject was and I'm sorry I brought it up." She took a sip of tea and carefully placed the cup back on the table.

"Why bring it up, then? You obviously had a reason. I mean, you brought me here under false pretenses. I can't believe this." She paced the floor, waiting for a response from her aunt. "Well?"

"How would you feel if your father came back into your life?"

Running her fingers through her short crop of auburn hair, Nia exhaled, her breathing labored. "Came back?" she asked. "That would imply he had been in my life previously, which isn't the case. Why would you ask me?" She stopped in front of her aunt and bent down to stare at her intently. "Oh my God, he's here, isn't he? He's back in Chicago?"

Her aunt looked down at the table and didn't answer.

Tears welled up in Nia's eyes and a million questions she couldn't speak formed on her lips. Nia grabbed the nearest chair next to her aunt and pulled it under her for support.

Several minutes passed before she uttered, "When did he come back? How long have you known he was here, Aunt Olivia?"

"Nia, I haven't known very long," her aunt whispered. "He contacted me a few days ago. Nathan wasn't sure you would want to see him, so I told him I would feel you out on the subject first." She tried holding Nia's hand in hers, but Nia pushed her away.

"I can't believe you didn't tell me about this." Nia paused. There may have been a time when she wanted to see her father, but she no longer believed in fairy-tale endings. "Well, you can tell him I have no desire to see him now or ever and he can take that to the bank." She started to get up, but her aunt stopped her.

"Wait a minute, Nia," she said, grabbing her arm. "I won't let you talk to me this way. I have raised you to be a better person than this. To be a tolerant and forgiving person."

"Tolerant?" Nia laughed. "When have you ever been tolerant of anything I have ever wanted to do? Except for my mother, you've never been tolerant of anyone that wasn't a churchgoer and Bible-thumper like yourself. Now that I no longer live under your roof, you've accepted my choices because you had no choice, because you wouldn't be a part of my life if you didn't."

Stunned, her aunt sat down. Her lips quivered and she blinked back the tears that welled in her eyes. She couldn't believe Nia had spoken to her with such disrespect.

Nia could see that she had hurt her aunt. Why was she taking her feelings about her father out on her?

"I can't believe you feel that way about me," her aunt said. "After everything I've done for you. I have loved and reared you like you were my own child."

"I'm sorry," Nia said, rushing to her aunt's knee. She hadn't meant to hurt her; it wasn't her aunt she was angry with.

"No, you're not. You meant those ugly words." Her aunt took out a napkin and dabbed at her eyes. "All I have ever done is my best and that wasn't good enough for you."

Nia sighed. She regretted having opened her big mouth. Aunt Livvie was not the most tolerant person in the world, but she loved Nia. She just wished her aunt hadn't opened up Pandora's box. Nia could only imagine how her grandfather would react if he ever got wind that her father was in town. There was no love lost between the two men. And while she was sure there was more to the story, she wasn't so sure she wanted to find out what that side was.

"I'm really sorry, Aunt Livvie," Nia said, leaning over to give her a big hug. "I'm not upset with you. I'm upset with my father for walking out on me and my mother. I shouldn't have taken it out on you." She gave her aunt another squeeze, which was returned. "But I do think it's best that we table this discussion, all right?" With the back of her hand, she wiped away the tears from her aunt's face. "I'm going to go now, but I'll call you later this week." Grabbing her purse from the cocktail table in the living room, Nia shut the front door behind her.

In a daze, she walked to her car and turned on the engine, but she couldn't move. A mixture of anger and fear paralyzed her. Learning that her father was in town disturbed her. On the one hand, she was curious to meet the man—he was her father, after all—but on the other, she was so angry at him.

Nia didn't know how long she sat out there, but when she was able to function again, the sun had already set and the sky had turned dark. Somehow she managed to put the car in gear and drive home.

Mentally exhausted, Nia finally made it through the door of her apartment. She was grateful for the solitude and quiet. Going back to her aunt's house always brought back bad memories. And this time was no exception.

Nothing could have prepared her for the turn their conversation had taken. Why would her father come back? It puzzled Nia as she noticed her answering machine blinking and pressed the PLAY button.

"Hi, Nia, it's Damon. I see you're not at home. Just wanted to let you know that I picked up those tickets for *Rent.* The show is Saturday at eight pm. I thought we could pick up dinner beforehand. I'll pick you up around six."

Exhausted, Nia dragged herself to bed and never once thought about how Damon got her phone number or knew her address.

# Chapter 4

Nia glanced down at her watch. It read five forty-five pm. She'd have to put a move on it. Damon would be at her house any minute to pick her up for a night at the theater.

Throwing off her thin robe, she slipped into the red sheath dress with spaghetti straps she'd bought last week with Lexie. Nia gave herself a cursory glance in the mirror. *My girl is right,* she thought, smoothing the dress down. *This dress is a knockout.*

After applying caramel foundation to even out her complexion, maroon eye shadow to highlight her eyes and a new shade of red lipstick to emphasize her lips, she was ready to go. The final touch was her favorite pearl-drop earrings, which accentuated each earlobe. Damon's eyes would fall out of his sockets, and for some reason she wanted that, wanted him to appreciate her—even though the scoundrel probably didn't deserve it, she mused. He had coerced her into this date, but she had to admit, she didn't mind.

When he put on the charm, it was almost impossible to resist him. He exuded a sexuality that was totally male. And Nia, like every other woman, was powerless to resist it, though in the back of her mind, she couldn't help wondering if she could trust him. Damon could easily have any woman he wanted. Why her? The last thing she wanted was to be another notch on his bedpost. She knew what it was like to be hurt and she didn't relish the thought of going through it again. Nia shook her head. She would not let negative thoughts ruin this evening. Like Lexie said, she needed to focus more on the positive, have fun.

The chime of the downstairs intercom announced Damon's arrival moments later. Nia buzzed him in and waited for his knock. Hearing him walk up the stairs to her second-floor apartment, she exhaled before opening the door. She was speechless when she did.

Damon looked absolutely magnificent in a black tuxedo and formal white shirt. Her reaction was just as strong as it had been each time she was within five feet of him. Tension formed like a knot in her belly and her heart pumped furiously. He was some specimen of a man and he was all hers tonight.

Nia didn't realize she had been staring at him for several moments until he spoke.

"I assume I pass inspection?" He spun around to give her a better view.

"I . . . yes," she stuttered, clearly embarrassed.

"May I come in?" he asked, walking toward her.

"Of course," Nia replied, moving aside to allow Damon entry. She closed the door behind him and caught him giving her the same appraisal.

Damon was having all kinds of wicked thoughts of what he'd like to do to Nia. The provocative dress she wore allowed him quite a view of her tantalizingly full breasts and the skirt clung to her hips, showing off her fabulously toned legs. Excitement was coursing through his veins and he could feel his manhood straining against his trousers. He didn't know how he was going to keep his hands off her tonight.

"Are you done?" Nia asked, watching him admire her.

"Not yet," he said, taking her hand and swinging her around. "My God, Nia, you look breathtaking!"

"Thank you. So do you." She smiled, looking up at him. When their eyes locked, Nia felt herself slowly sinking in those brown depths.

"Are you ready to go?" he asked, interrupting her thoughts.

"Yes." She looked away and opened her front closet to pull out her long wool coat. It was another wintry evening and she would need it. Damon helped her into her outerwear and she received an intoxicating whiff of his aftershave. It smelled clean and masculine, just like him. She lingered at the door before grabbing her purse and letting him walk her out.

Damon escorted Nia to the passenger seat of his black Lexus before walking over to the driver's side. Damon quickly turned on the heat and kicked the car into gear.

When they arrived downtown, traffic was backed up on State Street as everyone headed toward the Chicago Theatre. They inched along before Damon finally found parking in a nearby garage. Crowds of people were already lined up inside, wearing their finest minks and ball gowns as they waited for the show to begin.

The musical was fabulous and Nia said as much during the intermission. Damon had purchased excellent floor seats that allowed Nia an excellent view of the stage.

"So, you're enjoying the show?" he asked, handing her a glass of white wine from the bar. He was delighted that Nia was starting to relax. He had hoped that once she got to know him, she would feel more comfortable in his presence.

"Yes, very much," she replied, taking a sip. "Thank you, Damon. The show is wonderful."

"I'm glad you're enjoying it. If you don't mind my asking, where did you pick up your love of the theater? Are you a wannabe actress?"

"No," Nia said, shaking her head. "My aunt didn't allow me to pursue anything like that. She felt my head should stay in the books. I've always thought it might be biological. My mother was an actress, maybe that's why."

"You know, that's the first time you've mentioned your mother," Damon commented. "Didn't you say your aunt raised you? Where's your mother?"

Nia paused. "She's dead."

"Nia," Damon said, sympathetically, touching her arm. He felt like such a heel. "I'm so sorry. I didn't realize."

"It's all right," she said. "You couldn't have known. My mother died giving birth to me." Nia tried to keep at bay the tears that threatened to fall.

"Oh, baby, I'm so sorry." Damon pulled Nia into his arms and she let him, not caring that they were making a public display of themselves. She just wanted the comfort he offered.

Nia breathed in his masculine cologne. His arms felt so good, so strong, so protective, like nothing could hurt her as long as she was wrapped in them.

The overhead lights blinked, signaling that they

should take their seats. They separated and Nia took Damon's hand as he led her back inside.

Nia had no idea what Damon had planned for dinner and was surprised when he led her to the Signature Room on the 95th floor of the John Hancock Building.

Damon had immediately taken charge, ordering their entrees while Nia sat back and took it all in. He was not only attractive, but incredibly charming. A great conversationalist, he regaled her with childhood stories and anecdotes throughout their fabulous dinner.

Was this how the upper echelon lived, eating lobster bisque high above the city and going to Broadway shows? Nia thought, now staring out the window of the Lexus. She loved going to shows but with her advertising assistant's salary she could only afford half-price tickets at the Hot Tix booth.

Suddenly the car came to a stop in a parking space. Nia hadn't been paying attention to where they were going.

"Are you ready, sweetheart?" Damon asked, turning to look at her.

"Ready for what?" she asked, blushing slightly at her aloofness.

"To get your groove on." He gave her another one of his dashing smiles.

She looked around and noticed that they were in front of Millennium, a popular dance club on Chicago's north side. She'd always wanted to go there, but the cover charge was too outrageous for her meager salary.

"There is no way we're going to get in," Nia

stated, looking over her shoulder at the long line forming in front of the venue's main entrance. There had to be hundreds of people waiting, hoping that the bouncer would pick them to be one of the in-crowd for the night.

"Sure we will," Damon replied confidently. "*We* are not going in that way. We are going through the VIP entrance," he added, pointing to a side door.

He jumped out of the car and walked over to open her door. Damon took Nia's arm and folded it into the crook of his. "My friend Will owns this place. We won't have any problem getting in."

"Oh," Nia said, sighing and following him to the side entrance. An elegantly clad bouncer dressed in all black led them into the club.

Nia was amazed at the decor. The large dance floor in the center of the room was already packed with couples of all races swaying to the smooth R&B tunes being spun by the deejay. The easy laid-back vibe of the place was infectious and Nia could feel herself loosening up.

Damon was glad; he could feel Nia relax, too. He wanted her to feel comfortable with him, to be herself. If he screwed this up, he'd never get Nia to go out with him again. Tonight was a make-or-break night.

"Here's Will now," Damon said as a tall brown-skinned man approached them and enveloped Damon in a bear hug. He was equally as tall as Damon and just as good-looking. He had a smooth café au lait complexion, a square jaw and a well-trimmed goatee, and wore a sophisticated black suit with a matching tuxedo shirt and silk tie.

*He would be perfect for Lexie,* Nia thought.

"Why didn't you tell me you were coming?" Will asked, giving Damon a punch in the arm.

"Oh, I thought I'd surprise you, man," Damon replied with a laugh. He lightly put his hand on Nia's waist and pulled her closer. "Nia Taylor, meet my best friend and cohort William Kennedy. We go way back."

"Yes, *waaaay* back," Will said, smiling affectionately.

"It's nice to meet you, Will," Nia replied, extending her hand for a shake. "This place is great. The music is kicking and it has just the right touch of class."

"Thanks, Nia. I appreciate that," Will said. "Millennium is my baby. No one thought I could pull it off, so I had to prove them wrong."

"I'm sorry to hear that," Nia said. "But from the looks of it, the place is a success. Matter of fact, my girlfriend Lexie would love this place."

"You'll have to bring her here sometime. I'll leave a standing invitation for both of you with my bouncer."

"Thank you, that's very kind," Nia replied.

"I'll leave you to the rest of your evening. Here's your table," he said, indicating a small candlelit cocktail table on the perimeter of the dance floor. "It's the best seat in the house, right in the center of the room. I'll have my bartender send over a bottle of champagne and some of our best appetizers."

"I'll talk to you later," Will whispered in Damon's ear before departing.

Damon pulled out Nia's chair and she sat. "So, do you approve of my choice of after-dinner entertainment?" Damon asked, taking a seat across from her.

Nia didn't answer as the waiter came to the table,

uncorked a bottle of champagne and poured a glass for Damon and Nia.

"A toast?" Damon asked, holding up his champagne flute. "To more evenings like this."

Locking eyes with Damon, Nia clinked her flute with his. She wondered what he was thinking when he looked at her so intently.

Nia didn't have to wait long to find out.

"Would you care to dance?" Damon asked. After holding her earlier, he'd longed to feel her in his arms again.

"I'd love to."

Damon led Nia to the crowded dance floor and pulled her against his body. He had been waiting all night for the moment to feel her soft frame next to his. He inhaled the fresh smell of her clean hair and the intoxicating fragrance of her floral perfume.

She tried keeping their bodies at a distance, but Damon slowly inched her closer to his tall, lean, muscular form until their limbs were entwined as one.

Nia rested her head against his chest and listened to the erratic beating of his heart. She felt the heat emanating from his body as his hands surrounded her waist and guided her in step. They fit together like a hand and glove and easily moved to the rhythmic sounds of a classic Luther Vandross hit.

The song ended, but Damon didn't immediately let Nia go. A pulsing dance tune came on and still he held her. He wished he could hold her like this forever.

"Damon?" Nia whispered.

"Hmm?"

"The song ended."

He stepped back and looked into her big brown eyes and had to resist the temptation not to take her right there on the dance floor.

"Indeed it has." He led her back to their table. It was probably for the best anyway; he didn't want to scare her away. His body had become totally aroused just by holding her close. He hoped he hadn't offended her, but there was something between them and there was no disguising it. It felt so right.

The sexual tension crackled and Nia sought to put some distance between them before the situation moved beyond her control.

"I'm going to the powder room," she announced suddenly and bolted to the ladies' room. Damon was left staring at her retreating figure, hoping he hadn't pushed Nia too hard.

Nia needed breathing room. She was having a slew of lustful emotions that were unfamiliar to her. Most of the men she'd dated previously were either duds or leeches. She had never felt this way about any of them, never wanted to let them take her in their arms and kiss her until she begged for more. Her body was yearning for something she couldn't quite put her finger on.

It was like Damon had put a spell on her. All her senses were heightened, the music seemed louder, the strobe lights seemed too bright, the food smelled more delicious, the champagne tasted sweeter and Damon's touch excited her. When they danced, Nia felt like they were the only two people in the room.

*Oh my God. I am daydreaming in the restroom. I have got to snap out of this.* She wanted to splash cold water on her face, but she couldn't because it would ruin her makeup. Then how attractive would she be? Opening her purse, Nia found her powder and began to repair her face. When she looked in the mirror she discovered the statuesque beauty who had clung to Damon's arm the night of the Christmas party staring back at her.

"So you're his new plaything?" Kendall hissed, brushing her long black mane of hair. Her eyes narrowed as she swept Nia in from the crown of her head to the heel of her stilettoes.

"Do I know you?" Nia asked, feigning ignorance. She closed the clasp on her compact and turned back toward the mirror to apply her lipstick.

"Honey, let's not play games." Kendall cackled, tossing her hair. The curls flowed in layers down her slender back. "You and I both know who I am." She paused for effect. "I'm Kendall Montgomery, Damon's girlfriend."

Nia couldn't believe the gall of this woman, taunting her in the ladies' restroom. She didn't even know her and didn't care to. But that didn't matter to this woman who'd decided that Damon was off-limits to Nia.

"I believe that's *ex*-girlfriend," Nia said with emphasis. She would not let Kendall get the better of her this time.

"Listen, you little twit," Kendall sneered, jabbing her finger in Nia's face. "I will never let you have Damon. Hell, I've eaten girls like you for breakfast." She shook her hair and smoothed her body-hugging red dress to her slender five-ten frame.

"You've never dealt with me before," Nia countered defensively, applying a fresh coat of matte burgundy lipstick.

"You are no match for me," Kendall said, towering over Nia. "Damon and I have known each other for years and have been lovers for at least half that time. Matter of fact, I'm surprised Damon has even given you the time of day. You're a little too chubby for his taste. If you intend to sleep with him, you might want to join a gym and change that tacky shade of lipstick," Kendall added as she swept past Nia and slammed the restroom door.

Throwing the lipstick and other makeup items into her purse, Nia fought back the tears. She took quick breaths, forcing air into her lungs as she paced the bathroom floor. She couldn't believe Damon had actually dated such a person.

Kendall really knew how to hit below the belt with the chubby comment. Nia stopped pacing long enough to stare at herself in the mirror. She and her weight had always had a constant battle. She'd struggled at the local fitness center to lose those few extra pounds, and, to no avail, had tried all the latest diets from Weight Watchers to Slim Fast to Jenny Craig. Sometimes she wondered if she'd been cursed with bad family genes.

She definitely wouldn't win any beauty contests and was by no means statuesque. Standing at a whopping five-four, she had an average honey complexion, a round face, dark brown eyes, a button nose and full lips. Her smile and sparkling white teeth were her best features. As for her figure, Nia knew she wasn't like the latest fad of stick figures being perpetrated in the media these days. She was unquestionably voluptuous, but that wasn't a bad thing, was it?

But even that didn't explain Damon's interest in her. Unlike Kendall, she was no bourgeoisie black princess born with a silver spoon stuck in her mouth. And she most certainly was not a size zero.

Why was Damon with her tonight? She obviously wasn't his type. In fact, she was the exact opposite.

Perhaps she acted too quickly in accepting this date, she thought, stomping out of the restroom and flopping down in the chair across from Damon.

Although Damon had no idea what took place in those few short moments in the ladies' room, he knew instantly that something had changed. Before Nia had left, they'd had a connection. He hadn't imagined the attraction simmering between them, had he?

"Are you all right?" he asked Nia, his concern evident.

"I'm fine."

"What's wrong, Nia?"

"Nothing."

"Please don't insult my intelligence, Nia," Damon pleaded. "I know something is wrong, just tell me what happened. Did I do something?" He scooted his chair closer and took her petite hand in his large one.

"Not directly," she said finally.

He brought her hand to his lips and slowly kissed each fingertip.

"Damon, stop it," she demanded.

"Why, you don't like it?"

"Don't finesse me right now, Damon. Your ex-girlfriend sufficiently cooled any flames that may or may not have been burning between us earlier."

"What?" Damon sat up straight and peered across the room. "Kendall was here?"

"Correction, she *is* here," Nia said, pointing to the bar where Kendall was perched atop a stool. She was draped over some Latin stud, whispering sweet nothings in his ear, no doubt.

"Damn!" Damon muttered. "Listen, Nia, I'm sorry for whatever Kendall may have said to you in the ladies' room."

"At this point, I don't care." Nia stood up. "Just take me home, Damon."

"Nia—"

"This was a mistake. Things are moving too fast."

"And that's a bad thing?"

"Yes. I don't know if I'm ready to handle all this."

"You mean you're not ready to handle dating me?"

Nia didn't reply; she just headed toward the entrance. Damon followed her out of the nightclub and into the cold air. She stalked to his car and waited for him to open the door. He held it ajar and she sank into the plush leather seat.

The silence in the car as he drove to her apartment was deafening. Damon could feel Nia sitting tensely next to him, arms folded across her chest. Their progress was slowly slipping away and he didn't know how to stop it. She had positioned herself as far away from him as humanly possible without falling out of the car. Nia had shut him out and obviously had no intention of letting him back in.

When they arrived, Damon turned off the engine and got out of the car to open Nia's door. She walked up the stairs to the two-story brownstone that housed her apartment without saying a word to him.

Nia fumbled through her purse, trying to find the keys to open the front door. Finding them, she inserted the key into the lock before she turned around to face Damon. "Thank you for bringing me home," she said curtly.

"You're welcome," he replied.

Instinctively, Nia stepped back, but Damon moved closer to pin her body against the door. Nia looked back at him like a deer in the headlights and he wanted to die. Damon didn't want her to fear him; he wanted her to desire him as much as he desired her.

Nia felt the sexual energy emanating from his every pore. She knew what he was about to do as he pulled her near and anchored her to his body, knew that he was about to kiss her, and as mad as she was, she still wanted to feel his lips against hers.

Nia turned her head, but Damon wouldn't have it. With both hands, he grasped her face. She saw his lips descending and when they finally gently touched hers she thought she was going to melt. Slowly, he stroked her lips and increased the pressure, teasing them until they parted and she opened to him.

Damon softly growled as his tongue darted in and began to explore her mouth's soft recesses. He plunged deeper, stroking her velvety tongue with his. She leaned in farther to feel his hard, lean body and her chest was on fire as his lips continued to brand hers.

When Damon released her, they both took a deep breath.

"Good night, sweetheart," he whispered and bounded down the stairs, leaving Nia totally off balance with shaking knees. Minutes later, she was still standing in the same spot he left her, could still smell his aftershave on her clothes. Shaken, Nia finally closed the door behind her.

# Chapter 5

"Tell me, what have you been up to these days, big brother?" Damon's sister Jordan asked.

It was Christmas morning. The sky was overcast and rain showers were predicted. His father had cranked up the fireplace last night and their family home in Country Club Hills had a warm, cozy feeling. Damon had spent the night there so he could wake up to the smell of his mother's famous Christmas Day brunch. He was sitting with his mother and sister in their large eat-in kitchen while his mother cooked up the elaborate feast.

She was sure to include his favorite blueberry pancakes along with crispy bacon, cheese omelets, homemade biscuits with honey, croissants, fruit, fresh-squeezed orange juice and steaming hot coffee. When they were little, he and Jordan couldn't wait to wake up on Christmas morning, not just for the great gifts they were sure to receive from Santa, but for their mother's breakfast. He knew he was going to have to work out for a couple of hours at the gym to burn off the thousands of calories he was about to consume.

It didn't matter, though. He loved coming home and sitting in the big sunny kitchen. His mother had decorated it to allow for plenty of sunlight to come through the bay windows that overlooked their Olympic-sized indoor swimming pool. The kitchen was decorated entirely in cream and bright yellow and a huge island dominated the center. He and Jordan sat at an antique white pine table that could expand to accommodate a number of guests.

"Your father tells me you were quite taken with some young woman a couple of weeks ago at the Whitmores' party," Simone Bradley teased as she grated Colby cheese to put in their omelets.

"What?" Jordan perked up. "She would have to be some kind of female to capture *your* attention."

"See what you started, Mother?" Damon said, getting up to refresh his coffee at the island. He added a spoonful of sugar.

"Are you going to tell us about this woman? Have you asked her out?" his mother asked.

"Yes, please tell us," his sister chimed in. "Curious minds would like to know."

Damon stood back and stared at his mother and sister. He didn't enjoy the idea of having his family twenty-question him to death about his love life. They'd had plenty to say on his relationship with Kendall and he was determined that this situation would be different. He wouldn't let his family's opinion sway him one way or the other.

"Yes, I have," he replied finally.

"And?"

"And that's the end, Jordan. We've gone out a couple of times and I intend on seeing her in the future."

"That's great," she said, punching him in the arm. "And does she have a name?"

"Yes, darling," his mother joined in. "What is the

big secret? Are you ashamed of this girl or something?"

"Of course not, Mom." Damon sipped his coffee.

"She's from a good family, isn't she? You know, darling, you can't date just anyone. There will be many women that will be after you for the Bradley family name. You have to pick someone who will complement you, who's your equal."

"Mom, do you have any idea how snobbish that sounds? When did you become so status-conscious? Anyway, it's too early to tell just yet. But for the record, her name is Nia Taylor." He didn't want to give away too many details and jinx himself.

"All right, if that's the way you want it." His mother flipped over two omelets. "But please be careful. You have to watch out for gold diggers."

"Mom!"

"Damon, listen." His mother turned off the stove and came to grab him by the shoulders. "You know I only want what's best for you, someone who genuinely cares about you, for *you*. And not for your name. Just keep us posted, OK? You know your father and I like to know what's going on in our children's lives."

His sister, who had sat quietly during their interlude, rose from the table to rinse out her coffee mug. Damon hoped she wasn't under the same delusion that every woman was after him for his money. There had to be a woman out there who would want him for just him, he thought.

Damon believed Nia was that woman. She had a career of her own and was as quick as a whip; just the other day, they enjoyed a spirited discussion as they worked on the bank's ad campaign. Nia had suggested several clever ideas that would work in newspaper, television and radio spots to help increase business at Bradley Savings & Loan.

"Yes, we know, and sometimes a little too much," Jordan shot back at her mother. She ignored the glare her mother gave her as she went back to the stove to finish breakfast. "Damon, did you know our father set me up on yet another blind date?"

Damon laughed. "Who with this time?"

"It was Craig Garrett," his father replied groggily from the doorway.

"Awful Craig. Can you believe it? I used to make that kid eat dirt when we were little," Jordan said, turning around. "Listen, Dad, I'm just not interested, OK?"

"I realize that," their father replied. "Craig told me how horribly you treated him at dinner. All I wanted was to give you a little nudge in the romance department. When was the last time you had someone over for dinner?" he asked as he stifled a yawn with his hand.

"That's *my* concern, Dad. I won't have you interfering like you did with Damon."

"Now wait just a second, young lady. Did you forget who you're talking to? You would do well to follow Damon's example and get back into the swing of things. You're not getting any younger." Marcus Bradley gave his daughter a stern look.

"Hey, hey, how did my name get brought into this?" Damon asked from behind Jordan. He'd wanted a nice peaceful breakfast.

"Damon, c'mon," his sister said. "You remember how he was with you and Kendall."

"Please, let's not even bring that woman's name up in conversation," Damon said. Kendall had become a nuisance. Twice she had messed up things between him and Nia. He didn't want any more interference from her where his relationship was concerned. Although the Montgomerys had chosen Bradley Savings & Loan as their bank to help with the expansion of their supermarkets, Damon was not going to let her run roughshod over his personal life. As soon as he found the chance, he planned to have a long talk with Ms. Kendall Montgomery and put her in her place once and for all.

"Sorry," Jordan murmured apologetically.

"Speaking of which," their father said, "I wish you would tell us what happened with that girl. What could she have done that was so terrible? She's such a beautiful young woman. Your mother and I were so happy when the two of you became engaged."

Damon could feel his blood pressure rising. Why did Jordan have to bring up Kendall? She knew that was a sore spot between him and their father. He had no intention of spilling his guts to his family. What was done was done.

"Dad, as I've told you before, I am not discussing my private life with the family. Now or ever."

"Hmph." His father sighed and walked over to the counter to pour himself a cup of coffee. "Fine. All I'm saying is the Montgomerys would have been a great addition to this family."

Damon rolled his eyes. "If you'd had the Montgomerys as your in-laws, the whole world could have been your oyster and it would have solidified our presence in the black community."

"How typical of you, Dad," Jordan retorted. "To think of their engagement strictly as a business deal."

Damon smiled. His sister and their father were always at odds. If he said the sky was blue, she'd say it was green merely to be difficult.

"Young lady, where did you get such a big mouth?"

"From you," Jordan said with a laugh.

Damon's mother, who'd been quiet the entire time, finally spoke. "Enough of this. It's Christmas!" she said, pulling a pan of hot biscuits drizzled with honey from the oven. "Why don't one of you help me bring the food over to the table and stop fussing at each other?"

Damon rushed over first to gather the breakfast platters. His mother had been slaving away at the stove all morning while they bickered. "Sorry, Mom," he said, kissing her on the cheek.

"You better go help, too. You know you're not too old for me to swat on the behind," their father said, smiling at Jordan. He took a light swing at her backside.

Jordan missed it by running around the island. "You're getting too slow, old man," she said, laughing.

"Old? I'll show you old." Marcus Bradley chased his daughter around the kitchen. He narrowly missed colliding with his wife, who was carrying a carafe of hot coffee. Simone gave him a grim look and he stopped dead in his tracks, giving her a puppy-dog grin.

To Marcus, his wife was still the most beautiful woman he'd ever seen. With her auburn-colored hair and smooth brown complexion, at fifty she could still hold a candle to any twenty-year-old. Throughout their marriage, she had maintained her girlish figure by eating right and living well. Marcus considered himself a lucky man to have such a beautiful, supportive wife and a loving family.

"Here, carry the bacon and omelets," she ordered,

handing him two platters. He helped his wife carry the rest of the food to the table before taking his place at the head seat. Damon, Jordan and their mother followed suit. Before eating, they held each other's hands as Marcus said a prayer.

Nia was not having a pleasant holiday. The Taylor family was ensconced at her grandfather's home in Chatham, which was now full of parishioners from his congregation.

Why couldn't they have a normal, quiet family holiday? Why couldn't it just be the Taylor family? she wondered. She should have gone to Lexie's, but she'd promised her grandmother she would spend time with her relatives.

Unfortunately, her grandfather, the Reverend Samuel Taylor, had to be the center of attention. Wasn't it enough that they endured his three-hour sermon earlier this morning? Obviously not, because he was still at it in the living room. The strong baritone of his voice was enough to strengthen the weak and fragile, his commanding presence enough to scare the most disobedient of children. Once upon a time, Nia had been one of those awestruck people sitting at his feet listening to his every word, but she'd grown up a lot since then.

Nia escaped to the kitchen with her grandmother and aunt, who quickly put her to work stacking the buffet table in the dining room with paper plates, cups and cutlery so the guests could help themselves.

She fully intended to hide out in the kitchen for the duration of the evening while her grandfather held court. She wondered why she even bothered coming over sometimes. Did her grandfather even realize she was there? When she was younger, she knew she was the apple of his eye. Her favorite early memories were of sitting on his lap and twirling his beard or trying to braid his hair. She couldn't remember the last time she'd felt like she really mattered to him.

Her grandmother told her that her mother had been a daddy's girl, too. Maybe that's why he'd adored Nia early on. And maybe that's why he didn't now. Perhaps Reverend Taylor saw some qualities in her that were like her mother.

Whatever the case, right now he was ignoring Nia and the rest of the family, too, and she didn't appreciate it.

Nia rejoined her grandmother and aunt in the kitchen. They were warming up their traditional holiday feast of turkey and gravy, corn-bread dressing, pineapple ham, collard greens, homemade macaroni and cheese, candied yams, peach cobbler and sweet-potato pie. Her mouth watered in anticipation. Nia enjoyed the food at the holidays, perhaps a little too much. She would have to work out an extra few hours in the gym that week just to maintain her current weight. Tomorrow, she thought. Tonight, she would indulge.

"Here, Grandma, let me help."

Together they pulled the plump, juicy turkey out of the oven. Her grandmother basted it again before setting the bird on a big platter with a goblet of gravy. In unison, they garnished the table with the rest of the fixings.

"Grandma, is he ever going to stop?" Nia asked, inclining her head in the direction of the living room.

"You know your grandfather," she replied. "He

never changes. He enjoys spreading the Word to others."

"But on Christmas? Can't he rest from doing God's work for one day? I doubt God would mind."

"Don't be blasphemous, child," her grandmother admonished. "Why don't you go tell everyone dinner is ready?"

Nia reluctantly walked toward the living room, into the lion's den. She wondered how Damon's holiday was fairing. Was he having a good Christmas with his family? Since that kiss in the doorway, the handsome and sexy banker was never far from her mind.

His firm and skillful lips had sent an electric charge through her whole system. When she'd seen him at work shortly thereafter, Nia had tried to act completely unaffected, but she was sure Damon could see through her. He'd just sat there, looking amused as she gave her presentation. She doubted he even heard a word of it.

Making her way through a crowd of people, Nia found her grandfather sitting on the couch. She recognized several parishioners from the church gathered around him. They were sitting on the floor or propped against the wall or anywhere they could find space to listen to him.

"Sorry to disturb you, Grandpa, but dinner is ready," she announced loudly to grab the group's attention.

"Thanks, sweetheart," he answered. "Please, everyone, why don't you follow me. My wife, Melinda, makes the best turkey and dressing this side of the Mississippi." They all laughed and followed him to the dining room.

Nia stayed back. She didn't want to get immersed

in that crowd. She wanted to eat her Christmas dinner in peace. Noticing her absence, her grandfather turned around.

"Aren't you coming?" he asked.

"Not right now. I'll let everyone else get their helpings first."

"You're such a good girl," he complimented, coming over to give her a big hug.

"What was that for?"

"No reason, just because you're my sweetie and I adore you," he answered, still holding her and giving her shoulders a tight squeeze. "And I'm sorry if I've been a little preoccupied today, but I've been called to do the Lord's work and that never rests." He took her hand and led her to the couch. Nia sank down into its lushness. For once, she could actually feel the soft cushions. Her grandmother had taken off the plastic that usually covered the sofa because it was a special occasion.

"Tell me, what's been going on with my princess?"

Should she ask her grandfather the question that had bothered her ever since she left her aunt's last week? She'd been wondering what really happened between her mother and father. Was there more to the subject? Something they weren't telling her? Maybe it was best not to rile things up.

"Sweetheart, what's wrong?" her grandfather pressed. "I can see you have something on your mind. You can talk to me about it, whatever it is."

"I know," she murmured, avoiding his probing eyes. "It's just that I don't want to stir up trouble."

"Child, just spit it out. It couldn't possibly be that bad."

If that's the way he wanted it. "Grandpa, what do you know about what happened between my mom and Nathan Alexander, my father?" she blurted out.

"What!" he bellowed, abruptly standing up. "Why the hell are you bringing this up, child?"

Nia couldn't believe her grandfather actually cursed at her. "I knew I shouldn't have ever broached the subject. It's just that—"

"Just that what?" he yelled. "I want to know and don't you dare lie to me!"

"Grandpa, lower your voice. Do you want everyone to hear?" Nia whispered through clenched teeth. She knew he would be upset, but he was blowing this way out of proportion.

"I want to know now!" His voice was steadily rising. He stood at the doorway of the living room and yelled, "Matter of fact—Olivia, get out here!"

Her grandmother and aunt came running to the living room. "Dad, what's going on?" her aunt asked. "Mom and I could hear you all the way in the kitchen, not to mention the guests in the other room."

"Tell me, do you have any idea why Nia would bring up the filthy name of Nathan Alexander in my house?"

Nia heard her aunt's sharp intake of breath. She looked over and saw tears falling down her grandmother's cheeks. She was sorry she'd brought it up. Or was she? She'd wanted to know and maybe now she would finally have her answer.

"Well, I'm waiting."

"Samuel, please," her grandmother pleaded. "Let's just forget about all this and go in and have a lovely Christmas dinner. We do have guests."

"Don't try and placate me, woman," he responded. "Since Olivia seems to have a speech impediment, why don't you finish what you started?" He turned to Nia with his hands folded on his chest. He seemed so powerful and intimidating staring down at her.

"Fine," she replied, not backing down. "Aunt Livvie told me he's in town and wants to see me."

"You have got to be kidding me. Where the hell has the bastard been the last twenty-seven years?" He flopped down on the couch. "Probably writing more plays, I presume," he muttered underneath his breath.

"Dad, listen—" her aunt began.

"Don't you dare utter one single word," her father said, interrupting her. "I am very disappointed in you, Olivia Taylor. Lying, keeping secrets from your family." He shook his head. "How long have you been in cahoots with him?"

"I haven't been in *cahoots* with him, Dad," her aunt replied solemnly. "Nathan is a changed man and I thought Nia might want to meet him. He is her father, after all."

"There's no way in hell I am ever going to let that happen. Do you hear me?" He pointed his finger at Olivia. "You keep that man away from my grandbaby." He took Nia's hand and pulled her to him.

"Wait a minute, Grandpa," Nia said. "Don't I have some say in the matter?"

"Do you want to see him?" he asked, shaking her by the shoulders. "Do you want to meet the man that abandoned you and your mother at birth?"

"No, I don't, but—" Why was her grandfather behaving as if he had something to hide?

"Then that's the end of this discussion." He rose from the couch, pulling Nia with him. "Let's go get some grub. C'mon, Melinda."

Samuel turned around to give his daughter an evil look that spoke volumes.

Nia managed to eat some of her Christmas dinner, but everything was dry and tasteless in her mouth. She had almost turned the holiday into a free-for-all battle royale. Whatever it was her family may or may not be hiding, it was best left alone. If Nia never heard the name Nathan Alexander again, it would be too soon.

# Chapter 6

"Man, I had trouble keeping my hands off her," Damon said.

He and Will had just finished an intense game of racquetball at the Country Club Hills gym. Damon was exhausted from the workout, but after a shower and an hour in the steam room, he felt invigorated, like he could run five miles. Or was it just excitement that he finally found someone genuine that had him so amped? He'd had enough of women playing games, women who were merely after him for what his money could buy.

He hadn't realized Kendall was one of those types until it was almost too late. The only difference was she was a rich, status-conscious, backstabbing witch. Had Kendall even been interested in Damon, the man? He was lucky to discover her true ways before he'd married her. The only reason he even bothered with her these days was because their parents were still friends and Bradley Savings & Loan was loaning Montgomery Supermarkets money to expand. He had a lunch scheduled with Kendall later to finally put their business matters to rest.

Nia was so much more different than Kendall; she didn't care about his wealth or status. She liked him for him and that knowledge gave him an added kick in his step.

Will and Damon strolled through the tennis courts to the juice bar located opposite the large swimming pool. Will ordered a banana mango smoothie and Damon an energy bar.

"Some woman has finally got you sprung, huh?" Will laughed, handing the cashier a ten-dollar bill. "Keep the change," he said, taking a long swill of the smoothie.

"Maybe, maybe." Damon looked around for an empty table. The bar was crowded with the tennis set and singles on the prowl for a date. "I've never felt this way before. I mean, from the moment I first saw her, I knew I had to have her."

He found an empty table in the corner and sat down. Will joined him.

"I've heard that when you find the right person, it's love at first sight, though I never quite believed in it until now. Personally, I am content to live the single life."

Damon thought about Will's comment and took a bite of the energy bar. "But don't you want more sometimes?" he asked. "You know, the whole enchilada. A wife and some kids? A family?"

"Someday," Will said thoughtfully.

"Well, I'm ready now. And I think Nia could be the one."

"The one?"

"Yes, she could be the woman to become Mrs. Damon Bradley," he said with a silly grin.

"That's a powerful statement," Will commented. "I guess we'll have to wait and see."

* * *

Kendall gave her makeup a cursory glance in her compact before dropping it back in her purse. She knew she looked fabulous. This morning she'd spent well over a half hour picking out an appropriate business ensemble with just the right amount of sexiness and pizzazz. Then she'd gone to her beautician, who'd carefully coifed her hair until it gleamed in long cascades of curls down her back. And for good measure, she'd tossed in a quick manicure, too. She needed to look good and she knew Damon would take notice.

She had been thrilled when he'd called and asked her to lunch. She was sure he realized the error of his ways and was ready to resume their relationship. Kendall had known with certainty that Damon would quickly become bored with the timid mouse she ran into at the Whitmore Christmas party and Millennium. Really, what could he possibly see in her? *I am everything he could ever need,* Kendall thought. Sure, she'd made a mistake once with his friend, but that was water under the bridge. Damon had obviously come to see that they were made for each other.

Her father had been terribly disappointed when Damon had called off the wedding. Kendall hadn't the heart to tell him it was all her fault, that she was the one who betrayed Damon. Instead, she saved face and told everyone things were moving too quickly and *they'd* had a change of heart. It was a plausible story and her family believed it. A reconciliation would mean so much to her father. If she and Damon married, he would have no doubts about handing over the reins of Montgomery Supermarkets to Kendall. Then, she and Damon would be the toast of the black community. Together, they would be unstoppable.

"Are you ready to order, ma'am?" A waiter stood before Kendall, interrupting her thoughts.

"Um, um," she said, looking toward the entrance as Damon sauntered through the double doors. *The man sure knows how to make an entrance!* "No, no. That won't be necessary, my date is arriving now."

The waiter stepped aside and Damon moved in to sit opposite Kendall at the table.

"Well, hello, there," Kendall said. "It's good to see you."

"Let's dispense with the pleasantries, Kendall. You know why we're here," Damon said harshly. He nodded to the waiter, who took the hint and quickly moved away.

"I don't follow you."

"Don't play coy, Kendall. It doesn't become you. I'm not one of those boy toys you keep on the side to amuse you. I know just what a snake in the grass you really are."

"Damon!" Kendall was shocked he was speaking to her this way. She just knew he'd called to make amends. If that wasn't the case, she wasn't about to throw in the towel. "Well, if I recall, you used to be one of those boy toys and you loved every minute of it."

Damon recoiled at the thought of sex with Kendall. "That was another time and place, when I walked around with blinders on, but my eyes are wide open now, Kendall."

"Why can't you just forget the past? I've changed."

"I doubt that, Kendall," Damon replied. "You're still the same lying, manipulative woman you've always been and I want you to stop harassing Nia. Is that clear?"

A year had done nothing to change his position, but Kendall wasn't about to beg, at least not yet. "Harassing? Whatever do you mean?" she asked, bringing her club soda to her lips. Surely he couldn't mean the chat she'd had with Nia at Millennium. Did the girl scare that easily? If so, that could work in her favor.

"You know damn well what I mean," Damon hissed. "I want you to stay away from Nia. Matter of fact, stay away from me as well."

Kendall chuckled. "Might I remind you that you were the one that asked *me* out to lunch. Furthermore, I think it's going to be pretty difficult to stay away from each other when your bank is financing our expansion."

"Kendall, don't be dense," Damon replied. He was getting more and more annoyed by the minute, but he had to clear the air. He looked her straight in the eye so there could be no misunderstanding. "I meant that I don't care to see you outside of our business matters and as necessary at social engagements. Is that clear enough for you?"

"Crystal."

"Good." Damon stood and threw several bills on the table. "Enjoy lunch, it's on me." He dropped his napkin on his seat and strode toward the door.

Kendall stared at his retreating back. Somehow she was going to get him back. Someday he would realize exactly what he was missing, she would see to that. If he thought he had convinced her to give up, he would soon learn otherwise. Losing was not in her vocabulary.

* * *

Nia bit down on the pencil she was holding, awaiting Damon's next phone call. She had finally realized that ignoring him was completely out of the question. For the moment, Damon Bradley was a permanent presence in her life and somehow she had gotten used to it, even wanted it. She fully expected him to pop his head in at the office and was surprised when he didn't.

From her cubicle at the Dean, Martin & Whitmore agency, she looked outside and stared down at the dots of people ten stories below. Her small cubicle afforded her the one luxury most advertising assistants didn't have: a tiny window.

It was another brutally cold afternoon; forecasters predicted the temperature would fall twenty below zero later that evening. The wind from the lakefront was fierce, making everyone scurry inside. Nia was ready to go home. She had a splitting headache and was by no means ready to present her ideas for the Bradley Savings & Loan and Montgomery Supermarkets campaigns. After the meeting, Mr. Dean and Mr. Whitmore were deciding who would handle the supermarket campaign. She hoped it wouldn't be her group. The last thing she needed was to have to deal with Kendall on a daily basis. Life couldn't possibly be that cruel.

She grabbed her notepad, on which she had jotted some ideas, and headed toward the conference room. Chloe was already seated and Nia poured a quick cup of coffee before taking the chair next to her.

An hour later, Nia was not relieved. Luck, it seemed, had not been on her side. Mr. Whitmore had assigned the Montgomery Supermarkets campaign to her team. Was it too much to ask that she would have little contact with Kendall? God, she hoped so. Why would the Montgomerys want a lowly peon sitting in on the meetings anyway? Nia swiveled around to face her computer, but could only stare blankly at the screen. Working now would be futile. Five o'clock was looming and she was ready to go.

"Enough of this," she muttered, starting to clean up the sales orders spread out on her desk. She was eager to get home and check if Damon left a message for her since he hadn't called her at work. Pulling on her down coat and scarf, she bundled up to face the Chicago wind she would encounter getting from her office building to the parking garage across the street.

She raced down Sheridan Road in her Honda Civic, hoping to beat rush-hour traffic on her way home. Nia avoided thinking about the kind of drama Kendall could cause. The woman could single-handedly destroy her career. Somehow she had to find a way out of the campaign. Shaking the thought from her head, Nia paid close attention to the road. The last thing she needed was to get into an accident. Her Honda was only two years old and still in tip-top shape.

Walking up to her apartment, she was grateful to be home and out of the cold. She opened the door and looked around the modest one-bedroom, most of which had been decorated using pieces she'd found at garage sales in the northern suburbs. Her entire cherry-wood bedroom set, which included a headboard, dresser and hutch, cost Nia a mere fifty dollars.

The lamps and coffee table in her living room were picked up from a thrift store she and Lexie frequented. She'd deferred to a more contemporary style for her cream couch and matching love seat that she'd bought on sale at Rooms To Go. Her dining room harbored a lovely round mahogany stained pedestal table with four high-backed chairs for maximum comfort. Nia wanted her guests to be able to converse easily at one of her intimate dinner parties.

Dropping her purse and mail on the coffee table in the living room, she went to check the temperature on the thermostat. It read sixty degrees and she immediately raised the dial to seventy-five before checking her answering machine. There was no flashing light indicating a message from Damon.

Nia sat on the couch and flipped through the day's mail. The usual fare: bills, bills, bills, magazine, junk mail.

Making her way to her bedroom, she tossed her blouse and skirt in an empty chair before she threw herself down on her comfortable queen-size bed.

"Can't I just stay here forever?" she asked out loud, relishing the feel of the soft lavender comforter with matching pillows and shams. She closed her eyes and heard her stomach growl. Dinner beckoned.

Nia walked to the kitchen to see what she could scrounge up. Her refrigerator left her little options for supper: eggs, milk, cheese, tomatoes. Maybe she could make an omelet? It was light and enough to fill her up. She really must go shopping, she thought, but lately the bitter cold had kept her inside. She pulled out the necessary instruments and utensils from the cabinets to prepare her meal when the phone rang. She rushed to it, picking it up on the third ring. "Hello?"

"Hi, sweetheart."

"Damon," Nia replied, practically sighing his name. "It's good to hear your voice." It had taken him long enough. What was it with men that made them go for days without calling?

"You, too, darling," Damon answered. "How are you?"

His voice was rich and so yummy. Did he know the kind of effect he had on her?

"I'm great. What have you been up to?" She wouldn't let on that she had been anxiously awaiting his call. She twisted the phone cord around and around in her hands.

"Well." He paused. "I've been planning a little trip."

"Oh?" Nia's voice fell. Was he about to go away? They had only begun dating. "Where are you going?"

"*I'm* not going anywhere." Damon answered. "I was hoping we could go away for the long New Year's weekend together. My friend Will rented a place up in Alpine Valley. He has a huge cabin right by the ski slopes and he's invited a few friends down for the weekend. I was hoping you'd accompany me."

"Damon, I don't know," Nia responded, dropping the phone cord. "I think it's a little soon to be planning weekend getaways."

"I agree," Damon said. "Will has invited several other female friends, and if you want, you guys can share a room. Or I can sleep on the couch. Whatever you feel comfortable with."

Nia sighed. "I don't know."

"C'mon, Nia. It'll be a lot of fun. Will's parties are

the best." Damon could hear the reluctance in Nia's voice. Perhaps he was moving things too quickly. He wanted to spend more time with her and this weekend would be the perfect opportunity. He didn't want to pass it up. "Don't make me beg."

"All right, all right," she agreed. "I'll come, but I have to warn you that I've never been skiing before."

"That's okay. I'll take you on the bunny slopes," Damon said with a laugh. He was glad she agreed to come with him. "We'll have a great time. You'll see. Do you think you might be able to get off work a little early? It might help with the drive."

"Yes, I'm sure Chloe won't mind."

"Great, I'll pick you up Friday afternoon, say around three pm?"

"OK. I'll see you then."

"Agreeing to a weekend away—I'm so proud of you," Lexie said later that evening. She'd come by to return a scarf she borrowed for one of her many dates. They were sitting on the couch with a big bowl of popcorn between them, happily munching away like they used to in their college days when they would sit for hours shooting the breeze about classes, boys, clothes and movies.

"I know," Nia replied. "We didn't even settle the sleeping arrangements yet. I didn't want to sound like a prude by hounding him on the subject."

"That was probably a good idea. I mean, really," Lexie said, laughing as she slapped Nia's thigh, "when was the last time you got yourself some good loving?"

"Lexie!" Nia gave her friend's shoulder a light shove. "Sometimes you are truly too much. You know I'm not ready to become intimate with him."

Lexie threw some popcorn at Nia. When it landed in her lap, Nia tossed it in her mouth.

"What a wimp you are. Didn't you say you thought he was a hottie? That you wanted to jump his bones the other night? What exactly is the problem? There's nothing wrong with going after what you want. Damon's sure ready to jump yours or he wouldn't have invited you along."

"You think he has an ulterior motive?"

"Duh. He has the major hots for you, darling," Lexie said. "He can't wait to get you alone in that cabin so he can show you just how much." Lexie laughed. "Wouldn't he be surprised, though, if you gave it back to him just as good as you got."

"Wouldn't he, though?" Nia smiled and looked down at the empty bottle of white zinfandel on the table. She knew she would regret the heavy drinking in the morning.

# Chapter 7

The doorbell chimed the following Friday afternoon and Nia opened the apartment door to greet Damon. He looked very dapper, casually dressed in khaki pants, a blue pullover sweater and sturdy winter boots. Nia was glad she had dressed casually, too. She'd donned a large bulky sweater, some knit leggings and her hiking boots. She wasn't sure what the weather was like on the slopes.

Damon was checking her out as well. He didn't miss a beat, noticing how the leggings sculpted her thighs. It was probably a wise move on her part to cover those full breasts or he would be salivating the whole drive there. He hoped to make it to Wisconsin before a big snowstorm hit the Chicago area. He'd made sure the SUV he'd rented had been serviced and he put an emergency kit in the car that included flashlights, blankets and the like. The last thing they needed was to get stuck on interstate 294.

"Are you going to stand there or are you coming in?" Nia asked.

As Damon walked past her into the apartment, Nia got a whiff of his arresting cologne and knew it was going to be a long weekend.

"We better get going before the storm hits," Damon said, picking up her bags.

He was walking out the door when Nia said, "Before we leave I just want to say that I don't know any black people who ski."

Damon laughed at the comment.

"But I am willing to try anything once, just as long as I don't break my neck."

"I promise that you are in very capable hands." Damon leaned down to give her a kiss on the lips. It was very light and quick, but Nia wished it could go on forever. Damon, however, was already descending the stairs of her building. Nia grabbed her purse and locked the apartment behind her.

The drive to Wisconsin was uneventful, but Damon came prepared with a thermos of hot coffee and some light snacks. They only had to stop twice to fill up the gas tank before they arrived in Alpine Valley. Nestled between two gorgeous snow-capped mountains, the city was incredible. The SUV stopped in front of a huge cabin that looked more like a large castle.

Damon turned off the engine and got out to open Nia's door. "Well, we're here," he said. "What do you think?"

"Oh, Damon, it's so beautiful!" Nia exclaimed, taking his extended hand and climbing out of the truck.

Nia was stunned with the beauty of her surroundings. In all her twenty-seven years, she had never experienced this kind of luxury. Maybe Kendall was right. She was out of her league. Suddenly the door opened and a petite, brown-skinned woman wearing the latest in ski fashions stepped out of the lodge. Nia didn't realize his friends would already be there. She'd hoped for a chance to settle in first.

"Hi, I'm so happy to meet you," the woman gushed. "Damon has talked about nothing else. Anyway, Damon will grab your things. Come with me and I'll show you around." She took Nia's hand and rushed her inside the lodge. Nia turned to look to Damon for help, but he merely shrugged.

"By the way, my name is Paige Wilkerson. I'm a friend of Will and Damon. I've known them forever. All of us have been dying to meet the woman who has Damon's knickers in a twist."

Once inside, Nia had a better look at Paige. She had to be the tiniest thing Nia had ever seen. At less than five feet, her small figure made Nia feel like an obese monstrosity. Did the girl even eat? But she was as cute as a button with cinnamon-colored skin and a short bob framing her pixie face. Her cute dimples completed the picture of a perfect woman.

Dressed in skintight ski pants and a fitted ribbed fleece top, Paige proceeded to walk Nia through the lodge, showing her the gorgeous eat-in kitchen with oak cabinets. "Will had the whole place stocked, so whatever you want, it's probably here," she said. "Sometime during the weekend I'll whip up something special for everyone. I'm a great gourmet chef, if I do say so myself."

Nia nodded as Paige rambled, taking her through the informal dining room and a cozy living room where a huge moose head was nestled above the fireplace. Plenty of firewood was stocked in a nearby basket, probably to keep them all warm in case of a blizzard. Nia followed Paige up the stairs of the two-story lodge.

"This room is for you and Damon." Paige preceded her into an elegantly decorated bedroom. "There are three suites down the hall," she said, pointing to several other doors. "Of course, Will had to take the master suite, since he thinks he's master of ceremonies this weekend."

A four-poster bed with huge mahogany columns dominated the room. A rich red damask comforter covered the bed with various colored pillows tossed across it.

"So, what do you think?" Paige asked with a wave of her hand.

Nia was dumbfounded. The room was magnificent, with high ceilings and an enormous stone fireplace. The king-size bed was very imposing. Nia decided she wouldn't spoil everyone's weekend by insisting the girls sleep together. They were two adults. They should be able to sleep in the same bed, right? Nia had no idea what would happen with Damon this weekend and was nervous at the prospect. Her experience with Spencer left her ill-equipped for these kinds of situations.

"I think Nia and I will be very happy," Damon commented from behind her. He walked into the room and laid down their luggage. It thrilled him to know that Nia wasn't afraid and had decided to room with him. Maybe she felt the chemistry, too?

Nia was startled to find him standing behind her, giving off a look of such intense sexual heat. She instantly looked down at the carpet. Sometimes when he looked at her like that, it just made her shiver all over.

"I think I can read between the lines," Paige said, glancing at Damon and Nia. She made a hasty exit.

When Nia looked up, she found Damon standing in front of her. He had closed the door to the bedroom and they were all alone. His eyes were ablaze with fire as they searched hers.

Damon swept his arms around her waist, scooping her against him. "Look at me, Nia," he whispered softly, tilting her chin up toward him.

Her eyelids fluttered open and Damon was mesmerized by what he found in those brown depths. She had a need just like the one he felt growing in his loins. Threading his fingers through her hair, he pulled her to him.

Nia felt her body go taut with anticipation as she waited for his lips to descend upon hers. When they finally made contact, she was lost. His kiss was soft at first, his mouth barely touching hers. Then his tongue began a slow torturous outline of her lips before dipping inside to explore the inner recesses of her mouth with exquisite tenderness. She wiggled her bottom half to get closer to him and heard a guttural sound escape from him. Nia wanted him, needed him to give her what only he could.

It was no surprise to Damon that their bodies fit together like a hand in a glove. Perfect. "Do you have any idea what you are doing to me when you kiss me like that?" he asked huskily.

"Like what?"

"Kissing me so passionately like you can't get enough of me."

"I can't." Nia didn't realize she had spoken the words out loud, but Damon heard. He gathered her in his arms and his lips fell on hers with urgency, plundering her mouth as he dived in again and again. Damon ground his hips against hers; he wanted Nia to feel his arousal.

When his large masculine hands caressed her bottom, molding her firmly to him, there was no denying what was self-evident: Damon was fully aroused. To Nia, it was a jolt, knowing how excited he was and that she'd made him that way. Her breasts tingled with excitement when he ran his long fingers along the underside of them. They ached for his touch and when finally he cupped one in his palms, Nia thought she would die from pleasure.

Damon wanted better access to those full breasts that had captivated him from the moment he met her. In one fell swoop, he pulled the large sweater over her head and tossed it aside. Capturing one tiny bud between his forefinger and thumb, he squeezed it before taking it in his mouth. He laved the nipple with his tongue through Nia's bra, licking and teasing until it was erect and hard. When Damon was finished with one breast, he moved to the other to complete his ministrations.

Nia's head fell back as she let herself succumb to the sensations that washed over her. Unable to believe the primitive sounds that erupted from her mouth, she gasped in pleasure as he tongued her. Nia felt a sweet sensation start to form and grow between her thighs.

Damon trailed soft kisses along her collarbone, making his way up to her neck until he found a sensitive spot and began to suckle.

It gave Nia such delicious pleasure; she was caught up in the rapture and her body seemed to have a mind all its own. Her breathing became shallow and fast. Her heart was pumping wildly. Wrapping her arms around his neck, Nia brought Damon's mouth back down on hers. She tilted her head and parted her lips to give Damon better access as his tongue ravished her mouth. She feasted on him, savoring the taste. She could see how wanton her actions were, but she wanted to be closer to him. She wanted to feel the hard expanse of his chest against her breasts, and Damon, as if sensing her need, pulled his sweater over his head and threw it on the floor. Nia ran her hands down Damon's muscular chest, stopping at his washboard abs. They were hard and firm. Nia raked her fingernails over his nipples and felt Damon shudder. She relished the feel of his hairless chest, broad shoulders and corded back.

"Hey, guys, are you ready?" Will said, knocking as he entered the room.

They quickly pulled away from each other, but Damon still had his arm around Nia's waist, shielding her from Will's view. They both took ragged breaths as they sought to gather their composure, both a little stunned by the forced intrusion on their lovemaking.

"Sorry," Will said, grinning.

"Don't you know how to knock?" Damon asked testily. Nia pulled away from Damon to grab her sweater, which had fallen in a heap on the floor.

"I did, but I guess you didn't hear me." He laughed, taking a step backward when he saw the murderous look on Damon's face. Quickly Will looked away.

"Do you mind?" Damon asked, raising his brow.

"Of course not." Will smiled and closed the door behind him.

Damon looked over at Nia, who had been quiet during the exchange. Her back was to him as she fumbled, putting on her sweater that was turned inside-out.

He smiled because she had no idea what she had just done to him. He had completely lost control after he vowed that nothing sexual would happen between them this weekend. He felt like he was in a drunken stupor from her sweet drugging kisses.

Perhaps having two separate rooms would have been wiser. Damon didn't know how he was going to keep his hands off her the entire weekend. Obviously he had no will power when it came to Nia.

Nia was so embarrassed. Her behavior was scandalous, she thought. Grabbing her purse, she ran to the large master bath to splash cold water on her face, leaving Damon staring resolutely at her.

Looking in the mirror, she saw clear evidence of their lovemaking. Her hair was mussed, her eyes were bright and her lips were swollen from their passionate kissing. What was she doing? She hardly knew him. The situation had gotten completely out of control.

Her hands shook as she opened her purse to find makeup to repair the damage. She didn't want Damon's friends to think she was a brazen hussy, but how could she explain how she had reacted just now.

Damon had felt so big. When she grasped his buttocks, she'd felt him harden. She wondered what he would look like without any clothes on. Probably magnificently male and totally self-assured about his sexuality. For a brief moment, she wanted to delight in every pleasure his mouth had promised. *If Will hadn't come in . . .*

Nia feather-combed her short hairdo until the curls fell naturally in layers around her round face. She added a light glaze of lipstick and powdered her skin.

Exiting the bathroom, she found Damon putting his clothes in the bureau. Did he realize just how irresistible he was? Nia couldn't remember the last time she'd wanted or had the slightest inkling to make love. She'd dated occasionally, but none of those men remotely stirred up the kind of sensations she felt when she was with Damon; they didn't even come close. He'd awakened emotions she didn't know existed.

"Nia, listen," Damon began, turning around.

"Stop," she said, putting her hands up. "We just got a little carried away, but we're two adults who I'm sure are capable of being alone in a room together."

He took his cue from her. He didn't want her to feel uncomfortable in any way. If she felt better dismissing what just happened, he would let her. For now. "Of course we are," he replied. "Perhaps we should go downstairs so you can meet everyone else?"

"I think that's a great idea," she countered.

She took his outstretched hand and together they walked downstairs to the living room. His six friends were already assembled having cocktails. Nia felt she stuck out like a sore thumb. The other women were all elegantly clad in the latest ski fashions. Her leggings and pullover sweater seemed highly underdressed in this crowd. Perhaps she should have ransacked Lexie's closet before making the trip.

Damon hadn't noticed her discomfort and began to lead her around the room, making introductions. "Nia, you've already met Paige. I'd like you to meet her husband, Maxwell."

"Hello, nice to meet you, Nia." Maxwell extended his hand. Nia looked up at the tall, slender stranger with the dazzling, pearly white teeth and genuine smile. Distinguished-looking with an angular face, chiseled features and a tailored mustache, Maxwell appeared to be several years older than his wife, but was obviously quite smitten. He never removed his arm from Paige's waist throughout their introduction.

Damon led her to another couple standing near the living room fireplace. They were discussing the current conditions of the slopes and wondering if they'd be able to ski tomorrow. This woman obviously spent hours in the gym to maintain her athletic build. Her sculpted body easily fit into the tan ski pants and fleece top. She stood at about five-eight and was a perfect match for her boyfriend, or was it husband? Gorgeous shiny ringlets hung down her shoulders.

He was at least six feet and had a muscular build and a slightly crooked nose. Maybe he broke it while playing football, Nia thought. He appeared to have the physique for it, with his broad shoulders and muscular thighs. But his most arresting features were his eyes. They were the most interesting shade of green. He had to be of mixed race.

"Nia, this is my good friend Julian Masters. We went to Harvard together. He's a rising attorney at his father's law firm," Damon announced. "And this is his girlfriend Whitney. She's a whiz on the stock market."

"And soon-to-be wife," Whitney replied a little too quickly. "It's a pleasure," she continued, coming to give Nia a kiss on each cheek. Nia caught the look of disdain on Julian's face. Perhaps he wasn't ready to leap into marriage.

"Now you are officially part of the gang," Paige

said, smiling. "The young, the rich and the beautiful." Everyone chuckled.

"I don't know if I'd necessary call everyone beautiful, "Will quipped from behind the bar.

Paige turned to give him a glare. "Speak for yourself, you mutt."

"Now, now, there's no need for name calling," Damon scolded playfully. Ever since they were kids in private school, he'd had to referee the two of them. Paige and Will were sometimes like oil and water.

"What would you like to drink, Nia?" Will asked, playing the host.

"My baby makes the most fabulous drinks." A stunning-looking woman came forward and extended her hand. Was Nia supposed to kiss it? With a tiny waist, pert breasts and mane of long, straight auburn hair, she was obviously used to being the center of attention. Will must like very beautiful women, though Nia hoped they weren't always this superficial.

"Damon, darling, you forgot to introduce us," she admonished, fluttering her eyelashes. "My name is Carly Jones. I'm a model. You may have seen me in several commercials on television."

"Sorry, I must have missed them," Nia replied, shaking her hand. Were all Damon's friends young, rich and beautiful? What ever did Will see in her? "Uh, I'll have whatever it is you're creating back there, Will."

"Are you sure you're ready to try one of Will's creations?" Damon asked, coming to stand beside her. "They can be quite potent." He motioned for her to sit down with him on a nearby couch.

"C'mon, Damon," Will said, laughing. "If your girl thinks she can handle it."

"Of course I can handle it," Nia countered, sitting down. "Will, pour me a glass, please."

Will came from behind the counter and handed Nia a frothy mixture in a margarita glass. It looked delicious. "It's very sweet," she replied after taking a sip. "But I like it." She took another tantalizing taste.

"Just be careful with one of those things," Damon whispered in her ear. "They can really sneak up on you."

Nia leaned back in his arms and settled into the couch. She enjoyed watching Damon interact with his friends. He was a good conversationalist and easily included everyone. They discussed the possibility of Will opening a new club, Julian making partner at his father's law firm and even Carly's new commercial for Cover Girl. As Will's frothy drink began to work its magic, Nia felt herself loosening up.

After the cocktails, the gang decided to go to the main lodge for dinner and some dancing. Damon helped Nia into her coat. He wrapped her scarf around her neck and pulled her closer to him.

"Are you having a good time?" he asked. He knew his friends could be a bit much at first glance, but he hoped she liked them. They weren't always an easy bunch and often someone new felt like an outsider if they weren't familiar with the group's history or didn't know all the jokes and old college stories. Damon didn't want Nia to feel that way; he would stay close by this weekend.

"Yes, I am," she admitted. Damon kissed Nia full on the lips. "What was that for?"

"Just for being you."

"Let's go, lovebirds," Paige yelled from the door.

Damon and Nia were still standing in the foyer while the gang headed out the door. They soon followed suit.

The rest of the evening was a blur for Nia. Whatever Will put in that drink was some powerful stuff. All she could remember was laughing and talking throughout dinner with Damon's friends. She was sure the waiter was vexed with waiting on such a large group, but he kept the wine flowing. Carly, seated next to her, was surprisingly quite a hoot. Later on the dance floor she was even more so, giving Will an erotic dance.

Nia noticed Paige rolling her eyes at the intimate display. Although the others were equally inebriated, none of them carried on like Carly. She was a little too loud and perhaps a little too brazen for their subdued group. Nia could tell they weren't too thrilled with Will's latest choice of bed partners; they hardly spoke to her. Carly didn't seem to care, though—she was content to drool over Will.

Nia commented as much to Damon later in their room at the lodge.

"Well, Carly is a bit much," Damon agreed. "But you never know with Will. Who knows how long she'll last. We've seen them come and we've seen them go."

"So, Will's quite the ladies' man, is he?"

"He gets around."

"He's your best bud, right? Hmm," Nia wondered out loud. "And what does this make you? You know the saying, birds of a feather—"

"You have nothing to worry about, Ms. Taylor," he answered, coming to grab her by the waist and turn her around. "You are the only woman I want."

Nia, recognizing the look in Damon's eye, pulled away. It had been that very same look that had gotten them into trouble earlier. It was best not to start something they weren't going to finish, so she went to search the armoire for something nonsexy to wear to bed.

Damon was disappointed. He saw her fidgeting in the armoire. Didn't she know there was nothing she could put on that wouldn't make him horny as hell? Cold showers or no, it was going to be a long night. He didn't know how he was going to lay in the same bed and not make love to her. Who knew what would have happened if Will hadn't interrupted them. Damon wasn't sure at all if he would have been able to rein in his passion for her.

"Would you like to go first?" he asked, motioning toward the bathroom.

"Thanks," Nia said. Luckily she packed some flannel pajamas since she wasn't sure how cold it got in the mountains. The outfit would definitely not cause any trouble. She reached for them and scuttled past Damon to wash up for bed.

# Chapter 8

Over the next couple of days, Nia enjoyed spending time with Damon and his friends. Initially it was a little difficult to get used to their carefree lifestyle. She wasn't used to being able to order anything on the menu or buy whatever she wanted.

After the first night with Damon, Nia was a little uneasy about her wardrobe. She had never been skiing before and had only packed sweaters and jeans. The women must have recognized her discomfort because they offered to take Nia on a shopping spree in Alpine Valley.

Nia was immediately taken with the quaint town's cobblestone streets and small corner shops that housed a small grocery store, bakery, butcher and bookstore. They were there to pick up groceries so they could make a feast for their men. Nia and Paige were both great cooks and eager to show off their culinary talents.

"Before we go back, we have got to get you hooked up, girlfriend," Carly said. "These clothes"—she took some of Nia's sweater in her hand—"have got to go. They're dreadful and if you want to compete with Kendall, you're gonna have to do better than this."

"Aw," Paige moaned, embarrassed for Nia. Will had struck again by bringing a girl with absolutely no class. "What Carly meant to say is we just need to find you the appropriate skiwear." She nodded to Whitney for help.

Carly shrugged nonchalantly.

"Exactly," Whitney wrapped her arm around Nia's shoulder and led them to a nearby boutique. For the rest of the afternoon, they helped Nia select a colorful assortment of ski pants, vests, fleece shirts, a waterproof parka and lots of other goodies.

The ladies stood outside the dressing room while Nia decided which outfits she would put back. She couldn't possibly afford the whole lot of them. Her advertising assistant salary was modest and allowed her the *occasional* new outfit. She was sure that with Whitney being a lawyer, Carly a model and Paige a society wife, they could all spend such outrageous amounts on clothes. She couldn't. Coming out of the dressing room, Nia started placing several items back on the rack.

"What are you doing?" Paige asked.

"Paige, I can't afford all these things," Nia replied. "It was sure fun trying it all on, though."

"Nia, don't worry about it." Paige took the clothes from the rack. "I'll buy them." When the items rang up at the counter, Nia balked at the price. Paige insisted on paying and whipped out her credit card.

"Paige, I can't let you do this," Nia said. She felt really awful that she couldn't afford the clothes on her own. "You don't have to feel sorry for me."

"It's not pity. It would be my pleasure," Paige replied. "Please let me do this for you. You looked fabulous in everything. You shouldn't have to put anything back."

"Thank you," Nia relented, but inwardly she vowed to pay back every single penny.

Later they stopped for cappuccinos at a small café nearby.

"Thank you so much, ladies, for this outing," Nia offered as they sat themselves at a large table. "You have no idea how much this means to me."

"No problem," Whitney replied. "It was fun. We enjoyed every minute of it."

"Absolutely," Paige said, coming back to the table with a latte and a batch of homemade blueberry muffins.

"Darling, we can't have you looking like a pauper," Carly said, smiling. Whitney turned to give her a dangerous look. Nia took the comment in stride. She knew Carly meant well, even though the words that came out of her mouth didn't always agree with the sentiment.

"So, Nia, give us the dish." Paige sat down. "You and Damon are awfully cozy. What's the deal?"

"Paige, that's none of our business," Whitney admonished. She looked at one of the muffins and knew she shouldn't eat it but couldn't resist grabbing one. "Of course, anything you want to tell us would be greatly appreciated, Nia."

"What do you want to know?"

"Don't be coy," Carly murmured, sipping her herbal tea. "We want the dirt." She had to stay away from the basket of muffins on the table. She doubted Will would be as pleased with her if she didn't maintain a slender figure.

"Well," Nia said, "Damon and I haven't been seeing each other very long."

"How did you guys meet?" Paige quizzed. She had known Damon longer than any of them. When she was younger, Paige had a monumental-sized crush on him. But of course Damon always looked at her as a little sister, even after she blossomed into womanhood. Damon was actually the one who introduced her to Maxwell, probably to get her over him.

"We met at my company's Christmas party earlier this month."

"Was it love at first sight?" Whitney asked.

"Or, knowing Damon, more like lust?" Carly laughed.

"Something like that," Nia said. "At first I wasn't sure I wanted to date him. Some ex-girlfriend of his had usurped him that night."

"No!" Paige said. "Don't tell me. It was Kendall Montgomery."

"Yes, how did you know?"

"Just a feeling," she said. "All I have to say is watch out for that one. She has claws."

"You want to tell me the story on her?" Nia asked. Maybe she could glean some information from Paige so Kendall wouldn't catch her off-guard the next time. Damon hadn't been very forthcoming on the details of their breakup. Not that she had told him about Spencer Morgan either.

Whitney answered instead. "Sorry, babe, Damon never said why the two of them broke up. But I just know that bitch did something to him. I'd have to agree with Paige. Be careful around her."

"Thanks for the warning," Nia said. She would have to remember to be on her guard. Somehow she would find out what really happened between Kendall and Damon.

It was New Year's Eve and Nia was thrilled to be ringing in the New Year with Damon. Usually around this time of year she would sit at home dateless, listening to Lexie's plans for the evening. Tonight she would have someone to kiss when the clock struck twelve. Initially she'd had second thoughts about how wise it was to accompany Damon on this trip, especially when they couldn't keep their hands off each other on the first night. But since then, Damon had been the perfect gentleman. The last two days he hadn't so much as looked at her funny. Not one sultry gaze had come her way. She wondered if she had offended him. Nia thought she might turn up the heat a bit and make sure she hadn't scared him away.

After skiing on the bunny slopes, Nia took a quick shower, lotioning and spraying perfume on herself until she smelled good enough to eat. Damon needed a reminder that she was a woman.

While in town with the girls, she'd splurged and bought a pair of leather pants at an outrageous price. Carly claimed they were awesome, and, looking in the mirror, Nia had to admit that she was right. She accompanied the pants with a cowl-neck halter top that plunged low and gave a great view of her cleavage. Damon would be salivating.

Nia exited the bathroom and noticed that the room was empty. Damon was already in the living room with the others, getting a head start on the New Year's celebration.

It gave her a chance to make a grand entrance. Finding her bag, she left the room and walked slowly down the stairs, hoping Damon would look up from his conversation with Will.

* * *

"Why is it that women have to take all day to get dressed?" Will asked. He and Damon were playing a game of chess while they waited for Nia and Carly to come downstairs.

"I don't know, man." Damon laughed, moving a chess piece. He would have to stay alert. Will was an excellent player. "Maybe it's a conspiracy designed to keep us panting after them."

"Speaking of which, how are things progressing between the two of you? The last couple of days you guys have been awfully cozy," Will teased.

"They've been progressing, if you discount the fact that I've walked around with a permanent hard-on for days." Damon couldn't count the number of cold showers he'd had to endure after he slept next to Nia each night or watched her cute bottom in one of those tight ski ensembles. He was going out of his mind with longing.

Will laughed throatily. "I think you might want to keep that one to yourself." He punched Damon in the arm. "Though I am shocked to hear that Nia has you wrapped around her little finger." He knocked Damon's queen over and called, "Checkmate."

Damon smiled. Will had cleverly turned the conversation and he'd lost his focus.

Will saw Nia descending the stairs first and nudged Damon, who turned around to watch her entrance. He was mesmerized by her enchanting figure as she drifted down the stairs looking sexy as hell. He had never seen anything so lovely in his entire life. His heart welled with desire and he was pleased that Nia was his for tonight, and longer if he had anything to say about it. He wanted, no, he needed to be with her, to make her scream out his name as he was sheathed inside her wet heat. Something deep within Damon told him that having her for one night would not nearly be enough.

"Come here," Damon demanded. When she walked into his strong arms, he gave her a firm squeeze and a quick pat on the behind. He wanted to do more but they had an audience. "You look amazing," he told Nia.

Her heart skipped a beat. "Thank you," she whispered in his ear. "You look pretty good yourself." Nia sniffed his neck. "And you smell good, too."

"Thanks, babe. So, are you ready to ring in the New Year?" he murmured, pulling her close to him.

"Yes, with you." She gave him a kiss on his nicely chiseled jaw.

"Everyone ready?" Will asked when Carly finally emerged.

"Yes," they all agreed in unison, heading toward the door. Damon helped Nia into her coat and, hand in the hand, they walked to the nearby lodge.

The lodge was elaborately decorated with New Year's memorabilia. The staff had gone all out, placing balloons, streamers, hats, noisemakers and whistles on each table.

Damon had every intention of making it a night Nia wouldn't forget. Attentive during dinner, he made sure everything was to her satisfaction. When the band played a slow sexy song, Damon asked Nia to dance and she accepted. He held her firmly, grinding his body provocatively against hers so that Nia was in no doubt of his arousal for her. His hands stroked her back until finally coming to rest on her buttocks. Nia knew then that she had definitely hit her mark. Damon had most definitely not forgotten she was a woman.

Nia was breathless when they finally made their way back to the table. Out on the dance floor, all kinds of wicked thoughts came into her head. When Damon was holding her close, she was thinking of the things he could do to her. Her body was hot with longing and she ached to feel his hands over her entire body. Luckily the song ended the seduction and she was now able to think clearly.

Every time she was ten feet from Damon, her body reacted so strongly to him. She had never felt so aware of a man. Nia was thinking of their upcoming New Year's kiss when she saw her. Bold and big as day, Kendall was pretty hard to miss. Nia couldn't believe her eyes. Was the woman following them?

Damon followed the direction of Nia's startled expression and rested a furious gaze on his ex-fiancée.

He felt the tension mounting beside him; he could see that Nia was visibly shaken, and sought to thwart Kendall before she could attack. He stood, knocking his chair over. Everyone at the table looked startled by the murderous look on Damon's face.

"Wait." Will stood up, resting his hand against Damon's chest to keep him from killing the woman.

"Move," Damon said through gritted teeth.

Will looked at the intent in his eyes and stepped aside. Maybe he should let Damon strangle her and be done with it.

Damon stormed over to Kendall, who was standing with the hostess, waiting to be seated.

"I want to talk to you. Now!" he grunted. He grabbed her by the arm and dragged her out of the room.

"Damon, you're hurting me," she murmured coquettishly. He had that tone of voice and she knew he was furious with her, but she didn't care. Kendall would do anything to get him back; even if it meant making a public spectacle of herself. She had lost Damon once and she had no intention of letting that woman come and take her man.

Nia looked over her shoulder at the scene panning out and felt ill. She couldn't believe Kendall had shown up there of all places and of all nights. It was New Year's Eve and, to top it all off, Damon was embarrassing her by making a big scene. It's exactly what Kendall wanted, to make herself the center of attention and make Nia look like a fool.

The minutes ticked by and Nia wondered what the two of them were discussing. What could they possibly have to say that could take that long? It would be midnight soon and once again she would be left alone. But this time it was even worse, because she'd had her hopes up and thought things would turn out differently. Once again Kendall succeeded in ruining their evening on one of the most romantic nights of the year.

Nia began to twirl her napkin in her hand, tearing it into little pieces. She saw Damon's friends' sympathetic looks, but none dared speak to her, except Carly.

"Are you all right, darling?" Carly asked, picking up Damon's chair and scooting next to her. "Here, drink this." She had brought over a glass of brandy. "It'll soothe your nerves."

"Thank you, Carly," Nia replied. "They are rather frayed at the moment." She took a sip from the decanter, then spilled some on the table when she forcefully sat it down. No one seemed to notice.

"Don't let that woman see you sweat," Carly whispered in her ear. "She isn't worth it."

"I know that. It's just that—" Nia stopped. She didn't want to spill her guts at the dinner table. "What the hell is taking him so long?" She abruptly stood up and left the table, leaving everyone to stare at her retreating figure. She found the source of her anxiety outside the hall in a heated conversation with Kendall. They didn't even notice her presence in the doorway.

She coughed. Kendall turned around first to glare at her before rushing toward her, hair flying everywhere. "It's your fault he's treating me this way. He never used to be this mean to me."

"Step back, Kendall!" Damon warned. Kendall turned around and stared at him. "That's an order."

"Why are you doing this!" Kendall cried. "You know how much I love you. We're perfect together. This woman, this girl—she isn't right for you. You and I both know it and so does she. Look at her," she said, pointing at Nia. "She can see it, too. If you would just give me another chance, we could be good together again."

The situation was getting out of control and Damon didn't know how to handle it. Kendall was being outrageous and he knew this wouldn't help his budding romance with Nia.

"Give it to her," Nia replied. "Give her that second chance, Damon. Then both of you can get the hell out of my life." Nia turned and ran out of the lodge.

"Nia, wait!" Damon yelled. "Damnit!" He would follow Nia in a moment. But first he turned his wrath on Kendall. "Why can't you get that it's over between us?"

"Is it?" she asked.

"Yes, it is. You destroyed any feeling I had for you when you slept with Daniel. God, Kendall, he was one of my best friends and you betrayed me. With him!"

"I'm so sorry. If I had to do it all over again, I would never have succumbed to Daniel's charms."

"Don't put this all on him," Damon replied. "There were two people in that bed."

"Can't you find it in your heart to forgive me? We could begin again, make a new start."

"There is no starting over."

Kendall was getting nowhere fast. She had to use another tactic. "You and I both know what a marriage between our two families would mean, and not just for our businesses."

Kendall stepped closer, rubbing her body against his. She knew that when they were together, her body was her secret weapon.

"You are trying my patience," Damon said, pushing her away from him. "If you keep this up, Kendall, you're going to be the one to cause a major rift between our families and there won't be a deal at all." He turned on his heel and walked away.

Nia didn't realize she'd left her coat in the lodge until she was running through the cold night air. The wind was biting her face, but she eventually made it back to their cabin and slammed the door behind her. She was freezing and her teeth wouldn't stop chattering. She went over to the fireplace and saw that Will had extinguished the fire before they left. She ran upstairs to change into something warm and hide under the covers.

Moments later, she heard the front door slam. She figured it was probably Damon. It took him long enough! Didn't he know she just went out in the freezing cold without a jacket? It wasn't quite midnight yet, but if he had come back for a New Year's kiss, he was in for a rude awakening.

Finally, she heard the floorboards creak as Damon opened the bedroom door. He glanced at her under the pile of covers and was exasperated. What did she think he was going to do, attack her? He threw down his jacket and stormed into the bathroom.

The door reverberated and Nia was left alone. What was he mad about? Was she supposed to kiss his feet because he'd followed her? She heard the shower a few minutes later and rose from her bed to make herself a cup of hot tea before taking Damon on.

She padded down the stairs to the kitchen and put on the teakettle. He obviously didn't care what time it was. She opened the cupboard, found a mug and sat on the bar stool, waiting for the water to boil. The other couples picked that exact moment to come back, bursting in loud and rambunctious, singing "Auld Lang Syne." Why did they come back? Couldn't they have celebrated the New Year at the lodge?

Paige noticed her first. "There you are!" she exclaimed. "We have something you might be looking for."

Everyone turned to look at Nia and she wanted to scream. She saw the look of pity on their faces—poor Nia, caught in the middle of Damon and Kendall's love triangle. Or maybe they were thinking *Get out while you still can. You're no match for her.* Of course, Nia already had that very same thought.

"And what might that be?" Nia asked snippily. She was in no mood for Paige's perky persona right now. Paige heard it in her voice and turned beet red.

"Your coat," she answered, handing Nia her fleece jacket.

"Thank you," Nia said apologetically, accepting the jacket. Paige didn't deserve her wrath; the man upstairs did, for making a fool out of her and in front of his friends, no less.

"So, what happened between you and Damon?" Carly asked, coming over to join them. She obviously had no qualms about delving into their business. Nia turned around to give her a stern look. She saw the men fiddling around in the living room, looking for the remote. They were probably embarrassed by Carly's emboldened question.

"Carly," Whitney admonished, "that's none of your business."

"It's all right," Nia replied. "We haven't had a chance to talk just yet." She heard the whistle of the teakettle and went over to the stove to pour water into her teacup. She swished the tea bag around, resolving not to supply Carly with any more gossip. She took a sip of the hot tea to soothe her frazzled nerves.

"It'll be all right, sweetie," Carly whispered, coming up behind her and patting her back. "You're the right woman for Damon and he damn well knows it. In any case, the mood's been broken, so we're back here to celebrate the New Year properly. Ain't that right?" she asked Will, batting her eyes seductively at him. He growled in response.

Maxwell, meanwhile, turned on the television so

they could watch the countdown on "Dick Clark's New Year's Rockin' Eve."

"Come here, babe," Will murmured, "so we can start this New Year off right." Carly strolled over to join him in the living room and gave him a kiss full on the lips.

Walking out of the bathroom after his shower, Damon realized he was alone in their room. Nia obviously was very upset with him, and with just cause, but he didn't appreciate her running off like a spoiled child. He would have preferred her to stand up to Kendall and tell her exactly where to go. How could he have known that by telling his father he was going away for the New Year that it would leak to Kendall? It was an honest mistake and hopefully Nia would understand that. He had a few minutes to rectify things so they could start the New Year off right.

Damon dressed in jogging pants and a T-shirt and walked downstairs to join the others. Nia was standing apart from everyone else in the kitchen. His friends were over by the fireplace, happily chatting away or snuggling on the couch. Damon hated to see the distance between them and Nia.

"Hey, everybody," Damon said as he rejoined the group in the living room. He patted Will on the back.

"What's up?" Will inclined his head toward Nia in the kitchen. "You should go talk to her," he whispered in Damon's ear. "Tell her about what really happened between you and Kendall—that you were once engaged and she betrayed you, and that there's not a chance in hell you'd ever go back to her."

"I'm going to talk to her, but not about that," Damon said. "That's the past." He didn't want to dredge up how much he'd fancied himself in love with Kendall, only to have her break his heart. Damon wanted Nia to see him as the strong man she knew him to be. Taking a deep breath, he started to walk over.

"Did you send Kendall packing?" Paige inquired, usurping him first. She had watched Kendall worm her way into Damon's life, kissing up to his family at every possible opportunity. And she'd almost done it. Damon fell for her and offered her a big fat ring, but somehow luck prevailed and he rid himself of that manipulator. Kendall Montgomery was trouble and Paige could only hope that he put the issue to rest so he could move forward with Nia.

Damon watched Nia sitting quietly at the bar. "Of course I did. But you know Kendall." He gave her a knowing smile and pulled up a bar stool next to Nia. They sat face-to-face, but Nia appeared to have every intention of ignoring him. She was looking deep into her teacup like she'd found gold dust. When she finally sat her cup on the counter, Damon took her hand.

"Nia, can we go upstairs and talk, please?" He wanted to make amends and salvage the weekend.

She looked at him and saw the regret in his beautiful brown eyes and nodded her consent. Taking his hand, she let him lead her upstairs to their room. She didn't see the look of relief that was on everyone's faces.

Damon closed the bedroom door behind them and motioned for Nia to sit down on the lounge chair. He sat on the edge of the bed, wanting to be closer to break the ice that had formed between them, but he didn't want to push her.

"Nia, I'm sorry," Damon began. "I had no idea Kendall would show up here." He reached for Nia's hand and she allowed him to hold it.

"I know that. But you have to admit, it was rotten timing." She'd had sufficient time to calm down and knew that Damon had nothing to do with Kendall's presence at the resort, but it still hurt.

"But . . ." He paused seeing the doubt in Nia's eyes. "You still see Kendall as a threat to our relationship," he answered for her.

"Isn't she?" Nia heard everyone downstairs chanting the countdown to the New Year: ten, nine, eight, seven . . .

"No, she isn't," Damon rasped, his voice rising. "Listen, Nia, I told my father where I was going to be—he must have let it slip. You have to believe me when I say that Kendall and I are over."

"I know that here," Nia pointed to her head, "but tell it to here." She pointed to her heart. "Kendall wants you and she'll stop at nothing to have you, even it means hijacking us at this fabulous mountain resort. That woman is a barracuda."

"I know. That's why you shouldn't give anything Kendall says any credence. She's just being vindictive," Damon said. "Nia, you're amazing. You surpass any woman I've ever known. I don't care what my father may want for the family business. I only want you."

He pulled Nia to him, his lips lightly caressing hers. "By the way, Happy New Year," he murmured. Nia glanced at the wall clock and noticed it was just past twelve.

"Happy New Year." She kissed him back and whimpered when he twirled his tongue with hers in a deep sensuous kiss. She felt a stirring deep within her belly and pulled away.

Damon took the hint.

"Let's go to bed, okay?" he said. "And let's see if we can forget Kendall was ever here." Damon pulled back the covers and Nia joined him on the comfortable bed, and together they slept until the wee hours of the morning.

"Oh my God," Nia moaned as Damon carried her up the stairs of the lodge. Every bone in her body ached.

The entire weekend had been incredible. After the Kendall debacle, Damon had taken extra care to make sure the rest of their trip was romantic and uneventful.

Damon showed tremendous patience as Nia learned to ski, helping her choose the correct boots, skis and poles. At first Nia hadn't wanted to try anything other than the bunny slopes, afraid of breaking a leg or a limb, but Damon hadn't taken no for an answer.

She'd reluctantly agreed to go to ski school, but she felt like an utter fool, learning with a bunch of children. Nia couldn't even get into her skis, not to mention the countless times she'd fallen on her rear end over the last couple of days, but it was all good fun.

Nia was happy when her bottom finally hit the soft cushion of their massive bed. Damon smiled down at her.

"Do you know how incredibly beautiful you are?"

Damon inquired, leaning down to give her a kiss on the cheek. Since the Kendall fiasco, the time they shared that weekend had been bliss. He was thrilled she'd come with him and had kept his promise to keep his hands to himself. But right now, looking down into her big brown eyes, Damon wanted to lose himself in her.

Nia reached out and touched his cheek. "Thank you for saying so. Especially when every other woman in this house is stunning."

Damon got up from the bed and walked to look out the window. He rubbed his bald head. Why did she say things like that? Sometimes he could strangle her. She had apparently gotten the idea in her head that she wasn't beautiful like the rest of his friends. He walked back over to the bed.

"Nia, the only woman I care about is you," he said finally. "And I happen to think that you are the most attractive woman I've ever seen."

"But—"

Damon put his forefinger to her lips. "I'm not just talking about physical beauty. You're a beautiful person inside and outside," he said, pointing to heart. "You're warm and kind. Generous and caring. You've even taken to Carly this weekend and really included her when the other ladies shunned her. You're wonderful." He pulled her to sit up and face him. "And beautiful, too." He gave her a kiss on the lips. "Now, if you want, I would love to prove to you just how beautiful you truly are." Damon took her hand in his and kissed each fingertip. Nia blushed and put her head down.

Pulling her off the bed with him, Damon gave her a swat on the behind. "We'll table this subject for now. In the meantime, why don't you grab your swimsuit and let's hit the hot tub. It will help soothe your aching muscles."

"That sounds fabulous," Nia said. She opened the armoire to pull out her black one-piece bathing suit. Nia knew it flattered her figure without showing too much and she didn't feel comfortable showing skin in a two-piece ensemble, which had never flattered her generous hips.

Damon watched her as she scooted to the bathroom. Maybe one day Nia Taylor would let him into her inner sanctum. Then he would show her just how beautiful she was.

"Oh." Nia sighed seductively. "This water feels *sooo* good." She and Damon had gone onto the terrace to enjoy the hot tub while the other couples stayed at the lodge. It was so cold, Nia could make little Os with her breath.

She closed her eyes and leaned back against the tub to let the warm pulsating jets work on her tired, achy bones. When she opened her eyes, she saw Damon watching her. He seemed to never get tired of gazing at her. When he thought she wasn't looking, she'd catch him staring at her.

Underneath the warm water, Damon pulled Nia toward him. He settled her between his legs so she could lean back against his chest. When her soft thighs were nestled snuggly between his, he began to massage her shoulders and neck to help alleviate some of the tension.

If he couldn't make love to her, he wanted to at least touch her, to feel her soft, satiny skin against him. He was surprised earlier when she'd come out wearing a one-piece bathing suit. Most of the women he dated had no problem showing off their God-given assets, but Nia was different. She was very self-conscious about her figure, and even though she tried to hide behind the one-piece, there was no denying the sultry body underneath. Nia had the most deliciously curved bottom he'd ever seen and he could just imagine those shapely legs and scrumptious thighs wrapped around his waist while he plunged deep.

"Damon?" Nia asked, turning back to look at him. "Did you hear anything I just said?"

"Hmm."

"You were a million miles away," Nia said. "What were you thinking about?"

He doubted she really wanted to know exactly where his thoughts had led. "I was just wishing we could stay here forever," he said instead. "But unfortunately we have to go back home."

"I know," Nia commiserated. She turned around to face him. "But I want you to know that I don't regret our time here together. It was a great way to ring in the New Year."

"Do you mean that?"

"Absolutely." She gave him a quick kiss on the lips. He couldn't agree more and the best was yet to come.

"Good-bye!" Nia yelled from the car window the next morning. She had given each of the women—Paige, Whitney and Carly—a hug, thanking them for showing her such a wonderful time. She had even made plans to have lunch with Carly later in the week when she came back from her photo shoot in Hawaii. Nia had been shocked when Paige suggested they catch a movie or a play in the near future, but she happily agreed. Plus, she was determined to pay Paige back for the clothes she'd bought her.

Damon's friends had treated her better than she ever expected. She was glad she'd had a chance to meet them and to see a different side of Damon. He was quite the practical jokester and several times throughout the weekend he and Will had tried to one-up each other, Damon by putting snow in Will's boots and Will by hiding Damon's skis.

Nia rested her head on the car seat and settled in for the long drive back to Chicago. She didn't realize she'd fallen asleep until Damon tapped her shoulder. They were in front of her apartment building.

"Hey, sleepyhead," he said. "You're home, safe and sound."

"Hmm." She rubbed her eyes. Damon jumped out of the SUV and snatched her luggage from the back. Nia reached down for her purse and exited the SUV.

"I had a wonderful weekend and holiday," Nia said, smiling at her doorway. It was Monday afternoon and unfortunately they both were due at work on Tuesday morning. She opened the door to her apartment and Damon set down her luggage on the carpet. Then he bent down to give Nia a searing kiss that left her lips tingling. Slowly she walked him back to the front door.

"So did I, and hopefully there'll be many more such weekends," Damon murmured, giving her shoulders a squeeze. "I'll call you later, sweetheart."

He blew her a kiss and left her standing at her doorway, completely mesmerized. She finally closed her door and leaned back against it.

What a man, Nia thought. And he was interested

in her, flaws and all. Could this be true? Could she trust the feelings Damon had awakened in her? She could only hope. She picked up her luggage and shopping and was walking to her bedroom when she heard a knock on the door.

Did Damon forget something? Or maybe he came back for another kiss to seduce her into becoming his love slave. She just might let him. Dropping her bags, she rushed to swing open her front door.

It wasn't Damon. An older man who seemed oddly familiar, like she had seen him somewhere before, stood on the other side. He was quite distinguished-looking, with salt-and-pepper hair and a well-groomed mustache. At almost six feet tall, he had smooth honey-brown skin, an angular nose and large expressive eyes that shimmered. He was staring at her like she was some kind of alien that had suddenly beamed down to earth. For some reason, she just couldn't place his face.

"Can I help you?" she asked. Looking into his big brown eyes, recognition dawned on her. His eyes were a reflection of her own. Nia shook her head in confusion. But it couldn't be. Or could it?

"Hello, Nia," he said, finally speaking. "I'm your father."

# Chapter 9

For several long moments, they continued to stare at one another. He might as well have been an alien, because Nia was completely taken aback. Was this man really her father? Was this the man she dreamed of, longed for all these years to whisk her away from her humdrum life? She stumbled backward into her apartment.

She couldn't breathe; her lungs felt constricted. The stranger who'd called himself her father followed her inside and closed the door behind him.

"Nia, wait!"

She heard him too late as her legs went flying into the air and she fell hard on her bottom against the carpet. She kicked at the stupid luggage she'd carelessly left in the middle of the floor. She felt like a klutz and struggled to get up.

"Nia, are you all right?" he asked, grabbing her elbow to help her up.

She smacked his hand away. "I've got it," Nia hissed, standing up. Her father jumped back as if she'd scorched him.

Taking a deep breath, Nia studied his face. He looked surprisingly well, considering the fast life he'd led. It made her wonder what he had done with his life. Where had he gone? Did he ever marry? Have any kids? Maybe those questions were best left unanswered, Nia realized. She wasn't at all prepared for this moment. It wasn't every day you met your father for the first time.

"Why are you here?" she asked eventually, finding her voice. "What do you want from me?"

He didn't answer immediately. Instead, he stared at his daughter, tears brimming in his eyes. He was so proud. Nia had turned into such a beautiful young woman and he'd missed it. Reaching into his breast pocket, he pulled out a handkerchief and dabbed at his eyes. He would have to thank Olivia for doing such a great job raising his baby girl.

"Your Aunt Olivia told me you had no desire to see me," he said, his voice cracking slightly. "But I had to, though I probably shouldn't have just shown up on your doorstep. Seeing me must come as quite a shock to you."

It wasn't quite the truth. She'd told her aunt she didn't want to see him to avoid this moment, but there was no avoiding it now. He was here and it surprised her how much it hurt. She'd thought she'd exorcised any feelings she had for the father who abandoned her, put them in a locked box and buried them down deep. So why did she still care?

Could it be because he was a link to her mother? Or perhaps it was more? She was afraid to find out. Hadn't she endured enough during her childhood? The pain and rejection of those taunts about being a bastard were still fresh in her mind.

"You should have taken her advice," Nia replied sarcastically. Stepping away from him, she walked to the kitchen to compose herself; her throat was parched and she felt sick to her stomach. Pulling a clean glass from the cupboard, she went to the refrigerator to pour herself some water. Her father quietly followed.

"May I have some as well?" he asked to her upturned brow. "If you don't mind?"

Nia squinted at him. How many times had she thought that if he was a man dying of thirst, she wouldn't offer him a cup of water to quench it? Instead, she grabbed another glass from the cabinet and poured him one.

When he accepted it, his hand accidentally brushed hers and Nia snatched hers away instantly. She arched her brow, waiting in anticipation. For what? She didn't know. For an explanation she didn't even think possible? What could he say that would make up for not contacting her for twenty-seven years?

"So I guess you're wondering why I'm here?"

Nia stared blankly at him. "The more important question is, why now?" she asked, leaning against the kitchen sink. She stayed put because she didn't want to give him the impression he would be staying long.

He shrugged. "I don't know. I guess I just wanted to get to know my daughter and I was hoping you'd give me a chance."

"You're a little too late for family reunions, don't you think? The time for playing daddy has come and gone. You missed it." She couldn't believe his nerve. What right did he have to surface in her life after all this time? Where was he when she needed a father?

"Nia, I realize you are a grown woman and that you don't really need me. But I was hoping we could talk and sort things out."

"There is nothing to sort out," Nia said. Trembling,

she placed her glass on a counter nearby. "You walked out on my mother, leaving her alone and pregnant. You abandoned your newborn motherless child. What else is there to say?"

Her father looked genuinely hurt at the comment. Nia could feel the tears burning at the back of her eyes. She didn't want him to see how much meeting him hurt her. Storming out of the kitchen, she headed to the front door with her father in hot pursuit.

"You don't know the whole story, Nia," he pleaded, catching up with her at the door. "There's so much more you don't know."

"I don't need to hear your version of the story. I've heard it all from my grandfather. Right now I just want you to leave!" she yelled. The tears were starting to come down in full force. Nia was unable to keep them at bay. Brushing them away with a quick swipe of her palm, she yanked the door open for him to exit. She didn't want to hear any of his excuses. There was no way he could justify his actions. "Why did you have to come here? You had to know no good would come of this."

"Nia, I'm sorry," he cried, opening his arms to embrace her, but Nia kept her distance. The little girl inside may have wanted a fatherly hug, but the woman in her couldn't stand it.

Lowering his arms, he said quietly, "I didn't mean to hurt you by coming."

"Then go!" Nia shouted. "And don't come back. I don't ever want to see you again!" She'd gone this long without a father and she reckoned she didn't need one now.

Nathaniel saw how much his sudden appearance upset her and prayed that one day she might forgive him. With his shoulders slumped and his head hung low, he walked toward the door. "Maybe one day you'll be ready to listen to my side of the story," he replied before descending the stairs.

Nia slammed the door and crumpled to the floor. Wrapping her arms around herself, she let the sobs overtake her whole body. To have the father she'd never known suddenly show up on her doorstep was just too much.

She had always wondered who she looked like more. Her father or her mother? Having her father standing at her doorstep, her questions were finally laid to rest. She definitely looked more like him. In those few short moments, she memorized every feature. They had the same round face and the same eyes. She'd always known her big brown eyes didn't come from her mother. Her mother's eyes were almond shaped just like the rest of the Taylor family.

She didn't know how long she stayed there, but she knew she didn't want to be alone. Gingerly lifting herself off the carpet, she walked to the living room and grabbed her keys.

Twenty minutes later, she stood outside Damon's condominium. Should she have come? Maybe. Maybe not. She needed someone to talk to and he was the first person she'd thought of. Hesitantly, she knocked on his front door.

Damon opened the door wearing nothing but a pair of black silk pajama bottoms. Nia stared openmouthed at him. The blatant sexuality emanating from him was oftentimes overpowering. If his look of bewilderment was anything to go by, he was equally shocked to see her.

"Nia?" he asked. "What are you doing here?"

The last thing he expected when he opened the

front door was to see Nia standing on the other side. He'd hated to leave her earlier, but he knew they both had an early day tomorrow. Yet he was thrilled to see her. Looking at her tear-stained face, he knew something was wrong. She looked like she was in some sort of daze. He pulled her forward into his apartment and closed the door behind him.

"Are you all right?" he asked, seating her on his leather couch in the living room. He walked over to his minibar to pour her a glass of sherry. With a shaky hand, Nia accepted it. He sat down next to her and waited. She would talk when she was ready.

Nia had confided in him about some of her childhood and how hard it was growing up without a father. He hurt for her, knowing how cruel children could be. He craved to learn more about her, about her past, and now she had turned to him.

She took a sip and winced. "Very strong."

"It's meant to be," Damon said, smiling. "So, do you want to tell me about it?"

"You mean what brought me here hours after you just left?" She chuckled, her voice cracking slightly.

"Something like that."

She sighed. "I just didn't want to be alone." The tears were starting to form again. Damn them, she thought. Damon leaned over to grab a box of Kleenex from his end table. "I just want to stay here for a little while. If that's okay?" She took his hands in hers and pulled him down with her on the couch. She needed to feel his strong arms wrapped around her.

Damon didn't know how long they were spooning like that, with her bottom tucked into him. All he knew was that he was going crazy with longing for her. His body kicked into high gear and he could feel his arousal hardening. He shifted. He would never take advantage of her and he didn't want her to regret that she'd come to him.

After a short time, Nia finally spoke. "You know how I told you my Aunt Olivia raised me? Well, I left out a few facts. Like the fact that my father abandoned my mother when she was carrying me."

Damon sat quietly. It was a breakthrough, Nia deciding to confide in him.

"Anyway, to make a long story short, my father showed up on my doorstep right after you left. *Poof,* just like that," she continued, snapping her fingers. "After twenty-seven years, he just showed up."

"That's incredible. Did you have any idea he was in Chicago?"

"My aunt told me he slithered into town, but I never expected him to show up. Uninvited."

"It must have been quite a shock."

"To say the least. You see, my grandfather told me everything," Nia began. "My father, Nathaniel Alexander, was quite the ladies' man and he took advantage of my mother. She was a preacher's daughter whose only wish was to see her name in bright lights. My mom had big dreams."

Nia's eyes misted and her voice choked up, but she went on. "Big dreams. Dreams that may have cost her her life," she cried. "If she had never met my father—"

"You would've never been born," Damon finished. He pulled Nia to him and held her close to his heart. He wished he could take away some of the pain she was feeling, but he couldn't. Facing the past was inevitable. Nia was going to have deal with it one way or another.

"It's OK, baby." Damon rubbed her back.

Nia nestled close to him and let the tears flow. She didn't care if she was embarrassing herself. She just needed the comfort Damon provided.

"I know that in my head," Nia murmured against his chest. "But how can I reconcile the fact that she died bringing me into the world? How do I live with the guilt? She could have had such a rich life. Everyone said she was a great actress. She could have been something great."

"Nia." Damon tilted her chin up to him. "You can't blame yourself for her death. Things happen sometimes that are out of our control." Nia's eyes were bloodshot and her face was soaked with tears. He wiped them away with his hand.

"But it's not fair! She should have lived a long life," she wailed.

"I know, baby, I don't have all the answers," Damon replied. "I wish I did, though I doubt it would ease the pain you feel on having missed out not knowing your mother." He gave her shoulders a gentle squeeze. "But what about your aunt, she's been like a mother to you, hasn't she?"

"Yes, of course she has. But it's not the same."

"I know, but she loves you and she sacrificed a lot to care for you, her niece. She's raised you as if you were her own."

"Oh, God, you make me feel like such a heel. I've treated her so horribly."

"Nia, I'm sorry, I didn't mean to make you feel worse. You've been through enough tonight already."

"It's not your fault that I didn't have a father," she replied miserably.

"But if you want—"He paused, unsure if Nia

wanted to hear what he was thinking. He'd say it anyway; they wouldn't always agree. "Your father is here now and you could get to know him."

Nia jumped off the couch. "Are you serious?" She was furious. She couldn't believe Damon would think such a thing, let alone say it.

"Baby, listen—"

"You don't understand," Nia said, looking around for her purse. She couldn't stay there. Obviously she made a mistake in coming to Damon. He didn't understand. She should have called Lexie. Lexie would listen. Lexie would be on her side.

"No!" Damon shouted. "I will not let you run away from me and you're certainly in no condition to drive." He grabbed her arm. She tried yanking it away, but it was futile. He had a strong grip on her forearm.

"Please come back. You need to sit and calm down." He pulled her back down onto the couch. "I'm sorry if I offended you. I just thought it might help if you talked things out with your father. You know, clear the air."

"I have nothing to say to him," Nia said. "He walked out on my mother and thereby me. Never once in twenty-seven years has he tried to contact me. He left me with my aunt without a backward glance. He just went on living his life like I never existed. Like he never had a baby girl that needed him." Nia couldn't help it, the tears were forming again. "God, I can't take this." She tried to get up from the couch, but Damon wouldn't let her.

Reaching out, Damon hugged her tighter. Even when Nia pounded her fists against his chest, he didn't budge. He just let her fight him until she couldn't fight anymore. He knew she wasn't upset with him, but with her father. He had to let her release the rage she'd held inside for so long. Finally Nia quieted and he eased up, reaching over her to grab more tissues.

"Thank you." She took one and blew her nose.

"I have one final comment," Damon said. Nia threw him a murderous look. "You should hear him out. It can't hurt and it might help. Would you at least think about it?"

"Sure, but it doesn't matter." She sniffed.

"Why is that?"

"Because I told him to go to hell."

He laughed. "Now that I can believe." Suddenly everything seemed a little too dramatic. Nia threw a pillow at him and laughed, too. Damon threw a pillow back at her and the next thing she knew they were embroiled in a huge battle. To prevent one of her shots, Damon tackled her to the floor.

They looked at each for several long moments, neither sure of what to do next. Then at the same moment, they reached for each other. He kissed her and her anguish turned into a passion that matched his. Nia pulled him closer, for once becoming the aggressor.

Her lips teased his in a searing kiss. Easing her tongue between his lips, she explored his mouth. She wanted to feel his hard body against hers and curved her arm around his neck, pulling him forward. She trailed moist kisses down his face and then to his neck. She could feel him responding to her. There was no denying his arousal as she pressed her thighs firmly against him.

She'd never felt this way before. Every time she kissed him, she wanted more. Her body literally ached for him. She didn't know it was possible to feel this way, like her whole body was ready to explode. Those few moments with Spencer had never felt like this.

Nia let her hands roam down the strong contours of his back, finally resting on his firm, round buttocks. Nia heard his sharp intake of breath. She reveled in the hard feel of him as his silk pajama bottoms left very little to the imagination. More than anything, she wanted to be near him, wanted to feel the passion only Damon could quench. She started to unbutton her blouse, but Damon stopped her.

Damon knew kissing her was wrong, but he couldn't help himself. So he let her take charge, but he had to put a stop to it. Sex was not what she needed from him right now. What she needed was comfort and understanding, an ear to listen. Worst of all, he didn't want her to wake up tomorrow morning and regret having spent the night with him. He couldn't and wouldn't take advantage of her like that. When the time came, he wanted there to be no regrets and no recriminations. He wanted her to feel joy the morning after he'd spent all night making passionate love to her body until she quivered for more.

He eased himself off the floor, bringing Nia with him. Nia blushed. "I'm sorry," she murmured. "I shouldn't have come on to you like that. I don't want to be a tease." She started to rebutton her blouse.

"Don't be sorry," he whispered, bringing her hands to his lips and planting a kiss on them. "You know I want you, but I want to make love with you when the time is right, and now it isn't."

"You're right," she stated, smoothing her shirt. "I

think I should leave. I have to be at work in the morning."

"Are you sure you're okay?" he asked, helping her into her coat. He didn't want her driving if she was still upset. If anything happened to her, he didn't know what he'd do.

"Yes, I'm fine. I'm calm enough to drive home now. It's kind of funny though, because I don't remember how I made it here." She laughed.

"I don't even want to think about that," Damon said. "Just call me when you get home, okay?"

Nia stood on her tiptoes to give him a kiss before leaving. "I will."

Damon rushed to his balcony to watch her drive away.

# Chapter 10

Lexie called Nia at work the following day. "So, how was your weekend? Gosh, I didn't hear a word from you. Usually I can't shut you up. What gives?"

"Girl, you wouldn't believe it if I told you," Nia said, laughing. Her mind had wandered half the night. She'd tossed and turned until the wee hours of the morning. When she'd come in today, even Susan commented on the dark circles under her eyes. Of course, Susan had thought there might be another reason for her lack of sleep, namely a certain Damon Bradley. If only that had been the case, Nia thought wearily.

"The weekend was wonderful," she said, a little too cheerily. "The cabin where we stayed was absolutely gorgeous."

"Château." Lexie sighed. "Do tell and don't leave out any of the good stuff." Lexie was happy that Nia was finally letting go of the past and getting out and having some fun. She'd tried for years to get Nia to loosen up. That jerk Spencer Morgan had done some kind of number on her. When they went out for a night on the town, Lexie watched Nia turn down countless men. Many showed interest, though few actually made it to the finish line. She wondered what this Damon Bradley had that most didn't. A great body and fat wallet always helped, she thought. "So, did you share a room or what?"

"Slow down, Miss Thang," Nia said. "I can't get into all those details now. You do realize I am at work."

"You're holding out on me, but never fear, I'm coming for dinner and you can spill the beans." No matter how she tried to hide it, Lexie had caught the tone in Nia's voice and knew something was wrong.

"All right, what time?"

"Say, sevenish. You know I can never be any place on time."

"Sounds good to me. I'll see you then."

Nia processed some upcoming ad orders on her computer and didn't notice Chloe standing in her cubicle with a puzzled look on her face.

"Chloe," Nia said, startled. "What's up? Is something wrong?"

"Well," Chloe began, "it appears your presence has been requested in the conference room for that big ad campaign."

Nia's heart started pounding. She could hear it thumping. She dreaded asking the next question. "Which one?"

"It's not Bradley Savings & Loan, if that's what you're asking," Chloe replied. "It's Montgomery Supermarkets."

Nia muttered a curse word under her breath.

"What's going on, Nia?" Chloe asked, turning her employee's chair around to face her. She could see the distress on Nia's face. "Whoever this woman is, she requested you be involved in this project."

"Is that right?" Nia asked sarcastically. She couldn't

believe Kendall's nerve, to bring their personal lives into the workplace.

"Yes, as a matter of fact, she insisted on it, even after I assured her that the senior staff was capable of handling their campaign."

"Listen, Chloe," Nia started. She paused. Even though Chloe knew about her relationship with Damon, it wasn't a good idea to spill her business to her boss. "Although I appreciate the opportunity, I have a conflict of interest with both these campaigns."

"I know about Damon, but what do the Montgomerys have to do with this?"

"This woman, her name is Kendall Montgomery, right?" Nia asked. Chloe nodded. "Well, she's an ex-girlfriend of Damon's and has basically been stalking us." Chloe gave her a bewildered look. "I don't know any other way to put it. She showed up at the same nightclub we went to and even went so for as to follow us to Wisconsin to a ski resort."

"That could have been a coincidence," Chloe suggested.

"If this were any other person, I'd agree." Nia turned to face the window. "But because Damon's parents are close friends with the Montgomerys, it would have been very easy for her to find out our plans. Whatever the case, as you can see, I shouldn't be working on this campaign. Is there anything you can do?"

"I don't know," Chloe replied. "Mr. Whitmore is in there with her now. It's probably best that you make an appearance and I'll explain that you're working on another critical campaign. Okay?"

"You're a lifesaver." Nia threw her arms Chloe in a big hug.

Chloe smiled. "No problem. We'd better go."

Nia reached for a notepad and pen and walked with Chloe to the large conference room. Mr. Whitmore, Kendall and another man—Mr. Montgomery, she presumed—were all sitting around the conference table. Kendall was surreptiously nibbling on a croissant and giving Nia the once-over. Dressed smartly in a gray trouser suit and silk blouse, Kendall looked every bit the barracuda she was.

"Nia," Mr. Whitmore said, motioning for her to join them, "We've been waiting for you; the Montgomerys have expressed an interest in having you work on their upcoming ad campaign. It appears you're the woman of the hour, Ms. Taylor."

Nia hesitated. She wanted to make a quick exit.

"Please sit down," he said. "We have coffee and pastries."

Nia looked at Kendall and blithely ignored the daggers shooting from those oval-shaped eyes. Kendall was trying to make her uncomfortable, but Nia wasn't going to give her the satisfaction of looking away. Nia stared her directly in the eye.

Luckily, Chloe saved her. "Mr. Whitmore, if you remember, Nia is working on the Bradley campaign. As you well know, she was critical in coming up with the spot and I know I can depend on her to head it while I focus all my attention on the Montgomery campaign." Chloe smiled at everyone at the table.

"Of course, of course," Mr. Whitmore said. He turned to face Mr. Montgomery. "Chloe is our lead account executive, one of our shining stars." He winked at Chloe. "I believe your interests would best be served by having her work on your campaign while Nia handles one of our other clients."

Mr. Montgomery pondered this and nodded his head. He turned to his daughter. Kendall gave a dashing smile. "Of course, Father," she said. "If you feel that's best. We only want the best."

Nia let the snide remark pass. Kendall may have lost the battle, but Nia knew the war was far from over, as Kendall was a formidable opponent. "I'll get back to work, then," Nia said and left the conference room.

"If you'll excuse me, gentlemen." Kendall rose from her seat. "I'm going to go powder my nose." She exited and was hot on Nia's heels. Nia stopped dead in her tracks and spun around to face her nemesis.

"May I have a word with you?" Kendall asked. Not waiting to hear Nia's answer, she walked to the ladies' restroom down the hall. Reluctantly, Nia followed her.

"I have to hand it you," Kendall rasped, "you excellently maneuvered yourself off our campaign. Nice work."

Nia walked behind Kendall to stare at her reflection in the mirror and fluffed out her hair. "Why, thank you," she answered. Nia looked very professional in a slim, gray, Italian wool blend pinstripe suit with matching skirt and felt confident standing next to Kendall this time.

"But don't think it's over," Kendall responded, jabbing her finger in Nia's face. "I intend to win."

"I'm sure," Nia countered. She wouldn't let Kendall intimidate her. "But *this*, coming to my job. . . ? It's poor form even for someone like you. And if you're spoiling for a fight," Nia pointed her finger right back in Kendall's face, "I'll give it to you, but you may not like the outcome."

With that comment Nia stormed out of the restroom, leaving Kendall to stare after her.

Lexie arrived at Nia's apartment later that evening carrying a bottle of wine and their favorite veggie pizza: stuffed spinach. As usual, she looked stunning in a black miniskirt and lavender chiffon blouse.

"Thanks, girl." She took the pizza box from Lexie's arms and walked to the living room. "It smells delicious." Nia placed the box on the coffee table and threw some pillows down on the floor.

"I'll grab some glasses," Lexie said, heading to the kitchen and retrieving some wineglasses from the cupboard. "Your time is up now." She walked back into the living room. "Lay it on me." Lexie sat Indian style on the carpet.

Nia reached for a slice of pizza and took a bite. "Lexie, you would not believe how phat this place was," she began. "Damon told me we were staying at a lodge. But this place was no lodge. It was more like a palace, like one of those châteaux you see in Switzerland."

"Wow!" Lexie said. "It sounds like you've really snagged yourself a good one." She opened up the bottle of white zinfandel and poured herself and Nia a glass. "You know we all aren't so blessed to find a handsome and rich fellow."

"I'm sorry, Lexie," Nia said. "I have been a little full of myself these days, haven't I?"

"Yes, you have." Lexie handed her a glass. "But you need and sure as hell deserve it. I'm glad you've found yourself a man who appreciates you just as you are."

"Thanks," Nia said, reaching over to give Lexie a hug. "I can always depend on you to keep me sane and grounded. But, girl, there is more to the story. You will not believe who showed up at the resort."

Lexie held up her hand. "Please don't tell me. That skank of an ex-girlfriend that stepped up to you when you were in the bathroom at that nightclub."

"The one and only. I couldn't believe my eyes."

"So, what did you do?"

"I promptly scratched her eyes out," Nia said, laughing. Both women went into a fit of giggles. "No, seriously, I ran off like a big doofus. I'm sure Damon was real impressed. Anyway, we talked and hashed things out in spite of Miss Thang and salvaged the rest of the weekend."

"You should have put that witch in her place," Lexie said, munching on a slice of pizza. "You can't let her walk all over you."

"I know and I told her as much when she showed up at my job."

"You mean to tell me that hoochie showed up at your job?" Lexie asked. "Nia, it's time for the gloves to come off." Lexie put her fists up as if ready to box.

"Put your gloves down, Ali," Nia said, joking. "I told that chick she had a fight on her hands. I have no idea where things are headed between Damon and me, but I won't tolerate her continued interference." As an afterthought, she should have threatened Kendall that she would tell Damon. It would have sent the rat scurrying back to whatever hole she had crawled out of. Instead, Nia prided herself on how she'd handled Kendall. She'd walked out of that restroom with her head held high.

"Good for you," Lexie said with a smile, "'Cause you know if you need some backup, I'd be there to help you give that chick a beat-down she'd never forget."

Nia threw a pillow at Lexie.

"Did you know he was coming?" Nia inquired testily, standing over Aunt Livvie. She'd driven forty-five minutes to the south side just to confront her aunt, who was sitting on the sofa in her living room. "Did you know he was going to show up at my front door?"

"Yes, I did," her aunt replied. "Though I warned Nathaniel that it was ill-advised. I thought he would take my advice and give you time to adjust."

"Ya think?"

"There's no reason to be snippy, young lady. You don't know the full story about what happened all those years ago." She ran her fingers through her salt-and-pepper hair. "We were all so young and—"

"Then why don't you tell me, Auntie?"

"Because it's not my story to tell," her aunt Olivia answered. "If you spoke with him, then perhaps Nathan would fill you in."

"I am tired of waiting around for whatever it is all you are hiding from me," Nia said. "I am going to continue living my life and leave the past where it is, best left buried. Please relay that to Mr. Alexander."

Her aunt touched her face. It was an uncharacteristic movement for her. "Nia." She sighed when she saw the hard resolve in Nia's eye.

Nia saw the tears starting to fall down her aunt's cheeks, but she didn't want to be sucked into the past. Maybe she was afraid of what she might find there. Whatever the case, Nia knew she couldn't and wouldn't let Nathan Alexander walk into her life as if the last twenty-seven years had never happened. She patted her aunt's hand.

"I really have to go," she said. "I have plans this evening."

"With that Damon fellow again?"

"Yes, Auntie. I told you I've been seeing him."

"Is it serious?" her aunt asked. Judging from the smile beaming on Nia's face, she had her answer. Olivia had never seen that twinkle in Nia's eyes before.

As a child, when something was wrong, she could instantly see it on Nia's face. Then, Olivia could try to find a resolution. However, as Nia got older, it hadn't been as easy to decipher her feelings, especially about the opposite sex. Recently Olivia tried setting Nia up on several blind dates—until she'd been set straight. Nia had told her and whoever was listening (i.e. her grandfather) that she would not tolerate her family's interference in her personal life. She was a grown woman and could handle her own affairs or lack thereof.

Olivia had always hoped Nia would carve out a better life for herself, maybe meet a fine young man to settle down with and raise a couple of children. She didn't want Nia to end up like her: old and alone.

"I'm happy for you, dear."

"Thank you," Nia replied. "Who knows what will happen? We'll just have to wait and see." She held up her crossed fingers. "And whatever you do, please don't tell Grandpa. I don't want to put Damon through the Spanish Inquisition, though I'm sure he would jump at the chance."

Accepting the four introductory books for FREE (plus $1.99 to offset the cost of shipping & handling) places you under no obligation to buy anything. You may keep the books and return the shipping statement marked "cancelled". If you do not c about a month later we will send 4 additional Arabesque novels, and you will b billed the preferred subscriber's price of just $4.50 per title. That's $18.00* for all 4 books for a savings of almost 30% off the cover price (Plus $1.99 for shipping and handling). You may cancel at any time, but if you choose to continue, every month we'll send you 4 more books, which you may either purchase at the preferred discount price. . . or return to us and cancel your subscription.

* PRICES SUBJECT TO CHANGE

THE ARABESQUE ROMANCE CLUB: HERE'S HOW IT WORKS

PLACE
STAMP
HERE

THE ARABESQUE ROMANCE BOOK CLUB
P.O. BOX 5214
CLIFTON NJ 07015-5214

"All right," her aunt replied, crossing her heart. "But promise me you will bring your young man over for dinner so *I* can meet him."

"I promise," Nia said. "Anyway, I have to get out of here. I'll give you a call later this week." Nia kissed her aunt on the cheek and hopped in her car to drive to her apartment. It was odd that lately her aunt had become less reserved. For once, she actually looked happy.

A woman of her word, Nia brought Damon to Sunday dinner at her aunt's house the following week. It was a crisp afternoon when they arrived. The snow that fell the night before was slowly starting to melt from the afternoon sun. Nia appreciated that her aunt hadn't tattled about her new relationship to her grandfather.

"How do I look?" Damon asked, once they were out of the car and walking toward the house. He turned in a circle and Nia gave him a sideways glance. Damon looked marvelous, wearing a casual polo shirt that fit his well-defined chest, and khaki trousers that hung from his lean hips. Damon was the picture of masculinity and sexuality all rolled into one great package. With his glistening bald head and raw charm, her aunt would be toast.

"You look great as always," Nia said, brushing some imaginary lint off his shirt. She loved the feel of his strong shoulders. She may not be a small woman, but his arms had no problem holding her. "C'mon. My aunt is really a softie."

Nia fished in her purse for her keys and opened the front door.

"Mmm, what smells so good?" Damon asked, stepping inside. If he wasn't mistaken, it was some good down-home soul food. The aroma of fresh collard greens and smothered chicken wafted through the air. His mother only cooked soul food on the holidays or if either he or Jordan specifically requested it. Otherwise, she cooked healthy gourmet food. Whatever Ms. Taylor was cooking sure smelled delicious and he had come with a hearty appetite.

"Is that you, sweetie?" her aunt asked, walking into the hallway. She wiped her hands on her stained checkered apron.

Damon was surprised that Olivia Taylor was a petite woman. Somehow he had imagined a more domineering figure, from what he'd gathered from his conversations with Nia. Both women were short, although Nia was more curvaceous, and Nia's aunt had her same engaging smile, which she treated him to as she inspected him. He hoped he passed. Damon intended to make a good impression on the sole woman responsible for who Nia was today. Nia might still be in mourning for her biological mother, but Ms. Taylor was the one who'd been there when Nia needed someone.

"Welcome, Damon." Her aunt enveloped him in a hug he returned.

"Thank you for having me, Ms. Taylor. I brought these for you." He pulled a bouquet of roses from behind his back and presented them to her.

"They're lovely." Her aunt smiled, inhaling the fragrant blooms. "Thank you. Nia, go put these in some water while Damon and I have a talk." She handed Nia the flowers.

Nia looked back and forth between the two of them and figured that Damon would be fine alone with her aunt. She was relatively harmless, except when pushed.

"It's all right, girl," her aunt said. "We'll be fine." Damon inclined his head in agreement and Nia left the room.

Her aunt led him to the couch and patted the seat beside her. Damon obliged.

"So, tell me a little bit about yourself," Aunt Livvie started. She was eager to learn more about the man who had finally stolen Nia's heart. Damon Bradley must be a strong man with an iron will to break through the defenses Nia had put up over the years.

"Well, Ms. Taylor, I would have to say I'm a family man, first and foremost, and a business man second. I'm very close with my parents and younger sister."

"Family is very important," her aunt agreed. "I've tried to instill those values in Nia. And please call me Olivia."

"Of course, Olivia." Damon smiled. "Nia has talked of you and her grandparents often."

"Well, it's good to know Nia doesn't think of us too harshly. You see, her childhood wasn't that much fun."

"I'm aware of that, but what is important is right now."

"So tell me, Damon, what do you do for a living?" Olivia asked, offering him a plate of hors d'oeuvres that were sitting on the coffee table. Damon took a fried mushroom off the plate.

"I work for my father at Bradley Savings & Loan. I'm a vice president there."

"The bank on 87th Street? Oh, I bank there."

Nia's aunt nibbled on a chicken finger. "I have for years. How long have you worked for your father?"

"Hmmm, I don't know how long I've been working for the old man." He rubbed his chin. "Probably since some time in my early teens, though I would come in with my father when I was younger just to watch him in action."

"I'm sure your father must be very proud of you. He probably can't wait for you to follow in his footsteps."

"That's true," Damon answered. "He's grooming me to take over the business one day."

"So there's no reason for me to worry about your employment stability."

"Not at all, ma'am."

"I can tell by looking at you that my Nia is in safe hands."

"Thank you, I appreciate that," Damon said as he took her hand. "And I promise to never destroy the trust and faith you have in me."

She patted him on the back. "You're a good boy."

"Thank you, Ms. Taylor." Damon wiped his brow. "Whew! That was some interrogation. But I'm starved. Is it time to eat yet?"

Olivia smiled. She was so happy Nia had found a good man like Damon. "Yes, it is," she replied, standing up. "Let's go dig in."

# Chapter 11

The next couple of months went by in a blur for Nia. She and Damon spent a lot of time together, talking and getting to know each other. Nia loved the fact that they could converse on any given subject or just sit together quietly. Nia didn't feel like she had to keep her guard up all the time.

They had gone to several plays, which was just fine with Nia. The winter was prime theater season in Chicago and Nia looked forward to it every year. Just last week, Nia surprised Damon with tickets to the Chicago Bulls game courtesy of Dean, Martin & Whitmore. The more she got to know Damon, the harder she fell for him. It wasn't merely a physical attraction anymore. Their relationship had transcended that.

Tonight, Damon was playing chef. He professed great culinary talents, so Nia was eager to see if he was up to the task. She was sitting in the living room on Damon's black leather couch, sipping an excellent vintage white wine while Damon cooked up a delectable feast for her palate. She could smell the scents as they wafted to the living room.

Nia contented herself with exploring the rest of his condominium while he was in the kitchen. Damon had told her his mother decorated the place and she had outdone herself. His condo was situated on the lakefront of Lake Michigan, giving him a great view, and he loved his place, even though he had to travel almost an hour to Chicago's south side to go to work. Damon had put several logs in the built-in fireplace to give the place a cozy feeling.

The living room was completely decorated in black. A sleek, supple leather couch with thick padding and plump seat cushions was the main focus, along with an oval glass coffee table in the center of the room. Nia's personal favorite was a chaise longue where someone could sprawl out after a hard day's work.

Damon's mother used warm colors in the dining room, rich browns and mauves, and kept the artwork to a minimum. Several small pieces of African art were placed strategically throughout the condo. One in particular captured Nia's interest—it was of a mother holding her baby to her chest. The painting depicted a mother's love for her child. It was a very powerful statement.

"You like that one?" Damon asked, wiping his hands on the apron wrapped around his middle. He was standing in the kitchen doorway, staring back at her.

"Yes, it's very interesting," Nia said.

"It's one of my favorites, too," he said. "Mom has a great eye." He walked toward Nia. "Would you like a refill?" He nodded to her half-empty wineglass.

"Yes, thank you."

He handed the goblet back to her after he refreshed it at the minibar. "Are you ready for dinner?"

"Hmm, yes." She patted her stomach. "I'm starved. What did you cook?"

Damon took her hand and brought her over to the dining room. "I've cooked a masterpiece of perfection." He held out a chair and she sat down. Leaning over her, he lit the two candlesticks on the table with a starter. "Wait right here and I'll bring everything out."

Nia couldn't wait. She was famished. Since she started going out with Damon, she'd eaten decidedly less—she'd already lost ten pounds. The last thing she needed was to gain weight; she'd probably scare the poor man away.

She turned when she heard him behind her. "Can I help?" she asked, standing when she saw he was balancing a platter of food in each hand.

"No, you may not," he instructed. "Just have a seat and let me serve you."

Put in her place, Nia sat down and watched him put the steaming platters on the table. Damon had taken special care with everything, from the serving dish arrangement to placement of the candles and centerpiece. He went back to the minibar and brought another wine bottle to the table.

Damon wanted everything to be perfect. He had something very important to ask Nia and he was hoping she would agree. He leaned over to cut the main entree.

"It smells delicious. What is it?"

"It's veal loin with a peach glaze, parsley potatoes and asparagus." Nia clapped her hands in praise and Damon took a bow. He took Nia's plate and placed a generous portion of meat, potatoes and vegetables on it. Nia accepted it happily. Was he telling her she needed to eat more? Or perhaps it was a test to make sure she didn't eat it all. She resolved to make sure she left some on the plate.

Damon smiled. He followed her train of thought. He'd noticed that her hearty appetite had decreased and he was hoping it wasn't due to him. Didn't she know he wanted her to be herself?

Nia took a forkful of the succulent meat and sighed. "This is wonderful, Damon." She reached for a roll from the basket, lightly buttering it.

"Thanks. I'm glad you like it," Damon said, taking a bite as well. He pondered over whether to ask the question in the back of his mind. Should he ask now or later? Later won out.

They enjoyed the rest of the meal and managed to polish off the entire bottle of white wine. They rinsed off the dishes, placing them in the dishwasher before retiring to the living room for coffee and dessert. Damon had whipped up a couple of espressos to go along with a decadent pastry tart. He popped a disk into the DVD player and Nia snuggled into his warm, masculine arms. The movie was inconsequential because they probably wouldn't watch it anyway. Every time they were together, they couldn't keep their hands off each other and tonight was no different. Nia wanted to feel Damon's arms wrapped around her in a sensual embrace.

Now that they were settled, Damon felt he could broach the subject of sex and ask the question that was on his mind all evening. Over the past few months, he and Nia had spent a great deal of time together and he wanted, no, make that needed, to be with her. He hoped Nia was ready to take that next step in their relationship. He knew he was. His whole body ached every time he was with her. The slightest touch of her hand caused his whole body to go into overload.

He stroked her soft brown hair. She turned slightly to look up at him questioningly. "Nia," he began. He took her petite hands in his. "You know I enjoy spending time with you, right?"

She nodded in agreement, encouraging him to continue. "You know how much I care for you?" He turned her completely around to face him. He needed to see the look in her eyes to know for sure that this was what she wanted, too.

"Do you know how much I want you?" he asked. Nia's big brown eyes widened. Damon cupped her face in his palms before bringing it down to crush her lips beneath his in a mind-blowing kiss. She shifted slightly and felt his arousal against her belly. When his lips left hers, Nia was still hungry for more.

"Nia, I can't wait any longer," Damon groaned huskily. He ran his hands through her hair, pulling her close to him. "Please tell me I can have you?"

"Now?" she managed to croak out. She couldn't think with him touching her, stroking her hair, caressing her hot, fevered flesh. Now was not the right time. Hell, she didn't even have on sexy underwear.

"No," Damon said. "Not now." He trailed moist kisses down her neck and then licked her earlobe teasingly.

"When then?" Nia moaned in pleasure.

"What would you say to me planning a romantic getaway for the two of us?" His hands cupped her generous bottom and gave a gentle squeeze.

"Damon," she sighed, "that would be wonderful."

She wrapped her arms around his neck and planted a big kiss on his lips.

"All right," he said, gently extricating himself from Nia's arms. He didn't know if he could withstand just fooling around right now.

"Where are you going? I thought we were comfy." She smiled, curving her lips seductively with outstretched arms.

He couldn't suppress thoughts of taking her naked body in his arms. He was ready to have his cake and eat it, too. "I'll set things up for next weekend. Do you think you can take Friday off?"

Nia stood and answered him with a tender kiss.

"Easy now," he growled. "We'll have plenty of time for that in a couple of weeks." It appeared that Nia was as anxious as he was to move their relationship forward; soon she would be his completely.

"Lexie, this one shows way too much cleavage," Nia said, handing her a lacy nightie over the dressing-room door. She and Lexie were at Victoria's Secret picking out lingerie.

Nia had picked an assortment of lacy bras with matching panties and garter belts. They were now on a search for *the* gown as well as a teddy. Nia had always wanted one, but until now had never had the courage to buy one.

"Try this one." Lexie passed Nia a sexy black lace teddy. "This will knock him dead. He'll be imagining what you have on underneath all evening. It'll give him an instant hard-on."

"No doubt," Nia whispered from behind the dressing-room door.

"So, how does it look?"

"Lexie, it's perfect." She couldn't believe her eyes; she actually looked sexy. She pivoted around in the mirror.

"Let me see." Lexie knocked on the door. Nia opened the door and her friend scooted inside.

"Wow! Look at Miss Sexy Mama." Lexie laughed. "Girl, you look great. See, I told you. All you need is a little confidence and, of course, the right teddy."

Nia stared at the image in the mirror. She was no Kendall Montgomery, but she definitely looked hot in this getup.

"Now," Lexie said, "we have to get you some sexy black thigh-highs and the pièce de résistance." She threw her hands in the air. "Tall strappy sandals. Get dressed and be sure to put that teddy in your shopping basket. It's coming with us." Lexie walked out of the dressing room.

Nia hurriedly dressed and picked up her basket. Lexie was waiting on the other side of the door with the teddy's matching sheer robe. Nia gave her stern look, but Lexie threw it in her basket anyway.

"All I ask," Lexie said, pulling her aside, "is if you are going to have sex with Damon, you take this." Lexie handed Nia a box of condoms from her purse.

"Lex," Nia blushed, "put those away, we're in public."

"No." Lexie pushed them into her hand. "You're going to take these and protect yourself. You remember my pregnancy scare, don't you?"

"Lexie, I'm sorry. I didn't realize you still thought about it."

"Hey, I don't want to talk about my past mistakes.

This is your day. So let's get a move on it." She walked toward the checkout counter.

"Are you sure?" Nia asked, touching her arm.

"Absolutely." She smiled at Nia. "Listen, all I want is for you to be careful. No, make that responsible. You have no idea where he's been. Or whom he's been with."

"You're right," Nia said thoughtfully. "I guess I hadn't really thought about it. I know I haven't been sexually active, but Damon—"

"I'm sure he has a healthy sexual appetite just like every other red-blooded man," Lexie replied. "Just take those and use them."

"I will."

Later that evening in her apartment, Nia remembered Lexie's earlier comment as she packed for her weekend getaway. Getting pregnant was something she'd always feared, which was maybe why she'd postponed having sex since Spencer.

Growing up on the south side of Chicago, it had been impossible for her not to see teen pregnancy or single mothers in poverty. Even when she visited, she could still see it. Nia didn't want to end up like the women she saw in her grandfather's church. She wanted to be better than that, make smarter choices.

But she was human after all and she was ready to move her relationship with Damon forward. They had come so far and in such short time. She felt more safe with him than anyone else she'd ever known. Whenever she was with him, the sexual tension burned just below the surface and she was about ready to erupt. Nia knew Damon felt the same way. She knew that only kissing her was driving him mad. And her, too. She wanted to know what it felt like to have his arms around her as she took him inside her body. She was naturally curious after all these years to know the kind of joy she could experience with Damon.

Nia had no idea where Damon was taking her. He suggested that she pack light, nothing heavy. She assumed they were going someplace warm, away from the cold Chicago winds. Nia was sure Damon would wine and dine her, so she'd better be prepared with something fancy to put on. She wouldn't want to embarrass him by being inappropriately dressed like she had been on their ski trip. Looking in her closet for eveningwear, she found a nice cream sheath that would make her size-ten figure look generous rather than fat. For good measure, she threw in a beaded slip dress she'd managed to fit back into after all these years. The dress stopped above the knee and the spaghetti straps showed off her bare shoulders.

Closing the closet door, Nia walked into the living room to find her Victoria's Secret bag. She took her purchases back to the bedroom and carefully packed a mixture of new lingerie along with the necessary toiletries, shoes and such. Saving the best for last, Nia pulled a white silk gown and matching sheer robe out of the bag. The beautiful gown was made of satin except for an intricate pattern of interwoven lace at the bodice. She hoped Damon would enjoy seeing her in it, though he would probably have more fun taking it off.

Nia's appointment at the Red Door Spa was the finishing touch and had been exactly what she needed. She'd received the works: a massage, facial, manicure and pedicure, and thrown in a wax job for good measure. Now she felt ready to allow

Damon to see her naked. She imagined Damon running his fingers down her supple breasts.

Her phone rang. "Hello," she answered exasperatedly, irritated that her daydream had been interrupted.

"Hello, gorgeous," Damon replied. It was none other than the source of her fantasies. Did he have telepathy?

"Hi, Damon, what's up?"

"I was calling to find out if you were all packed and ready to be swept off your feet." He sounded eager with anticipation. He wasn't the only one.

"Yes, I'm ready. Can't you give me the slightest hint as to where we're going?"

"I'm sorry, darling." He laughed. "No can do. I want you to be pleasantly surprised. Don't worry, it'll be very romantic."

"I've no doubt it will be," Nia replied. She tossed a pillow playfully in the air and caught it. "I'm looking forward to this weekend."

"So am I," Damon said. "The two of us, alone together. It will be magic." Nia heard the glee in his voice and imagined him rubbing his hands together in anticipation.

"Until tomorrow, then."

"Good night, Nia, and sleep well, my darling," he whispered huskily. Placing the receiver back in the cradle, Nia fell onto the bed. She loved it when he used endearments. It made her feel special, like she was the only woman in the world for him. She perused her suitcase one final time before deciding she'd packed everything necessary for her trip. She'd make a final check in the morning.

Entering the bathroom, Nia completed her nightly ritual. She brushed her teeth, washed her face, changed into her pajamas and wrapped her hair in a scarf. Turning off the lights, she went to her bedroom and climbed into bed.

Not knowing what to expect from her lovemaking with Damon was foremost in her mind because she had no form of reference to compare it to. Her experience with Spencer had been minimal, leaving a sour taste in her mouth, and she hadn't been eager to repeat it. She remembered how Spencer had called her frigid and unresponsive. It was why she chose to remain celibate over the years. She'd wondered if there was something wrong with her, but when she was with Damon it was different—the exact opposite, in fact. One look or a feather-light touch from Damon and Nia instantly responded. Damon brought out her passionate nature.

What would it be like to make love to Damon? Would he be a good lover? Would he take his time, putting her needs before his own? Knowing the kind of person Damon was, Nia figured as much. He was always so willing to do anything for her; she didn't imagine he would be selfish in the bedroom.

Pulling the comforter close, Nia closed her eyes. Her last thought was that tomorrow at this very time, she and Damon would become lovers.

# Chapter 12

At the airport later the next afternoon, Nia was in for the surprise of her life. Tickets in hand, Damon led her to the counter for their departing flight to New Orleans.

"Oh, Damon," she exclaimed, throwing her arms around his neck and giving him a kiss on the cheek. "I can't believe you arranged this. You know I've always wanted to go the Big Easy." She would finally get a chance to try some of the local dishes like jambalaya, shrimp étouffée and gumbo.

"I know, I know," he answered, giving her a gentle squeeze. "I remember you mentioning it. Plus, it's one of the most romantic cities you'll ever see. Trust me, you'll love it." He leaned down to give her a kiss on the forehead. "And wait until you try the beignets and café au lait at Cafe du Monde."

They boarded the plane shortly thereafter and Nia snuggled in Damon's arms for the short flight. Damon arranged for a chauffeur to meet them upon their arrival at New Orleans International Airport. The chauffeur took their bags and escorted them to the limo, opening the door to allow Nia to enter. Nia ducked inside and Damon followed.

It was luxurious, with plush seats, a minibar and built-in television.

"Oh, Damon," Nia said, sighing.

"You like?" Damon asked, resting his arm lightly around the back of her neck.

"What do you think?" She smiled. "I can't wait to see what else you have in store." She laid her hand on his leg and felt it flinch. "Is something wrong?"

"No, sweetheart," he whispered. "It's just excitement." He couldn't say that her touch produced a chemical reaction. Instead, he leaned over her to push down the windows. "Look around you."

Nia did as instructed and peered out the limousine. She was amazed at the beauty and quaintness of her surroundings, the lush neighborhoods with the grand colorful mansions, Creole town homes and streetcars that lined the roads of the French Quarter. It was all so magnificent. She couldn't wait to see the hotel where they were staying, and when the limousine stopped, she was not disappointed.

Their hotel was cozily tucked in a quiet part of the French Quarter, away from all the noise and craziness of Bourbon Street, but close enough to walk. She took Damon's proffered hand and stepped out of the vehicle. Looking up at the historic inn, Nia instantly fell in love with the colorful nineteenth-century architecture. The lushly landscaped courtyard looked tranquil and intimate, hidden behind several large trees and blooming plants. They quickly checked in and the hostess led them to their bedroom with a private balcony.

A four-poster canopied bed with a paisley duvet cover stood prominently in the room, accompanied by antique cherry wood furniture throughout the suite. She wasn't sure what century it was but it sure looked historic as well as classy. Not that she'd expect anything less than the best from Damon.

The master bath was to die for. The spa bath could fit an army and the marble countertops gave the room a luxurious feeling.

"Damon, the room is absolutely lovely," she exclaimed, coming out of the bathroom. "You've thought of everything. I mean, spring in New Orleans—what could be more romantic?"

She threw open the terrace doors. Their balcony overlooked a huge pool. Nia inhaled deeply, jumping slightly when she felt Damon's presence behind her. He wrapped his arms around her midsection.

"I'm glad you like it, baby," he murmured. "This is all for you. And just you wait, there's more in store." Nia turned around to face Damon and saw the naked hunger burning in his eyes.

"I can't wait, but first we have to wash up for dinner." She smiled and ducked away into the bathroom.

"You look beautiful and sexy as hell," Damon commented when Nia emerged from the master bath a short while later. Dressing entirely for Damon's benefit, Nia wore a form-fitting, black, stretch lace dress with a plunging neckline. At the last minute she'd thrown the dress in her suitcase, a loan from Lexie. It was clearly the most provocative thing she had ever worn in Damon's presence, if his shell-shocked expression was anything to go by.

She was equally as smitten. Damon looked very dashing in a formal black suit and white tuxedo shirt. The saying was definitely not true about the clothes making the man. Her man did everything for the clothes that hung from his strong masculine body.

"Baby, let's get this evening started," he said.

"That lunch on the plane was horrid. I could eat a horse right about now." Nia laughed and linked her arm with his.

They dined at Arnaud's, a popular New Orleans restaurant. Nia had heard reviews about the place and had seen it on the Food Network, but nothing could compare to the dining experience. The intimate ambience and soft décor were breathtaking. The waiter had seated them in a secluded alcove where they enjoyed a four-course meal of Shrimp Arnaud as an appetizer, a mixed greens salad and spicy Shrimp Creole served over a bed of rice pilaf for the entree. The food was as beautifully decorated as it was delicious.

Later, after piping hot espressos and crème brûlée for dessert, Nia and Damon stopped at a local jazz club for some live music and took to the dance floor. Damon pulled her into his arms and meshed their bodies together.

Nia laid her head on his chest, wanting to dance away all her fears in his arms. Their bodies swayed to the rhythmic music and the rest of the room blurred. She was oblivious to everything surrounding her.

The warmth from Damon's body slowly invaded her senses. She could hear his heart thumping wildly, hear him taking deep, steady breaths. After tonight she would never be the same.

"Are you ready to go?" Damon asked. Nia had felt his growing arousal against her middle while they danced to the music.

Nia paused, faltering for a second. "Umm." Damon looked at her intently. Was he looking for doubt? She didn't have any. She nodded and answered firmly, "Yes, I am." She was ready to put them both out of their misery and experience bliss in his arms. He took her hand and together they left the nightclub.

Nia stared at herself in the mirror. The new white silk charmeuse gown with side slits hung elegantly down her narrow shoulders and flowed to her ankles. She'd already showered and lathered her body with peach-scented lotion, dusted her face with a light powder and moistened her lips with a sheer lip gloss.

Looking down, she noticed her hands shook. *Relax*, she told herself. Although Spencer Morgan was the past, he was having a profound effect on her present. Because of him she'd avoided emotional and physical entanglements with men. She'd allowed him to control her life for too long.

She wondered if Damon would be pleased with her body. Would his fascination with her end once they had sex? Now she was unsure of herself.

Nia shook her head. No, no, no. She had to stop this. *This* was something she was looking forward to. She had come a long way from that cramped dorm room many years ago.

She emerged from the adjoining bath, a little nervous, but with a lot more resolve.

Damon's hungry gaze drew her to him as she walked into his open, waiting arms. His eyes were so expressive and she saw the depth of emotion in them. It sent shivers down her spine to know just how much he wanted her. If she wasn't careful, she could easily fall in love with him.

"I've wanted you for so long, Nia." Damon took her hand in his when she approached him. "Your hands are shaking," he said. He brought her hand to his mouth and lightly caressed her palm until finally planting a kiss on each fingertip. Her eyes fluttered.

"I'm just a little nervous," Nia replied.

"Here, take a sip of this," he said, handing her a flute filled with champagne. She gingerly took a sip. "Nia, are you sure you're ready for this?"

As much as he wanted her, he didn't want to pressure her. Nia had confided in him about her first sexual encounter and how horrible it had been. He wished he knew the bastard who'd hurt her so he could strangle him for damaging her self-confidence. Damon hoped their lovemaking would erase her doubts about her body and her sexuality. Once he could show her how desirable she was, how hard she made him, she'd realize just how sexy she was.

"I just want to love you." He gathered Nia in his arms and her wrap fell to the floor. "Will you let me?" He tilted her chin.

"Yes," she whispered softly, her voice barely audible.

He didn't need any further invitation. He pressed his mouth against hers. Coaxing her lips apart, he dipped inside to taste her sweet nectar. He loved the feel of her, relished the honeyed interior of her mouth.

Nia responded by returning his ardor. His wet, erotic kisses were driving her mad.

"Baby, you taste so good," he whispered, his voice thick with desire. "I want you so much. Tell me you want me as much as I want you." Damon couldn't bear it if she pushed him away now. He searched her eyes for a sign of whether to stop.

When he didn't find one, he slid the satin gown down her shoulders and let it glide into a silk puddle on the floor. Only her tiny lace bikini panties shielded her from his intense scrutiny. Slightly embarrassed, Nia held her head down; she knew she didn't have the perfect body.

"Nia, don't be afraid," Damon crooned, cupping her face. She was more beautiful than he could have imagined in his wildest dreams. He didn't know how much longer he could control his acute hunger for her. Pulling her to him, he kissed her deeply. Nia moaned in protest when his lips left hers and licked his way to her chocolate-brown nipples.

Red-hot flames of desire engulfed her when he slowly drew one erect peak into his mouth. Applying intense suction, his fingers trailed a slow, leisurely path down to her navel. Nia was awash with pleasure as he bathed her sensitive flesh with his tongue and dipped his fingers inside to tease her belly button. Before she knew it, his fingers hooked on to her lace panties and slid them down her legs. She gasped when he slid one finger inside her moist center.

She was hot, wet and incredibly tight. He enjoyed the sweet friction as she bucked against his searching fingers.

When the sweet flow of her climax washed in waves over her, Nia grabbed hold of his shoulders for support. She had never experienced such a thing and marveled at the emotions that engulfed her.

The next thing she knew, Damon was lifting her into his arms as if she were as light as a feather. Gently laying her down, he pulled back the paisley duvet cover before joining her on the bed. He continued his onslaught by touching her stomach and planting moist kisses along her middle. When he parted her thighs and caressed with his tongue the tiny nub at the center of her womanhood, her spine arched and she panted in pleasure, moaning his name over and over.

She needed him inside her, she couldn't remember ever wanting anything more in her life. She brought his lips back to hers, loving the rough masculine feel of his mouth as it branded her. Then she felt that peculiar feeling again. Could it be another climax? She had read women could have multiple orgasms, but she never dreamed she would be one of them.

Damon looked into her eyes. He loved watching her reaction as he kissed, teased and caressed every inch of her body. He wanted to release all her inhibitions and banish all memories of the bastard that messed with her head and caused her to be so insecure. There were all kinds of sexual experiences and positions between a man and a woman. And he was going to show her each and every one of them. He wanted to possess her, make her completely his.

Standing up, he stripped himself of his pajama bottoms as Nia watched his every movement. She was mesmerized by his beautiful body. It was lean and hard. She swallowed as her gaze traveled to his sex straining against his briefs. Swiftly he removed them and knelt down on the bed beside her. Nia blushed when she thought of that very intimate part of him being joined with hers. She had never seen a nude man. With Spencer, they had been in the dark and he had jumped on top of her before she'd had a chance to look at him. It wouldn't be that way with Damon, she could see that now.

For Damon, Nia was his fantasy come to life. Just watching her had turned him on, so he allowed her to rove her hands over his broad chest, let her lightly stroke his nipples, all the while ignoring his body's demands to take her fast and quick and put an end to the torture. Nia deserved better than that Damon thought. He would take things slow and easy.

Rolling to his side, he reached for a condom on the nightstand and quickly protected himself. Nia watched him, feeling like a complete idiot. In the midst of her passion, she had gotten careless. Protection had been the last thing on her mind when Damon was doing all those incredible things to her with his hands and tongue. She was thankful his common sense prevailed.

Damon turned to find her watching him. "Next time you can help me put it on." He smiled knowingly.

"Next time? We haven't finished the first time."

"Trust me. The whole box will be gone before the weekend is over." He pulled her to him and lightly nudged her thighs apart with his knee. Balancing his weight on his forearms, he angled over her and pressed forward into her tight passage.

He felt her immediately tense up. She sheathed him, holding him inside her tightly. He became absolutely still, giving her time to adjust to his size. He didn't want to move for fear of hurting her, but a foreign feeling was gathering inside Nia's loins and she couldn't wait. She started to rock her hips, which sent a rocket of pure pleasure racing through him.

His hands slid down to grasp her bottom as he thrust deep inside her, filling her completely.

"Wrap your legs around me," he groaned. Nia did as instructed, completely beside herself as Damon slowly withdrew, only to thrust in again. In and out. In and out. The intimate feel of his thick manhood inside her was incredibly erotic, and before she knew it, tiny rockets shot through her head and her whole body exploded.

Meanwhile, Damon was close to the apex. Lifting Nia's buttocks, he thrust one final time and gave a shout as his body shuddered in climax and a wave of pleasure overtook him. Collapsing on top of her, he buried his face in her hair, loving the feel and smell of its coconut scent.

They hugged each other as they rolled over, still joined as one in a tangled mass of limbs. Leaning against his chest, Nia listened to his labored breathing. She felt completely like a woman now. After being joined in the most intimate way with a man, the way God intended them to be, she was in heaven.

When they finally separated a short while later, Damon cradled her in his arms. Her body felt so languid and sanguine. Was is possible to feel this good?

Damon smoothed her hair back from her brow and tilted her head upward with his index finger. He was greeted with tears streaming down her cheeks.

"Are you all right, did I hurt you?" He knew he had. She was very tight and he'd tried to remain gentle, but he'd wanted her too much.

"I'm fine," Nia murmured, looking away.

"Nia?" he turned her jaw to face him.

"OK, I'm a little sore, but that's to be expected, right?" She sighed. "I mean, it has been a while. But, Damon, sweetheart," Nia saw the anguished look on his face, "it was amazing. Being with you this way. I never knew—" She was unable to put into words how he made her feel.

He smiled. He didn't want to think of ever hurting Nia; she meant so much to him. "The two of us, we can't go wrong as long as we're together. We were meant to be together. You were made for me," Damon crooned in her ear. "The chemistry between us is so strong, so potent, so right."

He wasn't amazed that Nia was so responsive to him. The passion had always been there, right beneath the surface, lying dormant and waiting to explode. She had given herself wholeheartedly, holding nothing back. He was grateful she had allowed him to share this experience with her. He wanted to make love to her over and over again, but he didn't want her to experience any more discomfort than necessary. He would wait before taking her again.

He looked down and found that Nia had drifted into a blissful sleep. Cuddling next to her, he closed his eyes.

When Nia awoke the next morning, she found the bed empty with only an indentation of where Damon had lain. Where was he? She looked around the room and saw his pajama bottoms strewn across a chair. Then she heard the shower running and breathed a sigh of relief. It was a crazy thought; Damon wasn't going anywhere, but in the cold light of morning, everything looked different, felt different.

It was as if she had been in a dense fog and it had suddenly been lifted. Did everyone feel like this the morning after sex? Nia felt like she was on cloud nine and nothing could bring her back down to earth. She wished she could hold on to this feeling forever and never let it go.

Damon strolled through the master bedroom a few minutes later, wearing a towel wrapped around his middle. He looked absolutely spectacular. He came toward the bed, giving her an intense look of sexual heat. She blushed as she remembered that very same look last night when he'd made love to her for the first time. Looking down, Nia was right. His manhood was jutting forth and ready for action.

"Good morning, beautiful." Damon leaned over the bed to give her a kiss on the forehead. He'd loved her frank and open adoration of his body last night. It had excited him, knowing Nia found him equally attractive.

"Good morning, Damon."

"How do you feel?" he asked, pulling the covers away slowly to reveal Nia's bosom. Her breasts were as perfect as he remembered, soft and supple. He teased one nipple between his fingers until it stood out like a plump raisin. If he'd had his way, he would have made love to her all night long.

"I feel great." Nia smiled and reached for the covers. "Never better."

It amazed him that she was still self-conscious after their night of lovemaking. He'd thought of nothing else during the night and had woken up with a major hard-on that morning. Jumping into the shower diffused the situation somewhat. But seeing her now, he desperately wanted to be with her again and feel her sweet heat wrapped around him. He feared she was still sore, so he'd have to show some restraint.

"Ah-ah-ah," Damon murmured, slapping her hand away and retaining a firm grasp on the bed linen. "There's nothing you have that I haven't seen already. Or touched. Or kissed." He smiled when she blushed. He leaned in and softly began to kiss the nape of her neck, making his way to her belly button.

"Damon." Nia sighed, her head falling back onto the pillow. She accepted his weight as he joined her on the bed. Damon just loved the way she moaned his name. He wanted to hear her cry it out as he took her to the heights of pleasure, but there would be plenty of time for that later. Wrapping Nia's arms around his neck, Damon hoisted her off the bed and carried her to the adjoining bathroom where a luxurious bubble bath awaited. He laid her gently down in the tub.

Nia was touched by his thoughtfulness. She caressed his cheek and smiled. "You didn't have to do this."

"I know." He smiled back. "I thought you might be a little sore from last night."

"Mmm, this feels great," Nia moaned, lying back into the generous spa bath. The water jets pulsed through the water, soothing her sore, underused muscles.

"I want you to relax and enjoy this moment," he said, leaning down to give her a quick peck on the lips, "because I have a lot planned for us. New Orleans awaits you, my lady."

* * *

Thirty minutes later, when Nia emerged from her spa bath wearing nothing but a robe, she felt immensely refreshed. Nia noticed that Damon, always thoughtful, had arranged for beignets and café au lait from Cafe du Monde to be delivered to their room.

"Oh, Damon," she said, smiling. Nia had always wondered about the popular doughnuts. She rushed over to the table to join him for a late breakfast. Damon leaned over to give her a bite of the powdery doughnut and she took a nibble.

"Heavenly," Nia murmured, opening her mouth for another bite as Damon obliged her. He was already dressed in light khakis and a polo shirt and ready for the day. She'd thought they'd have more time in bed. Of course, there was always tonight.

They sat together at the small round table, eating their beignets and drinking coffee. Nia watched Damon read the paper, completely dumbfounded. He was very much at ease as if he did this every day. *Well, Nia, he is a thirty-year old man,* she told herself. *You're not his first lover, although I feel he's mine.*

"Darling, do you intend to stay in that robe all day?" Damon asked. "Or are you going to get dressed so I can show you the town?" As he read the paper, he noticed Nia surveying him over the rim of her coffee cup. "Of course, if you want me to take you back to bed, I would be more than happy to oblige."

"Damon," she replied huskily, taking a sip from her café au lait, "you're wicked!"

"Yes, I am," he replied. He wiped the foam from her upper lip with his finger and licked it off. "And you love it." Nia playfully threw her napkin at him and got up from the table to start the day.

Damon arranged for a carriage ride down the infamous Bourbon Street, allowing her to take in the sights, detailed ironwork architecture and sounds of the French Quarter. Nia was enthralled with the laissez-faire atmosphere that inhabited the streets.

And that wasn't all. Their day was fun-filled with a visit to the Pontchartrain Vineyard and Winery for a tour and wine tasting. Nia enjoyed the fruity and bold-flavored wines immensely. She was even a little bit tipsy afterward. Damon, being quite stalwart, said the wine hadn't affected him, but Nia could tell he'd had his fill, too.

They stopped for lunch at the Gumbo Shop and Nia got to try a true New Orleans po' boy, piled high with shrimp and served on crusty French bread with a side of fries and a pickle. It was delicious. They even had the opportunity to stroll through Mardi Gras World to look at the colorful floats and helium balloons that adorned the streets of the French Quarter during the festival.

They spent the next evening on a paddle-wheel boat for dinner with live jazz by a local band that was surprisingly quite good. Later, they enjoyed hurricanes at Pat O'Brien's, where the citrus-flavored drinks were very potent.

*New Orleans is amazing,* Nia thought on the last evening. They were riding back to the hotel after having had a fantastic time exploring the diverse city, meandering through the French Quarter and stopping to look in the antiques shops. Damon had even humored her and had her palm read.

For dinner, Damon took her to Club 360°, a revolving cocktail lounge on the thirty-third floor of the World Trade Center for drinks and dinner. They'd fed each other slowly, both savoring each bite.

It had felt good to be with Damon, just the two of them in a romantic city. She felt secure and safe and wished they could stay like this forever. The bond they'd created grew stronger with each passing day. Nia refused to put a name on her feelings, afraid of what she might discover.

"What's wrong?" Damon asked. He had been so in tune with her feelings and needs over this weekend. He seemed to know exactly what she wanted or needed at any given moment. It was intoxicating.

"I'm fine," she said. "Just a little tired."

"I hope not too tired for this." He imprisoned her in his arms and gave her a slow, torturous kiss, a promise of more to come once they reached the hotel. She couldn't wait either. Their lovemaking was intense and defied description.

The driver came around to open the vehicle door when their limo reached the hotel. They exited and walked hand in hand inside the hotel. Once she reached their suite, Nia headed to the bathroom to start a bubble bath.

Turning on the taps, she poured a generous amount of the Aveda bath solution in the water and watched the bubbles form. She was starting to undress, completely oblivious that she was being watched until she noticed Damon standing in the doorway.

"Would you like some company?" Damon queried. Nia raised her brow.

"What do you think?" she teased, dropping the

remainder of her clothing and climbing into the marble whirlpool. He let out a whoop before shrugging quickly out of his clothes and joining her in the tub. He moved to settle Nia between his thighs so she could lean against him and her round bottom could nestle against his manhood. He lathered her body with a soapy sponge and Nia sighed. She never knew such delicious ecstasy could exist and turned around to give him a sensuous kiss. Taking his tongue deep in her mouth, she sucked on it voraciously. He responded by pulling her firmly to him. She could feel his full arousal pressing against her belly and she ached to take him inside her body.

Nia reached down to caress his arousal and heard his sharp intake of breath.

He urged her to stroke his length. She was awed by the power of his manhood and the pleasure she derived from him. He knew just how and where to touch her to send her into orbit.

"Do you have any idea what you're doing to me?" he rasped. His tongue probed the inside of her mouth while his hands roamed the shape of her breasts and contours of her body. His finger slipped inside to tease her feminine core.

"Damon!" Nia cried out. She teetered on the edge of a mind-blowing orgasm as Damon continued to tease her with his hand. When he quickened the pace, she bucked against him.

Damon couldn't wait; her soft whimpers were driving him mad. He stood up, gently pulling Nia with him. He wrapped them both in huge fluffy towels, taking care to slowly dry Nia's body before picking her up and carrying her to the bed.

Nia was ready as she waited for Damon to part

her legs. Instead, he opened the drawer by the bed and pulled out some body oil. Slowly he drizzled massage oil down her shoulders, massaging it into her skin, starting first with her shoulders, making his way down to valley of her breasts. He molded and shaped them with hands and Nia enjoyed every minute. She wanted to reciprocate, but Damon pushed her back down on the bed.

"You'll have your turn," he said, continuing to rub the aromatic oil into her skin. His hands caressed her stomach, legs and finally ended at her feet. He stopped and took one red lacquered toenail in his mouth and sucked on it.

"What are you doing?" She started to rise, but he eased her back down.

"Don't you know I want every inch of you?" he said. "Relax, close your eyes and concentrate on how it makes you feel." He stroked her thigh, soothing her. He wanted her to enjoy the erotic experience. He wanted to see, touch and taste everything about this woman. He tongued her anklet, fingering the charm dangling from the jewelry.

Nia laid back and relaxed. And soon she felt a familiar warmth growing in her belly. She enjoyed the suction of Damon's tongue and wanted more of it and not just on her feet. His tongue left a line of fire, scorching her everywhere it had been. She savored it, surrendering herself to the passion that burned inside her.

Finally, when she could take no more, she pulled him up to her and licked her tongue over his mouth. He opened for her and she reveled in his husky masculine taste, but she wanted more. Quickly she grabbed a foil packet from the nightstand and protected them. Holding his hips, she pulled him deep inside, needing to feel all of him. His thrusts were equally as urgent and powerful, bringing them to a simultaneous release and then spiraling them back down to earth.

While Damon slept, Nia watched him. Reaching out, she caressed his head. When she was with him, she didn't feel fat or unattractive, but rather beautiful and desirable. He was so giving when they made love. He came right out and asked her, did this feel good and did she like it when he touched her there. She was discovering her body under his tutelage as something to enjoy. And as a result, their physical coupling was that more intense. She didn't think it was possible to feel this kind of overwhelming passion or connection with another person. She didn't know when or how it happened, but she had fallen in love with Damon Bradley. How was she going to live without him if something should go wrong? She felt vulnerable and totally exposed.

Damon must have sensed her anxiety and rolled over to face her. His soulful eyes looked back at her and she knew instinctively that things had changed forever between them. But she wouldn't ever regret becoming one with Damon.

He stroked her jaw. "Are you all right?" he asked, seeing something in her eyes he couldn't name. Could he dare think it was love? No, not yet, he thought. Nia was too cautious with her heart; she was still so afraid of risking it. He knew the word *love* had certainly come into play with him. He loved everything about this woman: her smile, her sense of humor, her intelligence and her amazing spirit. She was a phenomenal woman.

"Mmm," *Can he tell? Can he see the love in my eyes?* Nia

snuggled close to his hard, lean body, avoiding contact with his eyes. She loved it when he held her; she felt loved and appreciated in his arms. Unfortunately, they would have to go back to reality soon.

# Chapter 13

"Oh, Damon, I hate having to come back to the real world," Nia lamented, tugging on his arm in the limo that had been waiting for them outside O'Hare airport. "New Orleans was just so wonderful. Our own little paradise." Damon had made her happier than she could have ever dreamed possible.

"We'll have many more special nights together," Damon said seductively. New Orleans would not be an anomaly. His sexual appetite had reawakened and he had no intention of putting it back on hiatus. He wanted Nia safely ensconced in his bed tonight so he could ravish her luscious body all night long.

Nia could tell the direction Damon's thoughts had taken. He had a devilish grin on his face and she knew she would not be sleeping very much that evening. Not that she had gotten much sleep on their trip anyway. Just that morning, she had awoken to find Damon's hands roaming her body, easily teasing her into submission. They'd barely had enough time to make it to the airport.

Nia turned her thoughts back to the present. They were on their way to her apartment so she could put a few clothes in a bag. She planned on spending the night at his condo. Damon wanted to go straight there, but Nia insisted on picking up some fresh clothes for work tomorrow.

The engine stopped and Damon led Nia from the car. She looked at her brownstone and nothing looked familiar. It was as if her eyes had been opened and she now saw things in a different light. Opening her door, she heard the tail end of Lexie's message: ". . . Call me when you get in."

She flicked on the lights and took her luggage to her bedroom while Damon sat on the couch and turned on the television. Nia was sure Lexie wanted to know all the details about their weekend, but it would have to wait. She packed a blouse, skirt, hose, her black pumps and clean underwear into an overnight bag.

"Ready?" Damon asked, looking up as she walked into the living room. She nodded. He stood up to take the bag from her while she turned off all the lights. The chauffeur was still waiting outside her building to take them back to Damon's place for a passionate night of lovemaking.

Watching Nia sleep was the most beautiful thing Damon had ever seen. Snuggled against his big fluffy pillows, Nia seemed at peace and very comfortable in his king-size bed. He hated to wake her when she was sleeping so soundly, but he always tried to get in a quick three-mile jog in the morning before leaving for work, a trait he was sure he'd inherited from his father. Over the last few days, he'd missed his daily workout, though he enjoyed tremendously the other workout he was getting. It didn't matter what the two of them were doing, just as long as they were together. They couldn't seem to get enough of each other, whether they were sitting on the couch watching TV, or making love. They just had to be near one another.

He leaned over and whispered "Rise and shine, sleepyhead," to her sleeping figure.

Nia's eyes flickered open and she glanced at the clock on the nightstand. "Why are you up at this hour?" she asked, rubbing her eyes. "Do you realize what time it is?"

"I do," he said, stroking her hair. "And that's why we have to get a move on it." He threw back the covers and pulled Nia upright. She finally noticed that he was dressed in sweats and a T-shirt.

"You go ahead and get your morning run in while I go back to sleep," she murmured, lying back down on the bed.

"No, no, no. You're coming with me." He threw Nia jogging pants and one of his T-shirts.

Nia peered up at him, pushing the clothes to the side. "Are you serious? Listen, Damon, I don't jog. I can just barely manage the treadmill. Anyway, you'd leave me in your dust. Now, please, let me go back to sleep." She wanted to stay underneath the warmth of the covers and get another half hour of sleep before going to work.

Damon bent down. "You'll love it once you're out there in the fresh clean air. And I promise to keep a slow pace." He crossed his heart.

Nia pondered the idea for a minute. She could probably use the exercise. Reluctantly, she sat up. "Oh, all right," she muttered. "But you better not go too fast."

"Good girl," he commented, smiling.

Nia stood and went to the bathroom to brush her teeth. She washed her face and put on Damon's jogging pants and T-shirt. The pants didn't fit and were quite baggy, but they had a drawstring around the waist. She came out of the bathroom to find Damon stretching on the floor.

"C'mon, join me," he said.

They did a few stretches before going outside and jogging five miles. Nia was surprised that she managed to keep up with Damon. Maybe she wasn't as out of shape as she thought. When they made it back to Damon's condo, they took a long, leisurely shower together. It was an erotic fantasy steamy enough to keep Nia daydreaming for the next eight hours at work.

They finally emerged a while later and Nia set about finding the necessary items to make a pot of fresh coffee. Taking some whole-wheat bread from the fridge, Nia plopped two slices into the toaster and sat on the breakfast stool to wait for them. When they popped up, she buttered a piece of toast and watched Damon fiddle with his tie. Freshly shaved, he looked so magnificent. His head glistened and Nia wanted to eat him up with a spoon.

"I'm going to stay at home tonight," Nia stated while sipping on her coffee.

"Are you saying you're getting tired of me?" Damon inquired jokingly. He opened the refrigerator and took out an individual-sized carton of orange juice. He took a swig, never taking his eyes off Nia.

"Of course not." She smiled, munching on her toast. "I love spending time with you, but I told Lexie we would get together when I got back and it's been a couple of days."

"Nia, it's OK. You don't have to explain," Damon replied. "I know you had a life before you met me."

"I knew you'd understand." She stood up to give him a kiss on the cheek. "I really have to go, though. I have lots to do at the office." Damon walked her to door and she grabbed her bag laying near it. "I'll call you later, babe."

"It sure has been hard to catch up with you these days," Will commented to Damon as he bit into his Philly cheese steak. He was having lunch in Damon's office because Damon swore he was too busy to leave after coming back from vacation. "And if I didn't know any better, I'd say this woman has got you sprung." He wiped his mouth with a napkin.

"Will, please." Damon sighed, unscrewing the cap on a bottle of water and taking a long gulp. "I remember a time when you forgot you even had a friend when the right woman dropped into your lap."

Will laughed. "I remember no such occasion." He smiled and finished off his sandwich. It had been a long time since he'd seen his friend this happy. Even when Damon had dated Kendall, Will never saw a look of pure contentment on Damon's face. He had gotten to know Nia a little during their ski trip and he felt she was a good match for his friend. Warm and kind, Nia had just enough fire in her to keep his boy interested. "Whatever she's put on you is definitely working for you. You look like the cat that swallowed the canary."

"Oh, yeah, Nia is incredible. She's beautiful, intelligent and just plain fascinating. She has got me hooked—and completely satisfied," Damon replied as he took the last bite of his chicken parmigiana sub. "That was damn good." He wiped his mouth. "I appreciate you coming over for lunch. I was swamped and couldn't break away. My dad has me working on this big deal."

"It's fine. I needed to get out this morning." Will got up from the couch and walked over to the window to look out over the south side.

"Have a long night at the club?"

"Yeah, mon." He smiled. "Sometimes the ladies just won't let me go home." He gave Damon a wide grin. Damon knew how much Will loved the ladies. He could never just stay with one. Carly was one beautiful woman with a great body to boot, but he'd doubted that even she could curb Will's appetite.

Will loved the view from Damon's office and peered down at the pedestrians walking by. He needed to bite the bullet and make one wall of his office all windows, too. "I was going over the books with my accountant this morning."

"Business is going well, I hope?" Damon had been one of the first people to support Will's idea of opening a nightclub. And he hadn't just given the idea lip service. He had actually put his money where his mouth was and invested. Damon had wanted to do anything he could to help a friend's dream come to life. When Millennium came out of the red and began to make a profit, Damon happily obliged Will's request to buy him out so that he was the sole owner.

"Business is great," Will said. "Even thinking of opening up another one." He had been tossing around the idea of expanding for some time. "What do you think?"

"I think it's a great idea," Damon concurred. He

leaned over to grab both their plates and walked them over to the trash can. "Do you need any help or another loan to help get the ball rolling?"

"Not right now. I'm still scoping out the right location, but when I do, I'll let you know. Anyway, I've got to get going, I have a meeting with one of my liquor suppliers." Will came over to shake his hand. "I'll see you and your little lady soon, though?"

"You can bet on it," Damon said, giving him a pat on the back as he walked him out the door.

Nia kicked off her shoes and flung herself on her couch. She was exhausted and happy to be at home after a hard day's work. It was past six o'clock and Lexie was going to be coming over soon. She'd promised dinner, but at the moment Nia didn't feel like moving a muscle.

Reluctantly, Nia found some strength and made her way to the kitchen. Opening the fridge, she pulled out the fixings for a house salad and baked potato to go with two steaks.

In no time, she had the potatoes in the oven, the steaks marinating and the mixed green salad prepared. She rubbed her tired shoulder muscles and looked at her watch. Luckily she had a few minutes to spare and could shower before Lexie's arrival. She raced into the bathroom to strip and stand in front of the hot water. Her thoughts turned to her intimate moment in the shower with Damon earlier that morning. If she tried hard enough, she could still feel his hands lathering her body, caressing her womanhood.

Toweling off, Nia made her way to her bedroom, dressing in shorts and a T-shirt. She was headed to the kitchen to check on the steaks when the phone rang. She figured it was Lexie, calling to say she was running behind schedule and would be there shortly.

She caught it on the last ring. "Hey, girl, where are you?" Nia cradled the phone to her ear.

"Nia?" the masculine voice asked. It sounded oddly familiar but Nia couldn't place it.

"Yes, this is Nia. May I help you?"

"Nia, this is your father," he announced.

She waited with baited breath. What did he want? And what did he mean by father? He had no right to that title.

"Are you there?"

"Yes, I am," she replied. "What can I do for you?"

"Is this a bad time? I was hoping we could talk." He sounded very unsure of himself, like he was waiting for her to spew at him again. This time, Nia wouldn't give him the satisfaction. Since their last meeting, she had thought about hate; it was the flip side of love and he was undeserving of any kind of emotion from her, even that.

"No. It isn't." Nia switched to her cordless phone and walked to the kitchen. She opened the stove and felt the potatoes. Another few minutes, she thought. She would put the steaks on the grill when Lexie arrived. "I have a friend coming over for dinner."

"That's nice," he said, as if she needed his stamp of approval. "Listen, Nia, I know you're not anxious to see me, but I was hoping we could get together. I think we really need to clear the air."

"Why? What difference would it make?"

"The difference is that I think you need to hear some things from me almost about as much as I need to say them to you," he answered.

Nia thought about that comment. There were things she had always wondered about. This man had known her mother, even if it had only been for a short time. Perhaps he could give her more insight into what kind of woman she was. For that reason only, she would entertain the thought of meeting him.

"Listen . . ." Nia floundered for the appropriate way to address him.

"Nathan," he finished. "Just call me Nathan."

"I suppose that's a start." Her intercom buzzed. "All right, Nathan, let me give it some thought. I really have to go now, my friend has arrived." She'd given him five minutes and that was more than enough time.

"Okay," he said. She heard the relief in his voice that he'd made progress. "I look forward to your call. Good-bye."

After she hung up, Nia realized she hadn't gotten his phone number. She would have to call her aunt. Returning the cordless to the receiver, Nia raced to hit the buzzer Lexie was pressing furiously. "All right, all right, Lex!" she exclaimed.

A few moments later, Lexie climbed up the stairs and knocked on her door. "It took you long enough," she moaned as she sashayed in, looking positively fabulous. Wearing the latest Dolce & Gabbana springwear, Lexie looked every bit the fashion guru that she was.

"So what are you making for dinner—seeing as how you've kicked your girl to the curb and left me stranded ever since you got back from your romantic getaway."

"Oh, please, Lexie." Nia laughed. She went back to the kitchen to put the teriyaki steaks on the grill.

"There have been plenty of times you've kicked me to the curb for one of your stud muffins."

"Hmm," said Lexie, coming in to look over her shoulders. "Those look great. What did you put over them?"

"A honey teriyaki glaze. Trust me, it'll be delicious."

"I've no doubt," Lexie remarked, opening the cupboard and taking out two wine goblets. "You know me, I had to bring some wine." Lexie uncorked a bottle of red. "It'll go perfect with the steaks," she said, handing Nia a glass.

Nia sipped the wine while flipping over her steaks. She knew Lexie was waiting for her to spill the details. She would let her simmer for a minute. "How was work?"

"Girl, please, you know I didn't come hear to talk about no job or my trifling boss who is afraid I'm going to steal her job away," she said exasperatedly. "I want know about the trip. How was it?"

Nia gave her an innocent look as she reached into the fridge to grab the salad bowl and set it on the kitchen counter.

"Don't give me that look. I know you've been getting your freak on. I haven't seen you in days and you just returned my phone call. Give it up, sista."

Nia removed the steaks from the grill and put them on a platter. She motioned for Lexie to get the salad.

When they were seated at her round pedestal table, Nia finally let it all hang out. "Girlfriend, it was everything I ever imagined and then some." Nia watched as Lexie's eyes widened, eager for more details.

"Do tell, do tell! You've got me salivating in anticipation."

"The things this man can do with his tongue and fingers would blow your mind." Nia giggled. "Girl, he blew my mind. I had orgasm after orgasm."

Lexie spit out some of her wine. She wiped the spilled liquid with the back of her hand. "It was that good, huh?" Was Lexie ready for all the juicy tidbits?

"It was better than good. It was great," Nia replied, smiling. "I never knew what I was missing. I never knew sex could be so great and so . . ." she paused, searching for the right word, ". . . intoxicating. Being wrapped up in the another person, your minds and bodies as one—it's really quite incredible."

Nia looked up to find Lexie staring at her strangely. "What's wrong?"

"Sounds to me like you're in love."

"What?" Nia said. "Lexie, that's crazy. You've said a lot of wild stuff before, but this takes the cake." Nia wasn't ready to admit to anyone that she was in love with Damon. She thought it might somehow jinx it. Nia had decided it was better that she kept her feelings to herself and, when it was safe, would say the words out loud and risk her heart. "Love? No, this isn't love. It's just lust."

Lexie raised her brow. She wasn't buying it. She knew Nia. And Nia would never give herself so completely to a man, body and soul, if love were not a part of the equation.

"I do care a great deal about Damon. I just don't think I'm there yet." She put her head down, afraid that Lexie would see she was lying.

"If you say so," Lexie murmured. "Of course, methinks the lady doth protest too much. But I'll let it rest for now. I'm just happy you've found someone that makes you happy. Because I've never seen you look like this." She reached across the table to pat Nia's hand.

"Thanks, Lexie." Nia leaned over to give her a big fat hug.

"So, how was New Orleans?" Lexie cut into the juicy steak and took a bite. It tasted delicious and she was famished. She and Nia were devouring the steaks and potatoes like they were the last food on earth.

"Oh, it was great. New Orleans has so much character and history. And the Cajun and Creole food was to die for."

"Did you guys visit any voodoo priestesses, go to Anne Rice's house?" Lexie asked excitedly.

Nia felt bad; she knew how much Lexie would have loved going to New Orleans. Every year the two of them always took a trip to someplace new. They'd gone on a cruise to the Bahamas, whitewater rafting in Tennessee, and last year they had managed the ultimate trip: Europe. Two jam-packed weeks in London, Paris and Amsterdam and it had been well worth it. They discussed going to New Orleans someday, but Damon had beat them to the punch.

"It was everything I thought it would be. The room was luxurious with a huge four-poster bed and the bathroom was decked all in marble. Damon spared no expense." Nia took a forkful of her baked potato. "We visited a winery and a plantation, though I have to say I wasn't that thrilled with the latter experience."

"I can imagine. What else? Don't leave anything out."

"Damon and I went on one of those paddle-wheel riverboats for dinner that had real nice jazz. And do not let me forget the infamous Bourbon Street, a place that never seems to sleep. Girl, you would love this place. The bars are open till all hours and you can walk down the street with liquor in your hand. It's like a whole 'nother universe. And women flash their boobies all the time."

"It sounds fabulous, and don't you dare feel bad for getting treated to a romantic rendezvous," Lexie chastised her. She could tell Nia was trying to downplay her trip. She had known Miss Thang for a long time and knew when she wasn't being forthright, even about a certain subject called love. "Lord knows, I've had my share of romances and then some. I've probably had enough for the both of us. It's high time you had some good loving." Lexie gave Nia a huge grin. "Matter of fact," Lexie exclaimed, "I hate to eat and run, but I have to go."

"Lexie, you just got here." Nia put her hands on her hips. "Weren't you the one telling me we haven't spent enough time together?"

"I was," Lexie replied unashamedly. She rose from the dining room table and headed to the living room to find her coat. "But you don't fool me one bit, missy. I know you're dying to call Mr. you-know-who as soon as I leave."

Nia smiled knowingly as she followed Lexie into the hallway. Lexie was already putting on her coat. The thought had crossed Nia's mind, but she was content to spend time with her best girlfriend.

"I'll call you soon, sweetheart." Lexie gave her a quick kiss on the cheek before leaving.

After closing the door, Nia rushed over to pick up her cordless phone to call Damon. She knew he was having dinner with his sister and didn't want to interrupt their quality bonding time. The phone rang several times before Damon picked up, sounding breathless.

"Hello?"

"You're home," Nia replied, happy to hear his voice on the line.

"Hey, baby," he crooned in her ear. She loved when he called her his baby.

"When did you get in?"

"I just walked in." Damon shrugged out of his coat. "I was turning the key in the lock when I heard the phone."

Dinner with Jordan consisted of her interrogating him about the mystery woman he'd been dating that the family had yet to meet. He'd left promising to introduce Nia to the Bradleys, and he had just the night in mind: his family was going to the opera in a couple of weeks and his father always held a skybox that easily could seat five people. It would be the perfect occasion for him to show off his lady.

"How was dinner?" Nia asked, interrupting his thoughts.

"It was great," he commented. Should he broach the subject of meeting his parents? He had the distinct impression that Nia wasn't all that eager to meet them, though he couldn't much blame her. He often spoke of his father as a force to be reckoned with. Who wouldn't be afraid of meeting them? "Honey," he started, "Jordan and I were talking—" He paused.

"And?"

"And I think it's time you met my folks—you know, the whole family." His comment was met with dead silence. "So, what do you think?"

"I . . . uh." Nia hesitated. She was at a complete loss for words. She wasn't in any hurry to meet the Bradleys. For some reason, her female intuition cautioned her against meeting them, but she knew how important Damon's family was to him. *They can't be that bad,* she thought. Famous last words, an inner voice warned her. "I think that would be great. So when is this meeting going to take place?" Please God, let him say a month from now! Maybe even a year!

"How about in a couple of weeks?" Damon suggested. "We have a box at the opera."

"The opera?" Nia asked. "Now I'm really in for it."

"Yes, the opera." He heard her sniff in the background. "Hey, you might love it, honey, you never know. I think you can bear it for one night."

"All right," she conceded. "I'm sure I can. I guess I'll have to find something appropriate to wear to dazzle your family."

"Don't worry about my family," Damon assured her. "The only person you need to dazzle is me, and if you'll allow me, I'd like to buy something for you."

"Damon, you don't have to do that. I am capable of buying something for myself." Sometimes he was too much. Nia appreciated his generosity, but she wanted him to understand that she was a strong, independent woman capable of taking care of herself. "I can find something appropriate that won't embarrass you."

"I'm not worried about you embarrassing me,

Nia," he said, exasperated. "Please let me do this for you."

"Fine, but nothing too crazy, OK?" She sighed. "Do you need my size?"

"Honey, I know all your measurements intimately," he whispered. He knew every inch of her luscious body. Matter of fact, he wished she was there with him right now and he could let his hands roam all over every delicious curve.

"Yes, you do," Nia murmured. "What do you say to coming over right now and getting reacquainted with them?"

*Is she reading my mind?* "I'll be there in twenty."

Nia sure didn't need to ask him twice. She rushed into her bedroom to find something sexy to wear for his troubles. Lotioning her body, Nia slid into a lacy chemise, another purchase from a recent visit to Victoria's Secret. She was fast becoming one of Vicki's newest converts, now that she had Damon. She wanted to make sure she kept the home fires burning, and burn they would all night long. Nia spritzed on some of her favorite perfume to drive Damon wild.

Damon had a voracious appetite and she was anxious to match it this evening. She would tell him later about her phone call from her errant father.

Soon her intercom was buzzing and Nia rushed over to let him in. She slipped on a matching robe before opening the door with a flourish.

"Baby," he murmured, sweeping her up into his arms and closing the door behind him. His mouth came down on hers as he made his way to her bedroom. She barely had time to take a breath from the onslaught of his dizzying kisses before he laid her down on the bed.

"Mmm, now that was a hello."

"Yes, it was," Damon said, looking down at her. He fingered her new negligee. "Is this for me?" She nodded. "I like it, but right now you have much too much clothing on." Her robe and gown were easily removed from her warm, waiting body.

"So do you." She smiled. "Here, let me help you with that." She unbuckled his pants and they dropped to the floor. Damon stepped out of them and joined her on the bed.

"I missed you," Damon said, outlining the curve of her face with his forefinger.

"I missed you, too."

"How much?"

"Let me show you." Nia pulled his face toward hers in a searing kiss.

Their lovemaking was slow and sensuous and every bit as fulfilling as each previous time. Later, when she was wrapped up in his arms, she told him about the phone call from her father.

"What do you think about me meeting him?" she asked. She knew he had an opinion he was keeping to himself. Lately he was very closemouthed on the subject.

"Is that what you want?"

"Don't answer a question with a question!" she admonished. "I want to know what you think."

"Nia." He sighed and rolled over so he could face her. "I want whatever is going to make you happy. And if you feel you have some unresolved issues with this man, then, yes, I think you should meet with him."

She punched him in the arm. "See, I knew you had an opinion."

"Yes, I did, but mine isn't what counts. Yours is. And I will support you in whatever you decide."

"Have I told you lately just how incredible you are?"

"No, but you can show me again." Damon pulled her to him and Nia showed him exactly how much she adored him.

# Chapter 14

"Where have you been?" Nia's aunt inquired the following weekend. They were standing at the kitchen counter, rolling dough to make pies. Her aunt made the best crusts. Tender and flaky, her pies were always a success at the church bazaars. "I tried to reach you last weekend and this week."

Nia turned red. She and Damon had spent all their free time together since coming back from New Orleans. One of them was always staying the night at the other's house. It was like they couldn't get enough of each other. She loved making love with Damon, but she felt so wanton.

"Well, what ever you've been doing?" Olivia asked. "You sure do have a glow about yourself these days and I'm happy to see it." She leaned over to give Nia's shoulders a gentle squeeze.

Nia poured more flour over her rolling pin, not answering at first. "Auntie, you know Damon and I have been spending a great deal of time together," she started. She pulled the thin crust from the counter and placed it in several pie pans. How did one put into words that they were screwing each other's brains out? No, she couldn't tell her aunt that.

"Are things getting serious?"

"I don't know yet," Nia answered. "But they are progressing nicely. Damon even wants me to meet his parents. Though I'm not all that sure about it."

"Why not?" her aunt asked, pouring apple and peach filling into separate pans. Nia covered each pie with strips of crust and placed them aside for baking.

"Honestly, Aunt Livvie, I'm a little bit intimidated," Nia admitted. "Damon's family is very well off and I'm just a poor girl from the south side."

"Nia Marie Taylor, don't you dare stand there and tell me you don't think you're good enough for the likes of them." Her aunt grabbed her shoulders. "You are just as good, if not better than them and it what's here that counts." She pointed at Nia's heart. "Anyway, why wouldn't they love you?"

Nia sat down. It was great to be able to confide in her aunt about her fears. Why couldn't she have been more like this all those years ago? Her aunt had softened recently; she was a lot more affectionate and open these days. Nia wondered what or *who* caused the change in her. Not that it was any of her business; her aunt certainly was entitled to a life of her own.

She shrugged. "Well, Auntie, there's this ex-girlfriend in the picture that his parents approved of."

"But obviously their relationship didn't work out or he wouldn't be with you." Her aunt put her hands on her hips. "You have to remember that he chose *you*. His parents are just going to have to live with it."

"I know that." Nia groaned miserably. "But it would be nice if they actually liked me and thought I was the best woman for Damon."

"They will, Nia. Give it time." Her aunt sat down

at the table beside her. "You'll see. Time has a funny way of healing all things."

"Is that a hint, Auntie?" Nia wondered if her Aunt Olivia was referring to her father. Being with her aunt stirred up the pot, making her wonder what he had done with his life after leaving her mother pregnant and alone. Had he ever given a second thought to the child he abandoned?

"Of course not, honey," her aunt murmured. "I know where you stand on the subject."

Nia was silent on the ride to the Bradleys'. She was extremely nervous at the prospect of meeting Damon's parents for the first time. What would they think of her? What if they thought she wasn't good enough for him? True, she hadn't been born with a silver spoon in her mouth, but she was intelligent and pretty enough. She fought down the terror that sought to invade her over the upcoming evening. She couldn't let her past insecurities resurface.

To make matters worse, Damon had insisted on buying her a dress, right when she needed to look her best. He chose a long silk slip dress made with a floral pattern. It had a square neck and curved out to show off her hips. Damon bought it because he wanted to see Nia in clothes that showed off her curvaceous figure rather than downplay it. The finishing touch was a matching scarf she casually draped around her shoulders. The material of the dress hadn't allowed for much underwear, except minimal bikini panties and hose. Damon would be thinking about her braless breasts all evening and imagining what he would like to be doing to them.

The hairdresser had stylishly coiffed her hair earlier that morning and she'd added a pearl necklace and matching earrings that had belonged to her mother. Damon had told Nia she looked fabulous and incredibly sexy when he picked her up.

"Nia," Damon said, grasping her hand. "Everything is going to be fine. You'll see. They'll love you."

The Bradley home was more than Nia could have imagined. It stood out from the others in the small community of Country Club Hills due to the sheer simplicity of the brick architecture and the manicured lawn outside. Damon stopped his BMW in front of the three-car garage and stepped out to open Nia's door for her. She pulled down the mirror to check herself one final time before exiting the vehicle. Smoothing her dress, she took Damon's outstretched hand.

"How do I look?"

"Stunning." He smiled at her and took her hands. Noticing that they were ice cold, he gave them a gentle squeeze. Pulling his keys from his breast pocket, he opened the front door. Nia joined him inside the foyer and looked around at her surroundings. A huge bouquet of flowers sat on a side table. Nia had no doubt it was an antique, along with an enormous print on the wall and an Oriental throw rug strategically placed in the center of the foyer to match the beautiful chestnut cabinetry.

Damon helped her out of her trench coat and gave it to a uniformed butler who appeared out of nowhere. Mrs. Bradley picked that exact moment to make her entrance. She glided down the staircase before finally stopping on the last step.

"You must be Nia," she exclaimed, coming down to give Nia a quick peck on either cheek. Mrs. Bradley stood back to give Nia a thorough appraisal. Seeing the look on her face, Nia didn't appear to make a great first impression.

"Mrs. Bradley, it's a pleasure to meet you," Nia said.

Nia was struck at how beautiful Simone was for her age. Her brown eyes were bright and alive and her skin was still as smooth as a baby's bottom. Her careful makeup highlighted her tawny complexion and her thick, auburn hair was beautifully arranged in a sleek chignon atop her head. Diamonds and rubies were draped around her neck and dangled from both ears. She exuded class and understated elegance, wearing a beaded burgundy camisole and a long, paisley, taffeta ball-gown skirt that flowed to her ankles. She looked incredible for the mother of a thirty-year-old son and every bit the society matron. Nia was no hick and didn't consider herself from the wrong side of the tracks, but something told her she might be far out of her league.

"Welcome, Nia. Please come join us in the living room for cocktails before the opera." Simone Bradley motioned for Nia to walk ahead of her.

"Darling, don't you think you could have told her to wear something more appropriate?" his mother whispered, but just loud enough for Nia to hear. "And a little less sexy. We are going to the opera."

Nia blushed, but kept a straight face. She strode into the living room to greet Marcus Bradley and his daughter Jordan, keeping a polite smile plastered on her face. Nia would keep her head held high and act as if she hadn't heard his mother's insulting comment.

"Mother," Damon whispered, lightly grabbing her by the forearm, "don't start. I think Nia looks gorgeous."

"And we both know where your mind is, dear." His mother chuckled, patting his hand. "Don't worry. Everything will be fine."

"There's my big brother," a brown-haired beauty exclaimed, sweeping past Nia to give Damon a bear hug and smother him with kisses. No doubt, this was Jordan. Was she purposely being rude by not acknowledging Nia's presence?

Jordan Bradley was every bit as stunning as her mother. Nia noticed almost immediately that she exhibited the same superiority complex as well. A mass of golden ringlets framed her flawless face. Jordan appeared to be equally as tall as her father and Damon. Dressed in a black halter tuxedo dress with white satin lapels and black strappy sandals, Jordan towered over Nia. Her dress showed off her amazing athletic figure.

Mr. Bradley noticed the slight overture and came over to welcome Nia and shake her hand warmly. *Ever the diplomat,* Damon thought as he crossed the threshold with his mother. He returned his little sister's kiss, but he was going to have a talk with Jordan; he wouldn't have her disrespecting Nia.

"It's great to finally meet you, Ms. Taylor," Mr. Bradley stated. His lips thinned as he gave Jordan a stern look. "Forgive my daughter's exuberance. She and Damon are quite close."

"Sorry, Nia," Jordan apologized, trying to look contrite. The apology definitely was not genuine, but Nia nodded her head anyway.

"It's great to meet you, too," Nia replied, coming forward to shake his hand. A few inches taller than

Damon's six feet and one inch, Marcus Bradley dwarfed her. With his commanding presence and dark black eyes, Nia was sure his employees looked up to him as Damon implied, but feared him a little, too. Damon resembled his father, but Mr. Bradley had more lines on his angular face and narrow lips.

"Would you like a cocktail or appetizer before dinner?" Marcus asked, holding a platter of goodies to tempt her. Nia's stomach grumbled from the smell of the enticing aromas.

Nia looked at Mrs. Bradley, who was no bigger than a toothpick, and declined. "No, thank you, but a glass of white wine would be great."

"How about I prepare you one of my delicious martinis instead?" Mr. Bradley turned around to prepare the drink, not waiting for her answer.

"My father makes a great lemonade martini," Damon ventured.

"That would be lovely," Nia replied.

Nia accepted the drink and made polite chitchat with his family. Damon stood by her side the entire time, but sensed her uneasiness.

A short while later, Marcus announced it was time to head to the theater. "We wouldn't want to miss the curtain," he explained. "The limo I hired for the evening should be waiting for us outside."

They all filed into the foyer. Nia watched Marcus wrap a shawl around his wife and lightly kiss her on the shoulder. Simone looked up at him affectionately. It was great to see a couple still in love after many years, though to Nia it was quite unusual.

Her grandparents rarely showed public displays of affection. She wasn't even sure if they were still in love or whether they stayed together out of habit. She hoped that if she ever married, somehow she and her husband would manage to keep the flames burning.

As predicted, a black stretch limousine awaited outside the Bradleys' home. The men allowed the women to get in first before climbing in after them. Nia sat opposite Damon's mother and sister. She wanted to see their facial expressions and gauge their reaction to her on the ride to opera. Damon joined her, sitting opposite from his family. The limousine eased out of the driveway, making its way to the expressway and toward the Lyric Opera of Chicago.

"Damon tells me you work at Dean, Martin & Whitmore," Mr. Bradley began. "It's a great firm. Dan and I are old friends."

"Yes, I know," Nia said. "I remember seeing you at our Christmas party." Damon turned to give her an unpleasant look. Had she just stuck her foot in her mouth? "It's a great place to work and I love what I do," Nia continued.

"Ah, yes," Mr. Bradley said, ignoring her last comment. "Now I remember you as well." He turned to his wife and daughter. "Nia's the woman I told you about." His wife looked confused. "You know, the woman Damon made such a public display over in the Whitmores' living room at their Christmas party."

Damon sighed, rolling his eyes. "It wasn't a public display, Dad. I just introduced myself."

"Whatever the case," his father said, looking at his son, "Damon was quite enchanted with you, Nia, and could hardly concentrate for the duration of the evening."

"And that hasn't changed." Damon lightly kissed Nia's hand. "I'm as enchanted as I was that first night. Maybe even more now." Nia turned to give him a quick smile. She found confidence and assuredness in his sultry brown eyes and tried to convince herself to relax. This night meant so much Damon. He desperately wanted Nia to connect with his family and he'd forewarned her that his father could be quite blunt at times.

"That's great, son," Mr. Bradley replied. "It's great to finally see you happy again after that engagement fiasco with Kendall."

A hush fell over the limousine. Damon fumed sitting across from his father. He turned to find Nia's questioning eyes on him. She blinked several times, waiting for confirmation. The pain was evident in her eyes even though she tried to disguise it. Refusing to face him, Nia stared resolutely through the window.

He had expressly forbidden the subject of Kendall to come up in conversation and his father damn well knew it. He'd had a lapse in judgment and didn't wish to have it thrown in his face. Not to mention the fact that he hadn't told Nia about the engagement. It was so long ago to him, it didn't seem to matter. Whatever his personal agenda, his father had no right to make Nia feel uncomfortable.

Jordan, who'd been casually looking out the window, took the cue; maybe she saw the smoke billowing from his ears. Whatever the case, she changed the subject. "Well, I for one am excited to see *Carmen* again," she gushed. "The character is so sassy and no-nonsense. She's just my kind of woman and I hear it's going to be great with Anna Rossini singing the lead."

She smiled at Nia, who was frozen in anger. "You'll love it, Nia. Or maybe not, opera is an acquired taste." He could hear his mother's quick intake of breath; even his father put his head down in embarrassment. Damon felt Nia's hand ball up in a fist alongside him. Could his sister stick the knife in any farther?

Jordan looked apologetically at Damon. "I mean, not everyone loves the opera. Damon tells me you're quite fond of the theater and musicals." Jordan tried to backtrack, but Damon knew it was too late. Nia was furious and Damon didn't know what to do.

He was thankful when the limo came to an abrupt stop in front of the theater and they were able to disembark with no event.

Oblivious to the conversation swirling around her, Nia managed to put one foot in front of the other. From the start of the evening, everything had gone from bad to worse. First, his mother insinuated that she wore inappropriate attire for the opera. Then Damon's sister completely ignored her and spoke down to her as if she wasn't cultured enough to appreciate the opera, and all the while Damon stood by doing nothing to protect her from these attacks. But the worst was finding out from Damon's father that he'd been engaged to Kendall. Why hadn't Damon told her beforehand? He'd had ample opportunity, way before they'd even slept together. No wonder Kendall thought she had a right to him! How could he have kept this from her? She thought she could trust him. Had she made a mistake? Was he keeping more secrets from her?

The usher seated the Bradley party in their balcony theater box. Nia sat down stone-faced and looked directly ahead of her as the crowd of people below scrambled to find their seats. The lights flickered indicating the opening act was about to begin. Damon squeezed her hand when he sat beside her, but Nia snatched it away. She couldn't bear to look at him then, for fear of bursting into tears. Somehow she would make it through the rest of the evening with a modicum of decorum. She wouldn't give his family the satisfaction of knowing they had upset her.

"Here's some glasses," he offered, handing her a small pair of theater binoculars. "They'll help you see the action a little better." He stared at her, but she accepted them without looking at him.

*It's going to be a long evening,* Damon thought, sitting back rigidly in his chair. He'd hoped that night would be a resounding success and would've laid to rest Nia's fears about their different backgrounds. Instead, his parents cultivated her worst fears.

The rest of the evening proved uneventful. During intermission, while Nia was in the ladies' room, Damon took his family aside and had a word with them. He'd stressed that he wasn't going to put up with any more antics and would have their heads if they said one more negative thing about Nia's clothes, lack of culture or much less breathed the name Kendall Montgomery in her presence. After being dutifully chastised, they all promised to be on their best behavior, but the damage had already been done. The sparkle had gone out of Nia's eyes.

Over dinner, his parents played the eager hosts and Nia muttered the appropriate responses when asked a question. She talked at length about her job as an advertising assistant at Dean, Martin & Whitmore, even discussing her upcoming campaign, which pleased Marcus endlessly.

Damon noticed that she picked at her Caesar salad and barely ate her pecan-crusted salmon. He knew Nia to have a healthy appetite. He watched her move her food from one side of the plate to the other. This was all his fault. He never should have insisted that she meet his parents. He knew she wasn't ready yet and now they'd gone and embarrassed him, hitting on a sore spot between the two of them. He saw how uncomfortable Nia was around his display of wealth. Although she enjoyed the ski trip to Alpine Valley and the romantic weekend in New Orleans, he could tell she was unnerved by it. Of course, he couldn't blame everything on his family. Nia was angry with him for not telling her about Kendall, and justifiably so. But he'd been afraid to tell her about the engagement.

With their relationship still being so fragile, Nia was overreacting and probably looking on it as some sort of betrayal. This could completely destroy her trust in him and he couldn't let that happen. Nia meant everything to him. He didn't realize just how much until, when he thought he could lose her, he realized he loved her with all his heart. He'd tried to ignore those feelings but they were there. He'd known since New Orleans, but was afraid to admit it. Was Nia ready to let his love in?

He knew she wanted him to take her home, but he was taking her to his place. Somehow he would convince her just how much he cared for her. On the ride to his house, Nia stared out the window and sat as far away from him as humanly possibly without falling out of the car. All he wanted to do was pull her close and drown himself in her, but he didn't want to see the sad look in her eyes.

# Chapter 15

Damon opened the door to his condo and let Nia brush past him. She closed the door behind her, almost slamming it in his face.

"Why didn't you tell me!" Nia asked furiously, turning around to face him. She'd been holding the question inside the entire evening. She couldn't believe Damon had kept his engagement to Kendall a secret from her. To make matters worse, he'd stubbornly refused to take her home and had driven to his place instead.

"I'm sorry," Damon stated quietly. He loosened his tie and unbuttoned the top of shirt, ready to do battle. "I should have told you, but I didn't want you to overreact like you're doing now."

"Overreact? How could I not? I was completely taken off guard." Nia went over to the minibar to pour herself a glass of brandy. She needed something strong. She swirled the liquid around in the decanter before taking a sip. "Did your father enjoy embarrassing me? The old man must have gotten a real thrill out of sticking it to me."

Damon stood up. He'd had enough. Nia had hardly spoken a word to him on the ride home and the silence had been deafening. "Don't say another word," he rasped, putting his hand up. "I won't let you talk about my father."

"Why not?" she countered. "Your entire family tried to belittle me the entire evening. And you let them."

"I admit that they were out of line, but, Nia, they're not really who you're upset with, now, are they?" Damon asked wearily.

"No, they're not. They were only part of the problem. I'm upset because you lied to me."

"I didn't lie."

"Let's not play word games, Damon," Nia lectured. "A lie is a lie, whether it's one of omission or not. And you've yet to tell me why you broke off your engagement with Kendall. What's the big secret? What are you hiding from me?"

Damon rubbed his head in frustration. He shrugged out of his tuxedo jacket. "There is no big secret, Nia. It's simple. Kendall and I were engaged a couple of years ago."

"And what precipitated your calling it off?" Nia pressed. She waited for an explanation. Damon didn't appear to be forthcoming with the details.

"Do we have to talk about this?" Damon flopped down on the couch. It had been a long evening and he didn't want to think of the time when he'd been a fool, falling for Kendall's act. He didn't want to remember how she had come on to Will, who'd turned her down, before betraying him with one of his other friends. After Kendall, he'd thought he had lost the ability to love, contenting himself with celibacy until he'd met Nia. She'd single-handedly brought back his belief in love, the kind of love he saw in his parents' relationship and wished for in one of his own.

"Yes, I want to know what happened."

He gave in. "All right." He respected Nia too much to let anything come between them. "I let a long-standing friendship between the Bradleys and the Montgomerys precipitate a relationship between Kendall and myself."

"I know all this already."

Damon rolled his eyes. "Fine. What you don't know is that at one time I fancied myself in love. I was ready to settle down, start a family, and Kendall said and did the right things to make me believe she wanted it, too. But it was all a lie. She deceived me and I didn't notice her roving eye. Maybe I didn't want to see it. I always knew Kendall to be a flirt, but I never expected she would cheat on me."

Nia's eyes widened in astonishment. She couldn't believe it. Kendall was the one that ruined their relationship? She always thought it had been Damon who'd called off their affair because he wasn't ready for commitment. Nia never would never have guessed that Kendall was unfaithful.

"How did you find out?" She was utterly amazed. All this time, she had been so far off the mark.

"I saw them."

"Oh, Damon, I'm so sorry. I had no idea."

"No. Let me finish. You haven't heard the whole story." Damon took a deep breath. "Kendall didn't pick a stranger to sleep with." Nia's eyes widened in disbelief, but Damon continued. "She chose one of my best friends, Daniel Hollister. And I was the one who found them in bed together. I was stunned. Daniel and I went way back; we had known each other since kindergarten. I couldn't believe he could betray me with my fiancée, but there they were. It's hard not to believe something when you see it with your very own eyes. Afterward, they both begged my forgiveness, claiming that the other seduced them, but I didn't want to hear any more lies. Needless to say, that ended the engagement and the friendship."

Nia shook her head. "I don't get it. The way Kendall behaves, you'd think you were the one in the wrong, but it was her. She betrayed you. But yet she still thinks she has a chance with you?"

"Nia, you have to see that Kendall uses her body as a weapon. It's probably her greatest asset and she uses it to get what she wants, I know that now. Looking back, I can see that our relationship was all about the physical; she never really knew me. But then again, I was confused. I thought love and sex were synonymous and she was able to wrap me around her little finger."

"And now?" If Kendall could seduce anything with a pulse, what about Damon?

"Now, I know that love is about trust and mutual respect." Damon rubbed his head. "Listen, Nia. I'm sorry. I made a mistake. I should have told you about the engagement before now."

"God, Damon. You're saying all the right things. You're saying everything I want to hear, but how can I believe it? You were content to keep me in the dark about this Kendall business, even when she's been nearly stalking us. Would you ever have told me if your father hadn't mentioned it tonight?"

"I would have told you, but I didn't want you to think any less of me for being such a total schmuck."

"I would never have thought that."

"Maybe not, but it was how I felt. Nia, please tell me we can get pass this." He rubbed her shoulders, but she jerked away. "Give us a chance. Don't give up on us before we've really had a chance to start."

Nia rubbed her temples. She had been fighting off a migraine all night. "I'm not giving up on us. I'm just tired. It's been an emotionally draining evening. But don't for a second think I've forgotten about this." She pointed her finger at him.

"I just love it when you're all fiery and passionate."

Nia laughed at the comment. Sometimes Damon was too much; she was in no mood to fight with him. She just wanted to go to bed.

"Don't be mad at me," he begged, wrapping his arms around her. She struggled to get out of his warm embrace.

"Let me go," she said, pushing against his hard chest. It was no use. It was like pushing against a brick wall.

"No," he murmured into her ear. "Not before you forgive me." He took her face in his hands and kissed her forehead, her cheeks and her lips. She tried not responding to him. When he rimmed her lips with his tongue, seeking entry to her mouth, she kept them firmly shut and pushed away from him.

"Nia, I don't give a rat's ass about my family's feelings. They have to accept and love you, they won't have a choice."

"And why's that?" She looked up at him defiantly.

"Because I love you."

Nia stared back at him openmouthed. That was the last response she ever expected and Damon wasn't sure she was ready to hear it. He had hoped for a more romantic setting before he laid his heart bare, but there it was. She was quiet. "Nia, did you hear what I just said?"

She nodded, but tried to back away from him. He could see the fear in her eyes, but he wasn't going to let her walk away. He pulled her tighter against him.

"Nia, I love you. I have ever since the first moment I saw you at the Whitmores' party," he said. He knew that now was the most inopportune time to blurt out his love for her, but he meant every word. "And you've had me completely captivated ever since."

"Damon?" She stared back at him, wide-eyed. What she saw in his eyes made her tremble. He really did love her. She was beyond words; her heart was so full.

Nia desperately wanted to say that she loved him, too. Yet she couldn't seem to form the words and say what was truly in her heart. "Oh, Damon—"

He didn't give her the chance to finish. Instead, he kissed her fiercely. Massaging her lips until she parted them, Damon dipped inside to stroke her tongue over and over with his. She tried to rein in her response, give her mind a chance to catch up with her body, but the onslaught of Damon's kisses drugged her senses.

"Don't do that," he said, pleading. "Don't act like you don't want me."

"I can't think."

Bowing his head, Damon rained kisses along her neck before making his way to tease one pearl-dropped earlobe. Nia struggled even more; she needed time to let it all register, but he wouldn't let her go. When he found *the* spot and sucked on her neck, her legs buckled underneath her and she succumbed.

"Tell me you want me," he said.

She moaned. Damon was a master at knowing how to evoke a response from her, and at this moment, she didn't care if she didn't fit into his world, or if he was passing the time with her before going back to Kendall; she just wanted him.

Her defenses were weakened. "Yes, oh, yes. I need you now," she whispered urgently in his ear.

That was all Damon needed to hear. The hunger in him was as strong as Nia's, if not more so. They had only just become lovers, but she was a part of him now, a part he couldn't live without. They only made it as far as the couch before tumbling down in a mess of stripped clothing. Nia accepted his weight and her soft curves melted in his steel-like arms. She stroked his tongue with hers and Damon shuddered at the erotic caress.

His lips took a slow journey, tracing a path of wet kisses down the valley between her breasts, cupping them in his palms. Shaping them with his hands, he took one engorged chocolate nipple in his mouth and sucked on it voraciously. She felt feverish with desire as tension swelled in her body. His fingers made their way to the damp curls between her legs, parting the soft feminine folds as he boldly caressed the core of her womanhood. When he mimicked the thrust that his body would take, going in and out, Nia undulated against him. The sensations he evoked caused ripple after ripple of pleasure to envelop her. She was lost in it and Damon was the anchor. He tried to gather her close in his arms, but she wanted to take over. She smoothed on a condom before straddling him and guiding him inside.

He sank into her satin velvetness, letting her sheath him tightly. He shifted position so he could lift her hips off the couch and angle himself to thrust inside her more deeply. She tried to hasten the pace, wanting to feel that pulsating tension build within her.

"Easy, baby, or it will be over quickly," he said, groaning.

Slowly, deliberately, he found a rhythm. Welcoming her moist heat, he drove inside her hot, damp feminine cave and Nia contracted her muscles, tightening herself around him. He wanted to prolong their pleasure, but he couldn't hold back—his manhood screamed for release. Accelerating the pace, he quenched both their mounting desires. He gave a shout as his explosive release triggered her climax. He gripped Nia to him as he moaned her name in ecstasy. After the spasms subsided, Damon lay in her arms, feeling completely fulfilled. He'd never felt this strongly about a woman before or had such a powerful physical attraction. Could it be because he had truly made love for the first time?

Nia awoke feeling out of sorts, as though the world had suddenly shifted off its axis. She felt lost and out of control.

Wiping the sleep from her eyes, she found Damon staring down at her. He was holding a breakfast tray filled with bacon, eggs, toast, orange juice and piping-hot coffee. It smelled delicious and Nia sat up, pulling the sheet up with her.

"You didn't have to do this." She looked down from his penetrating gaze.

"I wanted to." He sat down and brushed his lips against hers. "Here, have some breakfast." He sat the tray in her lap and pushed some pillows up for her to lean back against. He loved watching her eat; she really enjoyed her food. Why couldn't she feel that way about life and love? She was ravenous and tore into the meal. She hadn't eaten much the night before at that horrible dinner with his parents.

"Thank you, everything was delicious," she said when she finished. She pushed the tray away, but held on to the coffee. Damon took the tray and placed it on the floor. Why was he watching her so intently? Had he changed his mind in the cold light of day about loving her? Did he want to take it all back?

Damon could see the fear in her eyes. "Nothing has changed, Nia." Taking the coffee cup, he put it on the night table and took her small, delicate hands in his. "I love you as much this morning as I did last night. I promise."

"No matter what your family thinks about me?" she inquired.

"Nia." Damon clutched her face in both hands and peered into her eyes. "Like I told you last night, I don't care about what my family thinks of you, or anything else that I do. I love you for who you are. Not how you were raised or what clothes you wear. I love you just as you are."

They were the words she had waited to hear all her life. Damon loved her as completely as she loved him. Could this be real and true and lasting? She hoped so, but only time would tell.

"Listen, baby," he began, "my father called while

you were sleeping. He has this big deal brewing and he wants me to handle the negotiations. It would be a great coup for Bradley Savings & Loan. I know this is bad timing, but I have to leave for a few days." He hated to go away now when Nia desperately needed reassurance about their relationship, but he had no choice.

"Of course, I understand." She didn't really, but she couldn't hold on too tightly or he might pull away.

"I promise to call you every day," he continued. "And every night. We can have all kinds of lascivious phone calls."

"Damon, you're a devil! But before you leave, I have a few lascivious thoughts of my own." She jumped off the bed and rushed into the bathroom with Damon hot on her heels.

Much later, they emerged from their shower, during which Damon had lathered her entire body with a soapy sponge while the stood underneath the pulsing tap water. Nia felt almost giddy as she got dressed. She put on a sleek burgundy sweater dress and matching cardigan. Since she had been dating Damon, she felt more comfortable about showing her shape. Now she wore clothes that accentuated her assets. Having Damon in her life had had a positive effect.

"Are you gonna miss me?" he asked as he packed his suitcase, adding toiletries and his favorite power suit.

"Terribly." She stood on her tiptoes to give him a kiss on the cheek.

"That means I'll be in for a real treat when I get back." He grinned roguishly.

"You betcha."

"So what do you have planned for the weekend?" Damon asked. This weekend without him would give her plenty of time to adjust to their newfound love and maybe one day soon she would be ready to allow him to put a ring on her finger. There wasn't a doubt in his mind that Nia was meant for him and that she would be Mrs. Damon Bradley someday. He only had to convince her of that fact.

"This and that," she said, making his bed. He loved that she felt comfortable enough to get domestic at his place. She smoothed the comforter down and plumped up the pillows.

"Are you still thinking about seeing your father?"

"Actually, yes," she admitted reluctantly. She hated to see her father and not know what was he was going to say. Generally she liked to see a train wreck coming, but she couldn't put off this meeting; it was long overdue.

"Don't chicken out." He closed his suitcase. "Nia, I think you need to do this. Maybe it'll give you the closure you need. You know—help you move forward."

"You could be right. I'll tell you all about it when you get back. Do you need me to drive you to the airport?"

"No, I hired a limo."

"All right. I'll see you when you get back."

"Give me a kiss," he demanded, pulling her into his embrace. Her arms encircled his neck and she gave him a deep, dizzying kiss for the record books. "I'll see you soon and don't forget to lock up." He gave her a gentle pat on the bottom before leaving.

# Chapter 16

It was midafternoon when Nia entered the door of her apartment. She loved staying at Damon's condominium; it made her feel close to him even though he wasn't there.

Last night, Damon had told her he loved her and she'd completely froze. She hadn't revealed to him how she really felt and she regretted that. The next time when he said those words, she would repeat them back. Of course, now she would have to wait a few days. Nia was going to miss him terribly. Being with Damon had become second to breathing.

Turning on her answering machine, she was stunned by what she heard. Simone Bradley had called and left a message, apologizing to her for her behavior the night before and asking Nia to brunch. Could she have been wrong about his family? They'd treated her so horribly, made her feel small and inadequate as though they judged her and found her wanting. Now she was calling? What gave? Had Damon put her up to it?

If she wanted the relationship with Damon to last, she didn't need to be at odds with his family. She wanted—no, make that needed—their acceptance. She owed it to Damon to find out. She picked up the receiver to accept, but faltered for a second. Was she really prepared for a lunch with Simone Bradley, housewife, mother and decorator extraordinaire?

She nodded her head. Yes, she could do this. She had to. It would make Damon so happy if she and his mother saw eye to eye. Nia would make every effort to ensure that it happened. Dialing his parents' home number, she was surprised when Simone answered on the first ring.

"Hello, Bradley residence."

"Um, hello, Mrs. Bradley. This is, uh—" Nia paused. The sound of his mother's voice triggered a wash of anxiety. "This is Nia Taylor." Great, now she was a stuttering idiot.

"Hello, Nia, I'm so happy to hear from you," Mrs. Bradley responded evenly. "I wasn't sure you would return my call after we behaved so abominably."

"Contrary to what you might think about me, I do know how important Damon's family is to him," Nia replied honestly. "And I felt like I should at least make the effort."

"That's very generous of you, dear. You could've caused quite a rift between my son and his family if you chose to, but I'm grateful that you have not. Would you please accept my deepest apology and join me for brunch on Sunday? My husband is out of town working on some business deal with Damon. It would be just the two of us and maybe Jordan if she stops by."

*Wonderful, the bitch on wheels,* Nia thought. "That would be lovely," she said. "What time?"

"Shall we say eleven o'clock?"

"Great, I'll see you then." Nia replaced the receiver in its handle.

One more call awaited her and now was as good a time as any. She grabbed the notepad sitting beside the phone and punched in the numbers. He too picked up on the first ring.

"Hello."

"Hello, Nathaniel," she started. She figured calling him by his first name was OK. He hadn't earned the right to "father" or "dad." Those were for parents that were actually a part of her life. "It's Nia."

"I know," her father replied. "I recognized your voice. I'm so happy to hear from you."

"Well, thanks," she murmured uneasily. How was she supposed to respond to that? "I've thought about what you said, and I think that maybe it's time we talked."

"Nia, that's great." He sounded genuinely pleased, though she wasn't sure why. She hadn't exactly received him with open arms. "Where would you like to meet? Would you like me to come to your place?"

"Um, no." She had to think quickly. Someplace safe and neutral. "How about Sunday at my aunt's? I'm sure it would be fine with her. About four?"

"That's fine. I'll see you then."

"Bye."

Well, that wasn't as hard as she had expected. Perhaps tomorrow wouldn't be so bad after all. Later she called her Aunt Olivia, who was ecstatic that Nia had finally agreed to meet with her father. She didn't mind them using her house as a meeting place; as matter of fact, she thought it was best—that way, she could play referee to the "fallout." *What did she mean by fallout?* Nia wondered later. Exactly what did her father have to say?

Nia was nervous as she drove her car up the Bradleys' driveway the following Sunday. She didn't relish going to this meeting, but it would mean so much to Damon and, like Simone had said, she didn't want to be the reason for a rift between him and his family, no matter how much they might deserve it. Hopefully this time she was more suitably attired. She'd chosen to wear a smart pink linen dress that came appropriately below the knee. Simple jewelry adorned her ears and she applied only a light touch of mascara and lipstick. She didn't want to look like a floozy and appear overly made up. Her short mane had just been relaxed and styled the day before at her favorite hairdresser. It was important she made a better impression than the first time.

She parked her car, walked up the driveway and rang the doorbell, waiting for the nightmare to begin. Nia was surprised when Simone Bradley greeted her at the door instead of their butler. This time, her perfect shiny auburn hair hung straight down her back while pearls adorned her neck and ears. She was casually sophisticated, wearing a cream cashmere sweater and long pleated skirt.

"Nia, darling," she exclaimed with open arms. Obligingly, Nia walked into them and returned the hug. "Thank you for coming."

"Thank you for having me, Mrs. Bradley," Nia replied when they broke apart.

"As I said on the phone, Nia, it was very gracious of you to come for brunch after our poor behavior last Friday night. Please allow me to make it up to you today."

"That really isn't necessary, Mrs. Bradley."

"Please, call me Simone."

"All right."

"I thought we could have tea first in the kitchen

and then afterward we can have brunch, which I've prepared myself." His mother gave her a warm, welcoming smile. "Please follow me."

Where was the ice-cold woman from the night before? Surely this couldn't be the same person. She expected that they would dine in the formal dining room, which would be as good a place as any to intimidate her. Apparently, she'd misjudged Simone Bradley. His mother had actually cooked for her.

Could those perfectly manicured pink nails have slaved over a hot stove? Damon told Nia that his mother was quite the gourmet chef and cooked a big meal on Christmas, but somehow Nia found it all so hard to believe. Smiling, she followed Simone down the hallway into the large eat-in kitchen. It was a lovely sunny and bright room; Nia saw why it was one of Damon's favorites.

"Please sit down," Simone said, motioning to a chair. She went to retrieve the whistling teakettle while Nia sat and took inventory of the decorating, name-brand appliances and huge indoor pool and patio. The view in the morning light was breathtaking.

Simone brought back two teacups and set the hot kettle on a coaster before joining Nia. She reached out to take Nia's hand in hers and looked her straight in the eye. "You really are a lovely girl," she stated simply, as if the thought suddenly occurred to her. *Am I supposed to say thank you?*

"Nia, I just want to say how sorry I am," Simone paused, "for the way my husband and I treated you the other night. It was horrible, really. I don't know what came over me. I know that maybe my husband may harbor illusions about a family merger with the Montgomerys, but I was under no such illusion. All

I can say is that I'm terribly sorry and beg for your forgiveness. You mean the world to Damon and I don't want to do or say anything that might hurt you."

Nia was stunned after his mother's speech. She appreciated the courage it must have taken for a proud woman to make that admission. She would accept it graciously and not rub salt in the wound. "Thank you, Simone." Nia patted her hand. "It means a lot to me to hear you say that. And I promise to try not to do or *say* anything that might embarrass you either."

His mother laughed throatily. "Dear, the only thing you need to do is be yourself and everything else will fall into play. And next time," she smiled, "please don't let Damon dress you. Please allow me to shop with you. I am very good at it. It's one of my favorite pastimes."

Nia laughed. "I think I can do that." There was still something on her mind and she hated to bring it up now, but she couldn't help herself. "Simone, is there anything you can tell me about Damon's relationship with Kendall?" Perhaps his mother could shed more light on the situation.

"Nia, are you sure you want to discuss her?" She was amazed the young woman had asked. "I thought this was a sore subject between the two of you."

"In a way, she is," Nia admitted. "But I need to know more because Damon hasn't been exactly forthcoming."

"Do you think my son is hiding something from you?"

"I don't know what to think," Nia answered honestly. She never knew what to expect next from Kendall. From the moment they met, she had been a thorn in their sides, constantly popping up where they were. "All I know is that he's been very tolerant of her shenanigans. Too tolerant, if you ask me." She went on to explain the stunts Kendall had pulled.

"Oh my, I had no idea," Simone said, clutching her chest. "Damon hadn't mentioned any of this to us."

"I guess he was embarrassed by her behavior and didn't want you to know."

"Well, that's no excuse. I will talk to her mother at once." Simone stood up. "I will not have her disrespecting my son or you. Deal or no deal."

"Really, Simone, that isn't necessary. Damon and I can handle Kendall," Nia implored, touching her arm. "Matter of fact, she hasn't been around much lately." Which could only mean that Kendall was preparing something devious, but that wasn't Mrs. Bradley's concern.

"Are you sure?"

"Absolutely." Reluctantly, Simone sat back down and Nia breathed a sigh of relief. The last thing she wanted was for Damon to find out she'd discussed their personal relationship with his mother. "And, please, let's keep this between the two of us."

"As you wish," his mother conceded. "But please let me know if there's anything I can do."

They spent the rest of the afternoon drinking tea and eating his mother's fabulous brunch. Simone sure knew how to make a meal. The fresh fruit, grilled lemon-dill salmon and salad of mixed greens with a light raspberry vinaigrette were delicious; Nia even indulged in a rich custard for dessert. His mother gave her a tour of the house while entertaining her with tales of Damon in his youth. Nia told her about her aunt and grandparents, who'd been a constant influence in her life since her mother had passed away. She was quite shocked at how happily she'd spent the afternoon with Damon's mother. After the last time at bat, Nia feared there would be a strikeout.

The time passed quickly and Nia begged her pardon; she was due at her aunt's for a family reunion of her own.

# Chapter 17

"I made a fresh pot of coffee," Aunt Olivia said when Nia walked into the kitchen half an hour later. It was four o'clock and Nia's father hadn't arrived yet. "I figured you and Nathaniel might need something a little stronger than tea."

"Thank you, Auntie Livvie."

It had been very smart to agree to talk to him so quickly or Nia might have agonized for days before finally canceling. She shifted nervously in the chair, anxious to get it all over with. When the doorbell chimed, signaling his arrival, Nia's heart lurched, but she reminded herself that she was in control of the situation. *She* was the one who had invited him to talk.

Her aunt walked in a few minutes later with Nathaniel Alexander right behind her. Nia allowed herself to really take a look at the man who was the reason she was in this world. Life must have been very good to him because he didn't look his age. He was fifty years old without the flabby stomach she saw in most men his age, and immaculately dressed in a blue sweater and tailored gray slacks. Leaving her mother must have worked to his benefit, Nia thought glumly.

He stood at the entrance to the kitchen while Nia

appraised him, not sure if he should enter the room. Her aunt nudged him inside. "Nia," he said, nodding his headed toward her.

"Hello," she whispered.

"May I?" he asked, pointing to the chair opposite her. She nodded and he sat down slowly.

"Nia, I am very grateful that you agreed to talk to me," he began.

"You indicated that I don't know the whole story. So let's hear it." She didn't want him to think anything was different between them just because she'd had a change of heart.

"I don't know where to begin."

"How about from the beginning?" she suggested. "Like when you met my mother."

"I'm going to give you two some time alone," her aunt said before quietly leaving the room. Nia hadn't realized she was still in the kitchen.

Nia watched Nathan wring his hands until he finally pushed away from the table. Walking to the back door, he stared outside her aunt's backyard. There was a long pause before he finally began again.

"I was a producer's assistant. It was a thankless job that paid very little money, with no real rewards except that every wannabe theater actress in the Chicago area wanted to be with me. They thought I was the easiest route to a plum lead role, and I admit I used some of those women. All I was interested in back then was the next pretty face that came along. That is, until I met your mother. Lily was like a breath of fresh air. She hadn't been hardened by the brutality of the business. She was so beautiful, warm and giving, and maybe a little naive, too.

"I'm sure," Nia said harshly. Nathan turned around at her sharp tongue.

She looked at him, eager for him to continue and tell her more about this side of her mother, yet angry at his callous treatment of women. She tried to sit and listen dispassionately as he continued to pace back and forth uneasily, wearing out the kitchen tile. She could see the distress in his eyes.

"Your mother and I met one night after a wrap party. I was smitten the first moment I saw her." His eyes filled with tears. "I can remember it like it was yesterday. . . ." His voice trailed off as he recalled memories of the past. "Your mother came in with a group of young actresses who had bit parts in the play. With her long black hair and tall figure, Lily stood out from the rest and I knew I had to meet her. Introductions were made. I could see that Lily was awed by me, and perhaps I took advantage of her naïveté. I'd been around the block, I knew the game. You see, Nia, I was used to jumping in and out of women's beds. With no thought or care about tomorrow."

Nia shifted in her seat. Maybe she didn't want to hear anymore. Her father was telling her to her face that he was a playboy and used her mother. It was more than she could bear. She put up her hand to silence him. "Please, no more."

"No," he stated adamantly. "You need to hear the whole story." Why did he want to continue? Didn't he realize that if there was a pedestal, he had just fallen farther off it?

"I wooed Lily. Taking her out for dinner, nightclubs and shows. I wanted Lily to be impressed. She didn't make me feel like a two-bit gofer who went around grabbing my producer's lunch or picking up his dry cleaning. When she looked up at me, I felt like a big man. We started spending more and more time together and one thing led to another and we became intimate. I didn't realize it at the time, but Lily wasn't ready for that kind of relationship. Brought up by a Baptist minister, Lily was very sheltered."

Nia listened. Little did he know that history could easily repeat itself.

"When Lily came to me and told me she was pregnant, I was flabbergasted. I was young, only twenty-two at the time, and I admit I behaved badly when she told me. I wasn't ready for marriage. I wasn't ready to be a father. I told her she needed to get an abortion."

He heard Nia's sharp intake of breath, but he continued.

"I offered her money, but Lily threw it back in my face. She told me she was a good Christian girl and she could never kill her baby. She begged me to do the right thing and marry her, make an honest woman out of her, but I refused. She was heartbroken. I told her she was acting childish and needed to grow up. 'Go back home to your father,' I advised her. I remember her crying uncontrollably. She didn't know how she was going to face her father and tell him she had failed him. She feared he would never forgive her."

"I guess I can take the story from here," Nia said, finding her voice. "She told my grandfather she was pregnant and he was devastated. He told her she was no longer any daughter of his. That's when my mother went to live with my Aunt Olivia—" She didn't get to finish.

"God, you're so bullheaded. You're like a dog

with a bone once you have an idea in your head, just as stubborn as your mother. Can I finish, please?" he asked, exasperated.

"Why should I let you finish?" Her voice rose and she stood up in defiance. "I know what happened."

"You know everything, do you? Do you know that I realized my mistake? Realized how much I was in love with your mother and that I was a fool to let her go?" he bellowed. "Do you know that I went to your grandfather's place to find your mother?"

Nia sat down, dumbfounded. She'd never heard any of this. Her grandfather never mentioned that her father came to look for her mother. He always indicated that Nathan left Chicago without a backward glance to her mother or the child she carried. Was this true? Or was Nathan lying to put himself in a better light?

"Yes, it's true." Her father responded to her silence. "I know you have every right to doubt my sincerity, but I am telling you the truth, Nia. In the weeks after Lily came back home and went to live with Olivia, I tried to go on with my life as if nothing had changed. I went through the motions at my job. I even tried picking up a few women and taking them home with me, but it was no use. I couldn't get the picture of your mother out of my head. I was in love with Lily Taylor and I had to get her back. I figured that she would have gone to her father for help, so I sought him out."

"If what you say is true, why did my grandfather never mention it?" Nia asked. She couldn't understand it. Her grandpa knew how much she yearned for a father. Why wouldn't he say Nathaniel had come back for Lily?

Nia looked to Nathaniel for answers. He looked

down at his feet as if guilty of something. But what? "I'm waiting," she said.

Nathan knew he had to tell Nia the whole truth, no matter how damaging it might be. He ignored her question and continued. "I found his address and I went to him. I told him I was ready to marry Lily and asked for her hand in marriage. He told me Lily was gone, that she went to live with a relative in Louisiana to get away from the shame I had caused her and the Taylor family. He told me you and Lily were better off without me. What could I possibly have to offer the two of you on a producer assistant's salary?"

His voice started to crack and it suddenly dawned on Nia that she really wasn't about to like what she was going to hear next. Alarm bells were going off in her head and a strange sense of foreboding washed over her.

"I'm ashamed to admit that I believed him. Your grandfather was very convincing and commanding; just being in his presence scared me. I could see why Lily wanted to get away from his strict rules and regimented life." His face contorted as he remembered shameful memories from the past. "But I can't put it all on him. I was the one who ran."

Nia's heart sank. This couldn't be true. Her grandfather couldn't be the reason why she grew up without a father. She shook her head in denial, putting her hands over her ears.

"Just stop, OK! I can't hear any more of this. I won't let you talk against my grandfather. No matter his faults, my grandfather loves me and he would never have done what you've suggested." She got up from the table. "This was a mistake. I should never have agreed to this meeting. If I had known you were going to place all the blame on my grandfather . . ." Nia's voice trailed off. "My God, have you no shame?"

"Nia," her father pleaded, "I know how awful all this must sound. I'm so ashamed of my actions, ashamed that I let your grandfather talk me into leaving the woman I loved and our unborn child. I wasn't man enough to stand up to your grandfather and I took the money he offered."

"Money? What money? What are you saying to me?" Her eyes widened and she blinked several times. Tears clouded her sight.

"I'm saying that I accepted five thousand dollars from your grandfather to leave Chicago and never come back, to leave you and your mother and never make contact with you again."

"Oh, my God," she cried. Horror engulfed her as the world she knew came crumbling down around her. The words coming out of his mouth weren't a comfort to her; instead, they were little daggers jabbing at her heart.

He accepted money, a bribe, to leave her mother pregnant and alone. Nia stumbled out of her chair and it crashed to the floor with a loud thud. "How could you have done such a thing!"

Her aunt rushed into the kitchen. "Is everything OK?" She looked back and forth between the two of them, saw the strain on Nathaniel's face, the streaked tears on Nia's. "Is there anything I can do?" she asked, moving toward them.

"No, Olivia, but thank you," her father replied, coming forward to block her aunt's path. "I have to hash this out with Nia on my own."

Her aunt looked at her, but Nia didn't say a word. Nia was beyond words at this point. Her aunt reluctantly left the room, leaving a deafening silence behind. Nia heard the ticking of the grandfather clock in the dining room as she waited for Nathaniel to finish what he started.

"Nia, I wasn't thinking clearly when I accepted that money." Nathan ran his fingers over his hair.

"Yes, you were," Nia retorted. "You said it yourself. You were young. You only thought of yourself. I'm sure five thousand dollars sounded like a lot of money at the time. It was enough to sell out the woman you claimed to love. How happy you must have been not to be burdened down by a wife and child. That money must have seemed like a real lifesaver."

"That's not true, Nia." He rushed to her and grabbed her by the shoulders. "Please believe me when I say that I loved your mother. Lily was one of the best things that ever happened to me. She gave me you."

"After everything you've just told me, do you honestly expect me to believe that?" She shook her head in amazement. "You must think I'm as naive as my mother once was. Well, listen up, Daddy, dear. I didn't just fall off the gravy train. And she didn't give me to you. I am not yours to have. Now, let me go!" she shouted.

He released her shoulders and stepped away. He didn't know how he was going to get through to her to make her see the truth. "I know this is a lot to take in and I've kind of sprung this all on you. But maybe in time, when you've had a chance to think this all out, perhaps you might give me a chance to be a father to you." At Nia's look of total incredulity, he rephrased his statement. "I mean, maybe we could find some way to be friends."

So this was his motivation all along, to try and form some kind of relationship with her. He was delusional; that was never going to happen.

"Friends? I have enough of those, Mr. Alexander," she stated firmly. "I don't need any more. And as for being a father, well, that time has come and passed. I don't recall seeing you when I needed a father. Where were you when I was sick? Or when I scraped my knees growing up?" She lifted her knee and pointed to a mark that could still be seen even through her sheer hose. "Where were you when the kids at school teased me and called me a bastard?" She turned to gauge his reaction. She had hit her mark. His eyes glistened and his shoulders sagged; at that moment he looked every bit his fifty years. "I don't recall seeing you then."

"I see," he replied, sounding completely deflated. He looked closely at her and knew he had reached an impasse. "You have no room in your life for me."

"No, I don't," Nia said. Her voice belied the inner turmoil that raged within her. She would not feel sorry for him. He didn't deserve her sorrow or her pity. What he had done was reprehensible. Even in her wildest dreams, she would never have conceived that he would tell such a story.

"You have no idea how I've regretted the choice I made all those years ago."

"Regret?" Tears were falling down her cheeks in waves as she wiped them away with the back of her hand. "You can keep your regrets. What good are they to me now?" Her father tried to walk toward her to comfort her. "Don't come near me!" she yelled. "I don't want to hear another word."

Walking to the back door, Nia fumbled with the lock. She wanted him out, out of her aunt's house and out of her life. What was she thinking? What had she hoped this meeting would accomplish? It most certainly hadn't given her closure. Instead, it had her questioning everything she believed to be true about her grandfather, who she knew adored her to tears. He would never hurt her, she thought, not hearing her father come up behind her

She held the door open and he started to walk through it, but turned back momentarily. "No matter what I've done or what you may think of me, I want you to know that I love you, Nia. I always have."

He left, leaving Nia sagged against the door. Hearing the door close, her aunt came rushing in and enveloped her in a huge hug. Nia clung to her.

"Oh, baby," her aunt murmured. "I know how hard that was for you to hear."

Nia pulled away from her embrace. "You knew about this?"

"Yes, I did. Nathaniel told me when he first came to town."

"You've known this all along and you didn't tell me!" She couldn't believe it. Now her aunt was in on the lies, too.

"It wasn't my story to tell, Nia. You told me to stay out of your life."

"So for once you actually followed my advice?" Nia gave a sarcastic half smile. "Now, that's surprising," Nia sighed.

Her aunt was right. Nia couldn't be mad at her for her father's choices, but there was one thing she needed and that was confirmation. And there was only one place she was going to get it.

"I've got to go, Auntie."

Her aunt released her from the embrace and Nia

searched for her purse, but couldn't find it. Her aunt found it lying on the floor and held it up.

"Thanks," Nia said, taking the purse and heading toward the door.

"Nia, I know where you're going." her aunt stated. "Do you want me to come with you?"

"No. This is something I have to do on my own." Nia gave her a kiss on the cheek and made a quick exit through the door.

# Chapter 18

Nia was a maze of conflicted emotions as she drove to confront her grandfather. It was no easy task, but she had to know the truth. She would need nerves of steel. Samuel Taylor was not an easy man to stand up to, and in the back of her mind, Nia could see how he could easily have intimidated a young man. Dismissing the notion, she parked the car and walked up the steps to her grandparents' house. Nervously, she rang the doorbell and waited for someone to answer.

Her grandmother opened the door and greeted her. "Hi, sweetie. To what do we owe this visit? Not that I'm not happy to see you, of course."

"Hi, Grandma." Nia went inside and gave her a quick squeeze and peck on the cheek. "Is Grandpa around?" she asked, leaving the foyer.

"Did I hear the doorbell?" her grandfather bellowed. Nia followed the sound of this voice and found him sitting in the living room in his big recliner, watching his favorite Sunday night program, *60 Minutes*.

"Grandpa," Nia said firmly, sitting on the couch opposite the recliner.

"Baby doll. What are you doing here?" Using the remote control, he clicked the television off.

Nia stared back at him and searched his face for a sign that Nathan was right. Nia couldn't imagine that her grandfather would ever do anything to hurt her. Now she was preparing to accuse him of the unthinkable when all he had ever done was love her. She shouldn't have come. She started to stand, but her grandfather stood up and sat down beside her on the couch.

He sensed her reluctance and grabbed her by the hand. "What is it, baby girl? I can see you have something on your mind. Tell your grandpa what it is."

Nia ran her fingers through her hair. There was no easy way of finding out if Nathaniel was telling the truth, except to ask the question. There was no skating around the issue; she was just going to have to say it. She looked her grandfather straight in the eye.

"Grandpa, did my father come to you looking for my mother? Did he ask for Lily's hand in marriage?"

Her grandfather sucked in his breath. He dropped her hands and stood up. "Nia, what is all this about? Have you been talking to that man behind my back after I warned you not to?"

Nia's heart fell. That wasn't an answer. Matter of fact, it was admission of guilt. She tapped her fingers against her knees, willing herself to calm down. "Yes, I did. And I was shocked by what he told me."

Nia waited for him to stop her but he didn't, so she finished. "He told me you paid him five thousand dollars to leave town and never come back. To leave my mother, leave me." she said, her voice becoming louder with each sentence.

Her grandmother came running into the room. "Samuel, what's going on?"

Nia wouldn't turn away from her grandfather. She was determined to look him in the eye and know for sure.

"Please tell me what he said isn't true! Please, Grandpa," she implored, looking to him for reassurance. Her grandfather shifted his weight from one foot to the other. Nia looked to her grandmother, but she looked down at the ground. They both looked guilty as hell.

"Please tell me you didn't lie to me all my life. That you didn't deprive me of the father I longed for." Her knees buckled and she dropped to the floor. Nia's heart lurched and tears racked her entire body.

She felt her grandmother's hands on her, stroking her back, trying to ease her grief, but Nia pushed her away. "Don't touch me!" she yelled. Finding some inner strength, she rose to her knees. "I want an answer. Is it true what my father said, that you paid him to leave town?"

"I know exactly what I did," her grandfather responded finally. "And I would do it all over again."

Nia gasped. "Oh, my God, do you know what you've done?" She shook her head, unable to believe the words that were coming out of his mouth. "Have you no shame!"

"Listen, Nia." She heard the change in his voice. He was giving her the stern voice he'd given when she was being chastised as a child. "I did what I felt was best for my daughter at the time. She didn't need a good-for-nothing like Nathaniel Alexander. He had nothing to offer her. She deserved better than him."

"Nothing to offer her?" Nia was furious. Her hands shook. She laid one over the other to steady them. "He was ready to marry her. To be a father."

"That's what he's claiming now, huh," he huffed. He paced the living room floor, kicking up the plastic covering the carpet. "The young man that came to my house that day was in no way ready to be a father and a husband to my Lily."

"Who made you judge and jury?"

"I was her father. I knew what was best for her," he stated simply. She stared at him. He honestly believed he was right. The Reverend Samuel Taylor had appointed himself God. She shook her head in disbelief.

Her grandmother finally spoke. "Nia, your grandfather is right. Nathaniel Alexander was a young man with no future. He didn't have a steady job. How was he going to support your mother and a baby? After talking with your father, he realized he was in love with the idea of being in love. So he did the only thing he could, he took the money and left."

"Condemning my mother to a life of loneliness. Because that's what she had in her final days. She thought my father didn't want her. That he used her, and then deserted her. You have no idea what that must have done to her. It killed her spirit."

"How would you know anything?" her grandmother asked quietly. "You weren't even born yet."

"I know what she lived through because I've lived through it myself. I know what it's like to be used and discarded." Nia noticed her grandparents' shocked expressions. It dawned on her that her family knew so little about her. Nia pointed to her chest. "I made those same bad judgment calls in the past. But the difference is that unlike my mother, I was able to rectify them. She never got the chance, and the sad part about it is that she never will."

"Baby girl, I don't know what more you want us to say," her grandfather said soothingly as if quieting a small child who'd had a tantrum. "Nothing will bring Lily back."

His dark, wistful eyes spoke volumes. He thought he could placate her and she would fall back in line, but he was dead wrong.

"I guess there's nothing more to say." Nia stood and grabbed her purse off the side table.

"Please don't leave like this," her grandmother pleaded, standing in her path to the doorway as Nia hurtled past her. "You're angry and you have every right to be. We should have told you sooner, but . . ." She tried to find the right words.

"Don't apologize, Melinda," her grandfather said. "We did what we thought was best."

"That's because you're always right." Nia turned around at the door to face him. "You're never wrong, are you, Grandpa? Why can't you admit that you made a mistake? And why do you always stand by him, Grandma, no matter what he does? Even when you know he's wrong?" Her grandmother lowered her head, tears falling down her cheeks. She waited for a response from either of them, and when none was forthcoming, Nia walked out of their lives.

The next morning, Nia awoke with a massive headache. She'd tossed and turned all night as nightmares about her mother haunted her with images of her fighting in the delivery room for the life of her unborn baby girl at her own expense. Nia had woken up in a cold sweat, her shirt soaked through. Around seven o'clock, she'd finally given up and gone for a jog. Damon would be pleased that his good habits had rubbed off on her.

Nia wished he were there. She needed him so much. When he was near, she could get through anything. But unfortunately she'd had to go it alone over the last couple of days. Even Lexie wasn't around. She was out of town at a fashion show in Milan. What she wouldn't give to have her best friend's shoulder to cry on.

Learning that her father hadn't abandoned her as she had thought left her mind spinning. How could she have known that her grandfather played a major part in his absence by paying him to leave town? It had all been so much.

In her wildest dreams she never would have expected her grandfather to admit that. He wasn't even ashamed or embarrassed about his actions. The worst part was when he'd told her that nothing would have changed the outcome of her mother's death. How could he know that? Knowing Nathaniel wanted to marry her could have made all the difference. Nia knew nothing would bring her mother back, but she could at least have had a father.

How could she forget what they'd done? Or forgive the lies? As much as she loved her grandparents, she didn't respect them now and wasn't sure she ever could.

# Chapter 19

Turning off the ignition, Nia jumped out of her car. She was so happy Damon would return that day. She didn't know how it had happened, but suddenly Damon meant everything to her. She couldn't imagine her life without his dashing smile, his engaging wit and their passionate lovemaking. After seeing the destruction lies could cause, Nia knew she had to tell Damon how she really felt. Time was too precious to waste a single minute.

Damon had been delayed for several days due to a setback in his deal. As promised, they'd called each other every day even if it was just for a quick chat. They talked about her day or how the campaign was going and each night Damon would fill her head with sexual fantasies, all of which he planned to fulfill once he returned. She let out a deep breath. *Easy, girl, gotta give the man time to get in the door.*

It was amazing, but she finally had the kind of relationship she'd dreamed of and envied when she saw other couples. Their relationship was nothing like her grandparents', where her grandfather ruled the roost. She wanted and craved more for herself, and with Damon by her side, Nia knew she just might achieve it. More than ever, she was determined not to let paranoia about Kendall take over. Damon had promised that there were no more secrets and she believed him. Nia was ready to tell him she loved him, to shout it from the rooftops to whoever would listen.

Together, they'd jumped over so many hurdles: his family, Kendall, even Nia's lack of trust in men. So there could be nothing but good things ahead for them now. Tonight she was going to tell him just how much she loved him and then they would fall into bed.

But first she would work her way up to the good stuff. Popping her trunk, she picked up two bags of groceries. She was going to prepare Damon a fabulous feast for the senses, as well as the body. Shifting her bags in her arms, Nia tried reaching for her overnight bag. *I'll have to come back and get it,* she thought, realizing she had too much to carry.

Walking up the stairs to his condo, Nia fumbled in her purse for her keys. Finding them, she opened the door to the dark apartment. She immediately made her way to the kitchen and turned on the lights. Emptying out her grocery bags, she placed the salmon steaks in the refrigerator to marinate and was looking for an ice bucket for the wine when she heard a noise upstairs.

Nia walked out of the kitchen and noticed Damon's suitcase sitting against the closet door. *Oh, my God, he came back early,* she thought, racing up the stairs with added anticipation. Nia burst through the bedroom door in a hurry.

The room was dark, but Nia heard the shower running. *Maybe I'll join him.* She reached for the light and flicked it on, and was shocked at the sight that lay before her.

Kendall was sprawled out on Damon's bed as if she belonged there, wearing nothing but a sexy black teddy. Nia closed her eyes in disbelief, but when she opened them all she saw were Kendall and Damon's clothing strewn across the room.

"Hello, Nia," Kendall purred. "I warned you I would be back in Damon's bed someday, didn't I."

"Oh, my God!" Nia exclaimed. Wide-eyed, she stared at Kendall.

"You could never take my place," Kendall sneered from the bed. "Did you honestly think that Damon would want a fat cow like you when he could still have me? You were merely a stand-in. And a bad one at that."

Nia couldn't move. She was frozen and her feet felt like they were stuck in cement. The bathroom door opened suddenly and a cloud of steam followed before Damon emerged with a towel draped across his waist. He stopped dead in his tracks as soon as he saw Kendall sprawled out on his bed.

Nia balled her hands into fists at her side as she stared back and forth between the two of them. She wanted to strike out at someone, but who? Surely her eyes were deceiving her. She blinked again to make sure she wasn't dreaming. Reopening her eyes, she saw Kendall's self-satisfied smile. Somehow, someway she kept the tears from falling; she wouldn't give Kendall the satisfaction of seeing her cry.

Nia looked to Damon for reassurance. Her eyes brimmed with tears and pleaded with his. "Please tell me it isn't true, that this is all a mistake."

"Nia, I know what this must look like." He gave Kendall a venomous look. "I have no idea what Kendall said to you, but whatever it is, it's all lies, Nia."

Nia looked back at him as if he had suddenly sprouted horns.

"Baby, listen," he said, taking a step toward her. Although her legs felt like jelly, she found the strength to step back.

For the first time in his life, Damon was scared. The way Nia was looking back at him was frightening. He prayed he could somehow explain and Nia would believe him. He knew how bad this looked. Him naked and Kendall lying in his bed half dressed.

"Listen, Nia, I swear to God, I've never cheated on you. You're going to have to believe me when I tell you this, but I came home early from my meeting and Kendall showed up. I didn't ask her to come over. She came over of her own free will. Just like she did when she followed us to Wisconsin, remember?"

He was desperate, his eyes pleading with Nia to believe him. Kendall didn't move a muscle. She was content to watch the drama unfolding before her.

"I told her I loved you and there was no chance we would ever reconcile. I thought she understood. I told her I was exhausted and I was going to take a shower before you came over. I told her to let herself out, but, Nia, I had no idea she would pull something like this." He held out his hand to Nia. "Baby, I'm telling you that when I went into that shower, I thought Kendall had left."

"Is that all you have to say?" Nia managed to utter.

"It's the truth," Damon replied. Stalking toward Kendall, he grabbed her by the shoulders and pulled her off the bed. "Tell her, Kendall. Tell her nothing happened." He wouldn't lose Nia over this woman.

"Why would I do that?" Kendall smiled. She stood unashamedly, wearing nothing but the sheer teddy.

"Because I'm going to strangle you if you don't?" Damon bellowed.

"I'll do no such thing. I'm not going to lie for you anymore, Damon. The lies have got to stop." Kendall turned around to face Nia. "Damon and I have been seeing each other for months. We've never stopped."

Nia put her hands over her ears, trying to drown out the words coming out of her mouth. Instead Kendall kept baiting her.

"Don't you get it, Nia. We've been lovers all along. Every time he's come to your bed, it was after he'd just made love to me."

Nia couldn't take it anymore. She rushed at Kendall, smacking her hard across the cheek, leaving a red welt.

"You bitch!" Kendall yelled, holding her face.

When Kendall moved to retaliate, Damon blocked her path. "Get the hell out here!" he ordered, pointing to the door. Somehow he would have to get through to Nia on his own, make her see through Kendall's lies.

Kendall didn't move immediately until she saw Damon take a step toward her. Quickly she picked up her clothes and headed to the adjacent bathroom. "You'll both thank me for this one day," she said, closing the door behind her.

Damon couldn't stand the sight of the woman and he would make sure Kendall paid dearly for her duplicity. He waited until she was out of earshot before continuing to plead with Nia, who stood in the corner of his bedroom like a lost child. "She's lying, Nia. I swear I never touched her."

Nia shook her head in amazement. "Please don't insult my intelligence. I have eyes."

"You're emotional right now. You're not rational or thinking clearly right now."

Nia wasn't buying it and when he tried to pull her to him, she wrenched herself away and ran down the hallway. The pain was unbearable. She felt as though her heart were being ripped in two.

Stumbling down the staircase, she reached the door just before a wave of nausea caught in her throat. Nia held on to the door for support. She didn't want Damon to touch her ever again. She couldn't bear to think of his hands on her after being with that woman. To think she had been about to risk her heart and tell him how much she loved him. How he would have laughed at her! She couldn't keep the tears from streaming down her face. What had she done wrong? Hadn't she fulfilled his sexual needs? Apparently not, if he'd run back into Kendall's all-too-willing arms, a woman he claimed to despise.

Damon raced down the stairs after her, careless of his appearance. He found Nia kneeling by the door, but she put her hands up in defense. "Keep away from me!" she screamed at him, plastering herself against the door. "Don't you dare come near me!"

"Nia, please look at me," he begged, kneeling down beside her. She refused to look at him. "Please believe me when I tell you nothing happened."

She shook her head. "How could I have been so blind to think that you loved me?"

"Nia, baby, I do love you. I love you with all my heart," he pleaded. He wanted so much to make her believe him.

"Why did I even try? From the start I knew we were so different, from totally different worlds. But I convinced myself otherwise. Hell, even your parents saw it. I'm not like that pencil-thin figure in there." Nia pointed upstairs. "But you, you made me believe it. You made me believe we could be together. Why did you do it?" She pounded his chest. "Why did you make me believe you? Why did you let me get my hopes up?"

"Nia, stop this." He grabbed her firmly by the wrists. "You need to calm down." He hated to see her in so much pain.

"Fine, let me go."

He waited several moments, and when she quieted, he released her wrists.

Nia leaned against the door for support. "I was so stupid. I knew I wasn't like the *Vogue* models you're usually into. And I most certainly wasn't raised with a silver spoon in my mouth, but for some reason I thought I had a shot. But obviously I didn't. I can't compete and I don't want to, not anymore. If Kendall is who you want, then you should be with her. She wins. Kendall wins."

"Who I want?" he snarled. She hadn't heard a thing he'd said, totally dismissing his declaration of love. "I want the woman I've been living and breathing for the last six months. The woman I've made love to night after night until we're both weak in the knees. Exactly when do you think I had time to cheat on you and have an affair with another woman?"

"Were you fantasizing about her when you were making love with me?" she yelled back at him.

That hurt. Damon was shocked she would say such a thing. How did women know the exact thing to say that would cut so deep? He never thought of another woman when he was with Nia. Seeing the doubt in her eyes, he wanted to reach out and touch her, erase the bad memories, make love to her until she screamed his name, make her believe in him. But his pride forbade it. He needed Nia to believe in him and in their love on her own. "Nia, I've been committed to you and only you from the very start. You know that."

Nia was amazed at his gall even after she caught him red-handed. Was this part of the cheater's handbook?

"You don't love me, you're nothing but a liar and a cheat. How could you do this? I deserve so much better than this. I deserve a man who loves me, respects me, is loyal to me. You obviously don't think I'm it since you're still shopping at the market," Nia threw at him.

"Nia, this is getting out of hand. You're saying hurtful things. Things you don't mean and that won't be easily taken back," he said. Damon was holding on by a thin thread. Maybe if he approached this rationally, she would respond better. "Why are you letting Kendall get the better of us? She's tried breaking us up long before this and none of her ploys have worked. Not at the Christmas party, not at the club and not at the lodge. Don't let her come between us now. You know she can't be trusted. Don't let this woman tear us apart."

"You would just love for me to believe that,

wouldn't you? Dumb, stupid, naive little Nia. You must have gotten a kick at stringing me along all these months. Is that how you get your jollies?" She heard his ragged breathing, but she continued. "Or maybe not. Maybe you just like to have your cake and eat it, too."

"Enough." He put his hand up to silence her. "You want to hurt me, you're doing an excellent job of it. I don't know what more I can say to convince you. I didn't sleep with Kendall."

"And I'm the Queen of England," she shot back.

"You don't trust me, do you Nia? Maybe you never did. I thought I broke through that wall you erected and convinced you I was genuine, that I was the real thing, a man you could love, trust and respect. Perhaps I pushed too soon. Whatever the case, I see my love isn't enough. You have to trust me, because without it our relationship has no foundation."

"I did trust you and you just broke that trust!"

"Nia, I am imploring you this final time to not believe Kendall's lies and this situation she's fabricated. You have a choice to make, Nia." His voice sounded cold as he looked at her. Nia saw the change in him. "If you walk out that door, don't expect me to come chasing after you." He hated to say the words, but she left him no choice.

Nia stared back at him for a long moment. Without a word, she found the strength to open the door and walk out.

Damon slunk to the floor, completely defeated. Surely Nia hadn't walked out on him? Had he lost the woman he loved more than life itself? He felt drained as though he had been sucked into an emotional vortex. Out of the corner of his eye, he saw Kendall slowly creeping down the stairs, making sure the coast was clear. Her head hung low.

"Get out!" Damon yelled. "And don't ever come back!"

"But, Damon," she cried, tucking her shirt into her skirt, "she's gone now. Don't you see? We can be together now. There's no one keeping us apart." She kneeled down in front of him and reached out to touch his arm, but he flicked her away like the pest she was. "Oh, Damon, I know you're hurting now, but in time you'll see it was all for the best. It would never have worked between the two of you."

"You don't get it, do you, Kendall?" Damon grabbed her by the wrist. "I don't want you."

"You don't mean that."

"Yes, I do. I don't love you. I never did, you were nothing more than a convenient body." He flung her away from him and Kendall dramatically fell backward to the floor and began to cry.

He'd seen her crocodile tears before and he would not be swayed. Damon wanted her out of his life and out of his family's business for good. She had finally done the unforgivable. And there was no turning back.

"Please don't say that." She crawled on her hands and knees toward him. "I know you loved me once. I made one mistake, Damon. I never should have slept with Daniel. I know I was wrong, please forgive me. I'm begging you. I love you."

"No, Kendall! Your mistake was coming between me and Nia." Damon grabbed her coat from a nearby chair and threw it at her. "I've had enough of you, your lies, your schemes and your manipulations. Do you hear me? I've had enough! Your family can kiss the money from Bradley Savings & Loan good-bye."

Kendall's eyes widened in fear. "Damon, you have no idea what you're doing right now," she said, standing up hastily. She had to pull herself together. Losing this deal would kill her father. He would never forgive her if he found out she was behind it. "You're upset. Think about what this would do to my father. To your family. My God, you've known us forever. Please don't do this. Please give yourself time to think about your decision."

"I won't be changing my mind, Kendall." Grabbing her by the forearm, he walked her to the door. He didn't care if anyone passing by saw him standing there in nothing but a towel. He wanted to be rid of this evil creature who had caused him nothing but grief.

"Are you sure about this?" She hated to leave like this, but the firm tilt of Damon's chin told her it was over. The matter was no longer up for discussion. Reluctantly, Kendall walked out and Damon slammed the door behind her.

What had he ever seen in that woman? It was her fault Nia left him and he would see to it that she paid dearly. Damon sat down on his couch, stunned. Could Nia really have walked out of his life without a backwards glance after everything they'd shared? Didn't he mean anything to her?

His love for Nia was anchored deep within his heart. How could she think another could ever tempt him? There was no other woman for him.

Why did he do it? Why did he let her leave? He knew why; Nia didn't trust him, so their relationship was doomed.

# Chapter 20

Nia felt like a wild thunderstorm had thoroughly thrashed her about. Seeing Kendall in Damon's bed made her feel like a dagger had struck straight through her heart.

Nia tripped on the last step and almost tumbled to the ground. She dug into her purse for her car keys, but couldn't seem to insert the key into the lock. Fumbling, she finally managed to open the door.

She put the key in the ignition, but the pain she'd desperately been trying to hide forced its way through her. Sobs racked her small frame and she gasped for breath, clutching the steering wheel. She couldn't breathe.

The world felt like it was closing in on her. Nia looked around the parking lot. Was she having a heart attack? Would anyone hear her, help her? She forced air into her lungs and slowly her rate came back to normal. But she didn't move or start the car. Instead she watched Damon's condominium for some sort of activity. Was Kendall turning off the lights so the two of them could go to bed together?

Walking away from him was one of the hardest things she had to do, but she had no choice. She needed to get out of a volatile situation. She had let herself believe in him, but Damon had proven he was no different than Spencer.

Finally, her instincts took over, instructing her to start the car and leave before she was discovered. She was sure it would thrill Kendall to see her sitting there, utterly defeated. Turning on the radio, Nia drowned out all the thoughts and pictures that were going through her head: Kendall lying half naked on his bed, Damon standing there in nothing but a towel. Caught in her thoughts, she didn't notice Kendall leave Damon's apartment in tears a few minutes later.

On automatic pilot, Nia drove to her aunt's home. She had nowhere else to go. Lexie was still in Milan and she couldn't bear to go home to an empty apartment. Everything would remind her of Damon and Nia couldn't take that right now.

Going to her aunt's would be a safe haven, a place of refuge from the storm. It was funny, but since her father's reappearance, Nia felt closer to her aunt than ever before. Despite her shortcomings, Nia knew her aunt Olivia would always be there for her if she needed it. And that was infinitely more than she could say about her father.

Nia parked her car haphazardly and jumped out. After running up the stairs, she banged on her aunt's door.

"Just a minute," she heard her aunt say. When she opened the door, Nia rushed into her arms.

"Oh, Auntie!"

"Baby, what's wrong? What happened?" her aunt asked. When Nia didn't answer, Olivia tilted her face upward to look at her tear-stained cheeks, then laid Nia's head back down against her bosom and held on tighter.

"Who is it?" Nathan asked jovially, coming out of the kitchen. "Olivia, your dinner's gonna get cold." He found Nia and Olivia huddled in the foyer, with Nia clinging to her aunt like she was a lifesaver. "Nia?"

Nia looked up and saw her father standing in the hallway. She hadn't noticed another car outside, but then again, she hadn't looked. This day had really been too much. Life was too hard and she couldn't stand it another minute. She needed her father.

Without hesitation, she rushed across the room and into Nathan's outstretched arms. She let him wrap her in his arms, gaining strength from the love she saw in his eyes at that moment. Her aunt's eyes welled up with tears at finally seeing the two of them reunited, even if it was only for one night.

"C'mon, darling." Her father led her to the couch in the living room. They sat.

"I'm gonna get you some water," her aunt said, rushing to leave the two of them alone.

Nia didn't remember how long they sat there, only that her father remained next to her the entire time, even after she had several bouts of crying. "How could he do this to me? How could he make me love him and do this to me?" She bawled.

Nathan didn't say a word. He sat and listened, rubbing Nia's back until she was so exhausted, she fell asleep on his shoulder.

The next morning, Nia awoke at her aunt's house to find herself in her pajamas. The night before,

Aunt Olivia and Nathaniel had been wonderful. Her father must have carried her up the steps while her aunt had put her to bed. She noticed her clothes neatly folded on a nearby chair.

Not wanting to move, Nia stared at a crack in the ceiling. When she heard voices outside her door, she sat up, pulling the comforter to her chin.

"Should we wake her up?" she heard her aunt say.

"No, we should let her sleep," her father responded.

Nia glanced at a clock on the night table and saw it was already noon. Had she really slept that long? Her poor ravaged body must have needed it. "I'm up!" she shouted through the closed door.

Her aunt knocked before entering, her father close on her heels. They both stood by the door, afraid to come in. "How are you feeling?" Nathan asked first.

Nia shrugged.

"Are you up for some breakfast?" Her aunt moved past him and brought a tray of toast, fresh fruit and coffee to the bed.

"Actually, yes," Nia said, reaching for the tray. Covering a piece of toast with marmalade, she greedily took a bite. Her aunt went around the bed, fluffing her pillows for her to lie back against while her father stood uneasily at the door. "I'm famished. It's amazing how hungry you are after an emotional breakdown," she said jokingly.

No one laughed but her. "You guys really need to loosen up some. I'm all right now."

"Care to tell us about it?" her aunt asked, coming to sit beside her on the bed.

"No, not really," Nia said, shaking her head.

"Maybe later, after I've showered. I feel like a raga-muffin right now."

"All right." Her aunt patted Nia's thigh. "You talk to us when you're ready." She kissed her on the forehead and stood.

"Why don't we have that second cup of coffee, Nathan? And let Nia eat in peace," she said. Her father saw the determined glint in her aunt's eye and decided it was best not to fight her on the subject. He hooked his arm in her aunt's and they left the room.

Nia sighed, grateful that her parents had decided to leave well enough alone. *Wait a second, why did I just think of them as my parents?*

It was true, though. Suddenly Nia felt like a fog had been lifted and she could see everything much clearer. Her aunt was the only mother she'd ever known. All these years her aunt had lived in Lily's shadow, never once asking for anything but Nia's happiness. As for her father, he was no angel and probably didn't deserve the title, but he was all she had, and last night he'd proven he could be more if given the opportunity. Maybe she should give it to him. Could loving Damon have opened her heart to other things?

Placing the tray on the nightstand, Nia threw back the covers and walked over to the bureau to search for a few clothes she kept there in case she spent the night. Finding a bra, fresh underwear and some sweats, Nia headed to the bathroom.

She turned the shower on full blast and let it wash over her. The scalding water pounded away the kinks of the night before, but her mind kept going back to the times she'd spent with Damon. The mornings when they had languorously made love in the shower, slowly caressing each other as they washed each other's bodies. Nia felt her breasts tingle with excitement and a familiar warmth developed in the center of her womanhood. She was angry at her body's betrayal. Even now, after everything, her body still craved his. Damon had become a part of her whether she liked it or not. She scrubbed at her body furiously, hoping to rid it of the memories. When she finally felt cleansed, she turned off the tap and exited the shower.

Dressing, she went downstairs to join her father and aunt for coffee. As much as she wanted to, she couldn't stay in her room forever. She knew they were waiting for her, anxious to find out what had caused her meltdown. They would hit her with a barrage of questions that would require very personal answers.

Nia found the two of them sitting at the kitchen table reading the newspaper. Her father was reading the sports page, while her aunt perused the coupons. They both looked guilty when Nia entered the room, and Nia caught her father pulling his hand away from her aunt's. Was something going on between the two of them? She hadn't been blind to the change in her aunt's behavior since Nathaniel returned to town, and evidently he had slept over last night. Nia wondered if love was in the air for her aunt. If so, she sure deserved it, even if it was with her father.

"Good afternoon," she said breezily, trying to put on a good front. She walked over to the counter and poured herself a cup of coffee. Nia felt their questioning eyes burning a hole in the back of her head, so she took an extra long time adding sugar and cream before turning around to face them.

"I'm sure you're feeling better after a hot shower," her aunt said, staring at her. Nia sat beside her, opposite her father.

"Yes, I am." She sipped at the hot coffee. "Did you spend the night here?" she asked, looking at her father.

"I did," he murmured. "I hope that's all right. Your aunt Olivia didn't seem to mind too much." He smiled at Olivia, who smiled back at him.

"Why should I mind?" Nia asked. "It's not my house." The words sounded harsh coming out of her mouth and a silence fell over the table. "I'm sorry." She felt bad at the comment; she wasn't upset with him. "It's not your fault men can't be trusted."

"Mmm, I see." Her aunt rubbed her chin thoughtfully. "I understand now what this is all about. Oh, Nia." She patted her niece's hand. But the last thing Nia wanted to hear was pity over her fallen romance.

"Care to fill me in?" her father inquired.

"Aunt Livvie guessed correctly. Things between Damon and I have gone sour," she said. At his raised brow, she continued. "Damon's my boyfriend. I mean," she paused, her voice cracking slightly, "my ex-boyfriend."

"Did something happen last night to facilitate this?" her father asked.

"Yes, something happened," Nia responded evenly. "I found another woman in the bed of a man who claimed to love me."

"Oh, Nia, no!" her aunt exclaimed. "Are you sure? I just can't believe Damon would do something like that. I saw how much he cared for you. The man was head over heels in love with you."

That's what Nia had thought, too, until she'd seen Kendall in Damon's bed, their clothes strewn across the room. Nia could feel the bile rising in her throat again. It hurt so much to think about it, but the images were forever branded in her mind.

"Olivia, I'm sure Nia knows what she saw," her father said.

"What I saw was that he was head over heels for another woman and just using me," Nia stated bitterly.

"Nia, are you sure you didn't misinterpret things?" Nathaniel asked. He didn't want to upset the poor girl, but the situation begged the question. Sometimes women had a tendency to overreact and make snap decisions or judgments based purely on emotion. Maybe this young man deserved a second chance.

"Yes, honey," her aunt agreed, "you could have misread the situation."

"There was no misinterpreting Kendall lying half naked in his bed and Damon coming out of the shower." A lump formed in her throat and the monsoon of tears she was holding in flowed down her cheeks. Her father walked around the table and gathered her in his arms for a fatherly hug.

"Shh, shh," he crooned. "It'll be all right." She snuggled into the cocoon of his chest. "I just feel so betrayed," she cried, resting her head against his firm shoulder.

"Well, what did he have to say for himself when you found him in such a compromising position?" Olivia asked.

Nia sniffed. "He said he didn't know what was

going on, that whatever I thought happened didn't. He claimed he'd gotten back from his trip early and found Kendall leaving a note on his doorstep. He *claimed* he told her he wanted nothing more to do with her. How convenient for him." Nia accepted the handkerchief her father offered. "He told me he'd let Kendall show herself out and went in the shower. The rest, as they say, is history."

"You walked in and found Kendall in his bed and Damon coming out of the shower," her aunt repeated. "Hmm . . ."

"It sounds like a plausible story," her father said, turning Nia around to face him. "But you don't believe him?"

"Why should I? I know what I saw. Plus, he's withheld the truth from me before about this woman. I have to believe what my gut instinct tells me."

"Or perhaps you're letting your own insecurities get the best of you," her father said. Nia jumped out of her seat. Her aunt sensed that the discussion might be about something more than just Damon, so she quietly left the room.

"How dare you say that to me? You've no right." Their father-daughter truce was over just as quickly as it had begun. "You don't know the first thing about me."

"And who's fault is that, huh?" her father asked. "You won't let me in. You've kept me at arm's length for months and that's exactly what you're doing to this man—this Damon. You're happy to believe the worst in him because then it would confirm your worst fears about men. Then you could say you've tried that love thing and it didn't work out."

"You go to hell. I don't have to listen to this, and

least of all from you," Nia said before stomping out of the room, but her father followed her and grabbed her by the shoulders.

"That's right, Nia, run away from your troubles like that will solve them. Why don't you stand up and face them?" he countered. His mouth was firmly set, ready to do battle with his daughter. "You're so sure you're right. Did you ever think that you could be wrong? Did you stand up to Kendall and fight for the man you love?"

"Fight?" She spun around to face him. "I've been fighting this woman from the moment I met Damon and I plum don't have anything left in me. I'm worn out, OK? She's won. She can have the no-account, lying cheat."

"Wow, you don't hold back, do you?" Her father chuckled. She had never heard him laugh before. It was a rich, throaty sound.

"No, I don't," she answered haughtily.

"Darling, you've got to let go of all this anger."

Nia sighed. "I don't know how." The anger was all she had. She didn't know any other way to be.

Her father opened his arms. "Then let me help you," he stated simply. "I can be a father, Nia. If you would only let me."

Nia so desperately wanted to believe him.

Sunlight streamed through Damon's blinds, waking him from his slumber. He had passed out on the couch sometime during the wee hours of the morning after drinking himself into a stupor.

It had been several days since Nia had walked out on him and he still couldn't believe it. How could she leave when he loved her so much? He needed her.

His whole well-being and happiness were intertwined with having her in his life. How was he going to live without her? She was his rock, his home. She completed him in every way that counted. Over the last six months, his whole life centered on her, being with her, laughing with her, making love with her. He ached to be inside her; his body was going through Nia withdrawal.

He'd fallen hopelessly in love with Nia Marie Taylor and it wasn't going to be easy exorcising her from his heart. He didn't know if he could or if he even wanted to. Nia didn't trust him, so their relationship had no future. How could she think he would hurt her and lie to her face? It had been all too easy for her to believe the worst about him. Hadn't he tried as hard as he could to show her he was honest and that he would be faithful and true to only her? How could she doubt him?

He wanted to go to her now, but his pride wouldn't let him run after her. This time she would have to come to him. She would have to be the one to admit she was wrong and beg his forgiveness. He was tired of trying to prove his love and loyalty to her.

Damon didn't hear the knock at the door or the key turning in the lock as his mother and sister entered his apartment. They found it dark, hot and musty. The curtains were drawn and Damon was lying on the couch. Cartons of day-old pizza, Chinese food and empty beer bottles littered the room. They made their way to open the curtains and balcony door to let in some sunlight and fresh air.

"Look at this place," his mother said, amazed at the sight in front of her. "Damon, what in heaven's name happened to you? Your sister and I've been trying to reach you for days and we've only gotten your voice mail."

"I think I found the culprit." His sister held up several empty beer bottles. Damon glanced at her from his drunken haze on the couch and plopped his head back down on the pillow. The woman he loved was gone and he was in no mood for this mother-daughter duo.

"Damon," his mother admonished. "You turn over and look at me." He ignored her and kept his head down. "You look at me right now, Damon Bradley."

Slowly he turned to face his mother and she saw how ravaged he looked. His eyes were bloodshot and his face looked like he hadn't shaved in days. He was sure it was a shock to his mother to find him so unkempt, but at this moment he didn't care.

He watched Jordan unbutton her coat, roll up her sleeves and start picking up cartons of food and taking them to the trash in the kitchen.

"Jordan, just leave it!" he bellowed. "Matter of fact, why don't the two of you just go."

"Darling, what is it?" his mother asked, scooting him over on the couch. It hurt her to see her baby in this much pain and she wanted to know the reason why. "What happened?"

"It's Nia," he murmured into the pillow. "Mom, I've lost her."

"What—how could that be?" she asked. "Damon, please turn around and look at me. Please tell me this is not my fault. I thought I settled everything between the two of us."

"Mom, what are you talking about?"

"I asked Nia over to brunch last weekend and we hashed everything out. She forgave me for being such a snob. She told me everything was fine between the two of you. Did I misunderstand?" She sniffed. "Oh, Damon, I'm so sorry, this is all my fault. I should have left well enough alone."

Damon sat up. He had no idea his mother had met with Nia privately and apologized. Nia never mentioned a word of it to him in his phone calls to her. He reached over and pulled his mother into an embrace. "Mom, it's not your fault," he said. "It's me. Nia is angry with me."

"What could you have done so soon? You just returned three days ago. I don't understand this. Nia was so excited to see you, almost impatient. She couldn't wait for you to get back. She told me she was going to surprise you with a home-cooked meal."

"And surprise me, she did." He motioned for his mother to move over so he could sit up. He rubbed his bald head to soothe his splitting headache. "Mom, could you get me some aspirin?"

"Sure, darling." She left the couch and went into the kitchen. Jordan was already washing the dirty dishes in the sink.

"How is he?" Jordan whispered.

"Not good," her mother said. "He's not making much sense. Something about him and Nia breaking up."

"See, I told you that girl was going to cause my brother nothing but grief."

"You hush now," her mother said, scolding. "Damon would be furious if he heard you speak like that."

"Fine." Jordan turned her back and went back to washing the dishes. "I'll keep my opinions to myself."

Her mother leaned over her and pulled a clean

glass from the cabinet. Opening the refrigerator, she poured a glass of mineral water and took it and some aspirin to Damon, who hadn't moved one iota from where she'd left him.

"Here you go, darling." She handed him the bottle and he twisted it open, quickly popping several pills into his mouth and washing them down with water. "Better?" He nodded. "Did you have a fight with Nia?"

He took another swig of water. "Nia found me in a compromising situation with Kendall. She thinks I cheated on her."

"How could she think that?" his sister shrieked from the kitchen doorway. "You would never cheat on her, or any other woman, for that matter. You're much too honest and decent for that. You're a good man, Damon, doesn't she know that?"

"Nia believes otherwise," Damon said. "Not that I blame her." He put his hand up to prevent Jordan from speaking another negative word against Nia. "Listen, J," he explained, "Nia came by to make me dinner just as Mom thought. But Kendall came over before Nia got here. I told Kendall I was through with her games and if she darkened my doorstep again, I would have her arrested. Mom, the only reason I let things get as far as they did was out of respect for our family's history with the Montgomerys. I warned Kendall to stay away and she appeared to agree. Unfortunately, I told her to let herself out and I went to take a shower. When Nia arrived, she found Kendall sprawled out on my bed wearing next to nothing and me coming out of the shower looking suspiciously guilty."

His mother gasped. "Oh, my."

"So she jumped to the conclusion that you slept with Kendall?" his sister finished.

"Yes. I was wearing nothing but a towel and Kendall had of course thrown our clothes around to make it look as if we had been in a hurry to make love. God, when I think of that woman, I want to strangle her." He balled a fist and hit the side of the couch. "I tried to explain to Nia that she misconstrued the situation, but she didn't, or wouldn't, believe me."

"You've got to make her," his mother said, grabbing him by the shoulders. "Listen to me, you have to go to her, Damon, and make her believe you. You can't just let her go without a fight."

"Why not? She did." He stood up, wrenching himself from his mother's arms. "She ran away without fighting for us. For our love."

"Why should you go?" asked his mother, eyeing him. "Because you love her and she loves you. I saw it with my own eyes. That girl is crazy about you. You have to believe that."

"It's sad to say, Mom, but sometimes love is not enough."

"I agree," his sister chimed in. She had never been fond of Nia and was glad her brother was rid of her. "Nia clearly doesn't love you enough if she believes you could cheat on her with that slut Kendall. I mean, of all the things." Jordan was furious that Nia could think her brother was that slimy. Damon was a prince among men.

"J, just shut up, OK. Because you have no idea what you're talking about," he spat.

"A woman claims she loves you but walks out on you at the first sign of trouble. How do you expect me to react, big brother? Do you expect me to turn the other cheek? You need a strong woman. Someone who is going to stand by you, no matter what. A woman to complement you when you take over Bradley Savings & Loan one day. Nia Taylor isn't worthy of you. And she most certainly isn't good enough for you."

"Stop it, J. Do you hear me? I won't have you talking against the woman I love," Damon roared. "God, I can't take this." He rubbed his pounding head.

"Damon, I'm sorry," Jordan said, coming to kneel down in front of her brother. She reached for him, but he shrugged her away.

"Please tell us, darling, what can we do to help you?" his mother asked.

"Yes," Jordan agreed, looking up at him. "What can we do?"

Damon sighed. "First off, you can help me get out of here. Away from this place."

"That's a marvelous idea." His mother stood up. She walked over to grab her purse. "Why don't you take a shower and get freshened up? If you want, your sister and I can pack a bag for you?" Simone opened his coat closet to find his suitcase. "You can come and stay at the house. What you need right now is to be with your family. We'll help you get through this crisis."

Damon could see Jordan searching his face for acceptance of the idea, but all he could do was lie down again on the couch.

"Mom," Jordan said, interrupting their mother's gushing. "Mom, stop. I don't think Damon wants to be with his family right now. I think he wants to go someplace alone."

"Oh," his mother replied, turning around slowly. "I guess I got a little ahead of myself."

A silence fell over the room. "I have an idea," his sister said out of the blue. "Doesn't your friend Matthew have a cabin up in Wisconsin? You could go there and stay. You know, regroup. What do you think?"

Rubbing his chin, he mulled over the idea. Some time away from Chicago, from Nia and the memories that haunted him would probably do him so good.

"J, that's a great idea. I think I'll take you up on it."

It wasn't easy going to her mother's grave site; Nia hadn't been there in years. She'd stopped wanting to go and her aunt hadn't pushed. Now, she stood facing the tombstone. Her father and aunt were at a safe distance behind to give her privacy.

Nia needed to come and try to bury the past and embrace her future, a future that included her father and her aunt, the only mother she had ever known. Over the last few weeks, the three of them had spent a great deal of time together, talking and soul searching, and Nia had come to the conclusion that her mother's ghost was haunting her and she had to let her go. Everything wasn't hunky-dory now; it was going to take time and a whole lot of patience. She and Nathan still had a lot of work to repair their relationship, but Nia was willing try and that was the first step.

It seemed odd to her that the sky was so blue and cloudless as she stood at her mother's grave. Shouldn't it be dreary or raining? Cloudy and overcast?

Laying the dozen lilacs on Lily's headstone, Nia sank to the ground and wept. She cried for Lily's lost youth and her dreams that would never materialize. She didn't know how long she stayed like that, when she heard her father and aunt behind her.

"Are you ready to go?" her father asked, moving to comfort her. Auntie Livvie was standing beside him.

"Yes, I am." Blowing a kiss at the grave, Nia turned around to face them.

"This had to be very hard on you," Nathan said.

"It was, but I can't imagine it was easy for you either."

"No, it's not. This is the first time I've been to Lily's grave. Your grandfather wouldn't tell me where she was buried." The pain in his eyes was self-evident; her father was haunted by memories of the past as well. Somehow he would have to live with his own guilt and demons.

"I'm sorry, Nathan," her aunt said, squeezing his arm. "My father had no right to do that, but you could have come to me."

"I was so ashamed, Olivia. I didn't think I had the right to ask anything of the Taylor family." Her father's voice cracked under the pressure.

Nia could see that Nathan, a proud man, was holding back his tears.

"It's OK, Dad," she said reassuringly. The moment the words were out of her mouth, Nia couldn't believe her ears. She had never dreamed that one day she would call someone "dad," least of all Nathaniel Alexander.

Finding him at her aunt's after leaving Damon had been a breakthrough for them. She had been a mess and his being there had helped tremendously. Nathaniel had helped pick up the pieces; Nia hadn't known she needed a father until she had one staring her in the face. He didn't back down, no matter how hard she made it for him while all the pent-up emotions she'd held inside for so many years were unleashed.

Her father had made her see she had judged Damon unfairly. Somehow Nathan had gotten through to her, and as soon as she could, she was going to take off to find Damon and beg him to take her back. Damon had never given her any reason to doubt him, but she had. She was always so quick to believe the worst. Now she had to find him.

"Are you ever going to see your grandparents again?" her aunt asked. "I know my father may not deserve it, but he really misses you, Nia. He loves you so much, they both do. And you'll never find another person who could love and adore you more besides them and your father and me. You're his grandbaby."

Inhaling, Nia spoke. "Maybe one day soon, but not right now. What about you? How do you feel about it?" She looked to her father for an answer.

"Nia, I don't begrudge you a relationship with your grandparents," he replied. "Just don't expect us to be friends."

Nia smiled.

"Do you blame them for Lily's death?" Aunt Olivia, wondered out loud. "There was nothing he or the doctors could have done. Daddy made sure Lily had the best possible medical care."

Nia nodded. "I understand all that, Auntie. And I know that being angry with Grandpa won't change things. Just give me a little time to absorb it all, OK?"

"Sure, baby." Her aunt gave her an enormous bear hug.

Taking both their hands, Nia walked back to the car. As they drove away from the cemetery, Nia whispered, "Good-bye, Mama."

# Chapter 21

A few days later Nia walked through the glass doors of the law firm of Hamilton, Morgan and Gilbert with surety and purpose. Her feet sank into the plush forest-green carpet. She had come dressed to impress, wearing a black sleeveless sheath and matching red duster, armed with the knowledge that she wasn't going to back down. She knew Jordan Bradley would not be laying out the welcome mat for her.

She would have preferred to approach Damon's mother, but when she telephoned, the butler informed her Simone was at a charity event and Nia didn't feel comfortable approaching Damon's father. Jordan was the next best thing.

Nia stopped at the front desk. The receptionist, a young blonde, looked up from her work. She looked every bit the legal eagle in her Donna Karan suit.

"Jordan Bradley, please."

"Do you have an appointment?" the blonde inquired.

"No, I don't. But if you could let Ms. Bradley know that Nia Taylor is here, she will agree to see me."

On the contrary—she was sure Jordan Bradley

*wouldn't* want to see her, but she also doubted Jordan could resist giving Nia a piece of her mind when the opportunity presented itself.

"I'm not sure what she's doing here," Nia overheard the receptionist whisper into the headset. "All right, as you wish. I'll send her in." The receptionist turned back to face her. "You can go in, through the double doors, last office on the right."

Nia followed her instructions and found Jordan in a small corner office, sitting behind a large maple desk stacked high with files. Nia guessed that a lowly associate didn't rank too high when it came to getting a great office. Not waiting for an invitation inside, Nia closed the door behind her and took a seat opposite Jordan.

Nia nodded her head. "Jordan."

"Nia." Jordan replied, raising her brow. "I must say this comes as quite a surprise." She smiled sardonically.

"I'm sure," Nia retorted. She looked around the cramped office and noted the brass plaques of Jordan's achievements, along with her bachelor's and law degree. Family photographs adorned her walls, including some of Jordan and Damon. Nia had never known that kind of close-knit bond. Until recently it seemed everyone in her family kept love at arm's length.

"Very clever of you," Jordan said. "You knew I wouldn't turn you away at the workplace for fear of making a scene."

An awkward silence filled the room.

"Yes, I did, but I won't insult you by trying to cozy up to you. I know you'd see right through that so, let me cut to the chase. I want to know where Damon is."

Nia had tried unsuccessfully to contact him, calling his cell phone, condo and his office, with no results. She had to tell him she was wrong. She had to find Damon and she knew Jordan knew where he was.

"Do you honestly think I'm going to tell you where my brother is?" Jordan asked, whipping off her reading glasses.

At twenty-seven, Jordan was the youngest associate in her law firm. Her every action and movement exuded confidence that must have taken years to master. She probably had defendants quaking in their boots on the witness stand, but Nia wasn't going to give her that much power. She would not be intimidated and cross-examined. It seemed that letting go of the past and embracing her father had given her a newfound confidence.

"Yes, I do," Nia answered unapologetically. She scooted closer to the desk to look Jordan straight in the eye. "You're going to tell me exactly where he is because I know you want what's best for your brother." Nia held her hand up. "I know you don't think that's me." Jordan shrugged. "And I know you don't approve of me as the right woman for your brother."

"You're right. I don't think you're good enough for him." Jordan catapulted from her chair. "And it has nothing to do with where you come from, or how you dress, though I do think you need some help in that department. It has nothing to do with the fact that you've accused him of lying and cheating on you—and with that witch Kendall, no less. He's been through enough with that two-timing slut, especially when he caught her in bed with Daniel, but that's beside the point."

Nia stared back, shocked. She thought Damon would take that little piece of info to the grave with him. Apparently not.

"Yes, Nia," Jordan said at her shocked expression, "he finally told me what happened between the two of them, which is why he would never do what you accused him of. Damon is one of the best men I know. He's honest and loyal. Kind and generous to a fault."

"You don't have to list all of Damon's good qualities to me. I'm well aware of them and have experienced them all," Nia bounced back. "Listen, Jordan, I know I was wrong and I'm ready to admit that—to you and to Damon. But how can I if I don't know where he is?"

"And you expect me to help you? If there's a problem between you and Damon, you need to look closer to home because the reason is right at your own doorstep." Jordan turned her back on Nia to face the window.

Taking a couple of deep breaths, Nia held on to her temper. She had to get through to Jordan. She knew it wasn't going to be easy, but being hit with extreme animosity wasn't pleasant either.

"The blame lies entirely on my shoulders, I admit that. But it's not your place to judge me or my actions."

Jordan whipped around. "No, it's not. But I won't stand idly by and give you another chance to hurt my brother."

"You may not want to hear this, but it's not your choice to make," Nia said quietly. "It's his. And you need to give him that choice. Whether he slams the door in my face or takes me back with open arms, it's his choice."

"Damn you, Nia Taylor," Jordan said, stomping her foot on the floor.

Had she made a breakthrough? Was Jordan willing to tell her where Damon was staying? Would she get the opportunity to make things right between them? She waited for a response from Jordan, who'd turned quiet all of a sudden. Nia walked behind the desk to touch her shoulder.

"Please, Jordan," she pleaded. Jordan turned around and saw the tears in her eyes. "I love him. And I know he loves me. You know it, too. I can see it in your eyes." Jordan held her head down, but Nia continued. "We have that in common, you and I, our love for him. And that's why I am asking for your help."

After several long moments, Jordan finally spoke. "He's staying up at our friend's cabin in Wisconsin." Jordan moved past Nia and wrote down the directions to the cabin. She ripped the sheet off her legal pad and thrust it at Nia.

"You won't be sorry." Nia grabbed the slip of paper.

"Don't make me regret this, Nia," Jordan replied, grabbing her by the arm. "Or I'll make you eat those words."

Nia crossed her heart with her free hand and Jordan let her arm go. She wanted to give Jordan a big fat kiss, but doubted the wisdom of the move. Instead she walked back to her chair and threw her purse over her shoulder.

"Some free advice," Jordan offered as she walked her to the door.

"And what might that be?" Did Jordan know something that would convince Damon to take her back? She did know her brother better than anybody.

"Persistence is the key," answered Jordan. "My brother is about as stubborn as I am."

"Don't I know it."

It was an unseasonably warm and mild afternoon in Chicago. The skies were blue with puffy white clouds, the trees were rustling and the flowers were blooming, but Nia was miserable.

After talking to both her father and Lexie, Nia saw the situation completely differently. Lexie had called her a fool for ever letting a good man like Damon get away.

Unfortunately, she realized her mistake a little too late. Her father told her to listen to what was in her heart. He was right about her letting her own insecurities overtake her. Now it was up to her to put things right. She just wasn't sure Damon would give her the opportunity to tell him how wrong she'd been. To tell him she was sorry for ever doubting his love for her.

She had gone through a mental catharsis, releasing her past demons by forgiving her father and finally laying her mother's ghost to rest. Her aunt was her mother and it was high time she acknowledged that fact and gave her aunt the proper respect.

These were the thoughts that accompanied her on the drive up to the cabin where Damon was staying. Nia knew it wasn't going to be easy begging for his forgiveness, but she had to try. He would either reject or embrace her, but she would never know if she could have saved their relationship if she didn't put forth the effort. Jordan told her he had gone up to the cabin to "get over her." She was about to find out if he'd succeeded.

A while later, Nia stood at the front door of the cabin. "May I come in?" she asked Damon, who was looking at her with disdain.

"Why? I think you said all you had to say to me back in Chicago, don't you think?" Damon crossed his arms.

Nia prepared herself for an uphill battle. "No, I don't," she answered. "I think emotions were running high, and now that the dust has settled, there's a lot that hasn't been said that needs to be."

"You can come in and say whatever you need to, and then leave." Reluctantly, Damon stepped aside to allow her to enter.

Nia wouldn't let his harsh tone deter her. She walked inside and looked around the cabin. It appeared that she had disturbed him from reading because a book lay open on the coffee table along with the throw blanket he'd cast aside on the couch. Nia walked over to the window opposite the couch and peered out at the lake. The cabin was very quiet and serene with tons of trees lining the woods below. It was a good place to collect your thoughts and, if necessary, get over someone.

She turned to find Damon staring at her pointedly, waiting for her to begin. Nia looked into Damon's face, but it was unreadable. How was she going to reach him? He had built up a wall that seemed impenetrable, but she had to try. She had no idea how he was going to react to what she had to say. Her throat felt dry and a lump started to rise in her throat.

"May I have a glass of water?"

Without answering, he turned on his heel and walked into the kitchen. A few moments later, he returned with water for her and a beer for himself. He handed the glass to her, avoiding any physical contact, and sat down on the couch. She accepted the tumbler and stood by the window, taking a long gulp.

A silence formed for several long, tense moments before Damon broke it. "Nia, I don't have all day," he said finally, taking another swig of beer.

Slowly Nia moved away from the window and with heavy, wood legs found her way to a nearby chair across from him. She knew he wouldn't welcome her sitting beside him on the couch, even though she longed to reach out and touch him, feel his arms wrapped around her. When they were making love, they were so in tune with each other's feelings, but of course that wouldn't solve anything right now.

"Damon," she began, "so much has happened since we last talked." He looked at her strangely. "I mean, since we *really* talked." Nia felt anger emanating from his every pore. "You see, that day I came over to welcome you back home from your trip, I'd just had a very emotional weekend with my family."

He gave no response. He probably figured she was always having problems with her family. What made that weekend any different?

"I finally took the time to hear my father out," she continued. "I learned that my grandfather played a part in my mother's death." Damon's eyes perked up and suddenly he appeared interested in what Nia had to say for the first time since he'd let her in.

"What does all this have to do with you and me?" He hated himself for saying the words as soon as he'd uttered them. He wasn't a thankless bastard and he didn't know why he was acting like one now. He just couldn't afford to let Nia Taylor get under his skin again.

For days now, he'd tried to forget about her smooth, honey-colored skin, those delicious lips that were quivering with fear this very moment. He wanted to lose himself within her soft feminine curves, but he couldn't think with another part of his anatomy now because his heart couldn't withstand another blow.

"My father did not abandon my mother as I originally thought. After Lily told him she was pregnant, he reacted horribly. But later he realized his mistake and went to find her." She took a sip of water. "Unfortunately he went to visit my grandfather. Damon, he was ready to marry Lily and be a father to me." Nia stopped, tears forming in her eyes. Even talking about it now, she still got choked up. She pulled out a handkerchief and dabbed at her eyes. "But my grandfather discouraged him, told Nathaniel he wasn't good enough for his daughter. My father believed him."

"Nia, I'm so sorry," Damon said. It was heartfelt. He knew how much she loved her grandfather and how hard it must have been for her to hear such awful things about him.

She sniffed. "It gets worse. He paid my father five thousand dollars to leave town and never come back, to never make contact with my mother." Damon gasped. "My father took the money and ran. Lily went to her grave believing he didn't want her or me."

"I see."

"Do you really, Damon?" Nia asked, jumping out of the easy chair and coming to sit beside him on the couch. Had she made some progress?

She reached out to touch his hand, but he snatched it away. Her heart sunk. Maybe she was expecting too much too soon. She had to finish, tell him everything that was in her heart.

"I know you're wondering how all this relates to us, but—"

"There is no us," he replied bitterly, interrupting her. "You saw to that."

"Damon, please don't be like this," she pleaded, scooting toward him.

He moved away. He didn't want to be near her. It hurt too much.

"It's all right. I guess I can understand your reluctance to hear me out. But you're going to, Damon Bradley." Finding her voice again, Nia let her confidence flow and told Damon of the crazy events that preceded her arrival at her home.

Nia couldn't tell if Damon was listening and absorbing everything she said or ignoring her. He was looking at her, but she couldn't tell if he truly felt her pain.

"Anyway, what all this means is that I was an emotional basket case that day you got back. I needed you so much, but I didn't want to spill all this out on the phone. So I waited, eager for your return so you could take me in your arms and tell me everything was going to be OK."

"But you thought the opposite of me, didn't you, Nia? You thought I wanted Kendall. How could you think that? After I told you what she did to me? How could you think I'd want her back? I loathe that woman." He finally let the anger out. Nia needed to know how much she'd hurt him. "And to prove it, I told her to shop someplace else for a loan."

"Oh, Damon!" Nia exclaimed. "You did?"

"Yes, I did. And you would have known that if you'd just believed in me," he replied. "But you didn't. I loved you with my whole heart and you threw it back in my face. My love for you was a gift I gave you freely and you squandered it."

"I'm so sorry. In my defense I can only say that I wasn't thinking clearly." She reached out to touch his shoulder, but he shifted to the far side of the couch again. "Listen, Damon, I know this rift between us is all my fault. I should have believed in you."

"But you didn't. You were willing to believe the worst in me, Nia." He was tired. "You did this to us. Not me."

"Everything you've said is the truth," she agreed. "But it was not just about you, though I wish it were. It was about me."

"What are you talking about?"

"I'm talking about me," she said. "I had a lot of insecurities about myself, about being woman enough for you. You've been so wonderful, but the more you did, the more I felt way out of your league. I didn't feel like I was worthy of you. I thought I was too fat or not pretty enough or not from the right family. I felt completely inadequate and these feelings were reinforced by Kendall and by your family's initial reaction when they met me."

"Oh, Nia," he exclaimed. "Why didn't you mention any of this before?" He thought she had let go of her hang-ups about his family. After all, she had gone to brunch with his mother.

"I can't say, maybe I was unconsciously trying to destroy the one thing I wanted more than anything in the world."

"Why, baby? Why would you try and destroy our relationship?" His voice rose in disbelief.

"I don't know!" she cried. "All I have ever wanted is to be appreciated, valued, loved—but I thought I was reaching for the stars. That someone like you would never, could never love me. I guess I never felt worthy of love. I mean, if my own father could walk out on me, then maybe there was something wrong with me. Maybe I was unlovable." Nia dropped her head into her hands, sobbing openly.

Damon couldn't bear to see her this way, pouring out her heart and soul to him. He gathered Nia in his arms, absorbing the sobs that racked her body. They sat together in silence while Damon comforted her. It amazed her that he was still putting her needs above his own.

"I know that's not true now," she said sometime later. "I know my father loves me the best he can. We've made peace with the past and we're going to try to move forward and have some kind of relationship. I don't know what, but I guess time will tell."

"I'm so happy for you, baby," he crooned in her ear, and kissed her cheek. "I know how much you needed that."

"But that's not who I care about right now."

"Who do you care about?" His heart was beating wildly in his chest. Was Nia finally ready to let him in?

"You. I care that you support me, listen to me,

cuddle me and stand up for me against all those who might disagree that we're not absolutely made for each other. I know that when I'm with you, there's nothing you wouldn't do for me. You would go to the ends of the earth for me. You're what matters most to me. You've shown me what it means to love and be loved."

"Nia, you're right. I do love you, but what is love without trust?" He wanted to believe her, needed to.

"My whole life has changed since I met you, Damon. I never knew what it was like to be in a relationship with someone, to have their love and trust, and I'm sorry I abused that. I was a coward. I should have shown you just how much I value having you in my life. But I had to go through all that mess with my father to bring me to this point." Nia took Damon's face in her hands and softly stroked his cheek. "Damon, I mean every word I'm saying to you. You don't have to guess because I'm telling you without any doubts that I love you and you're the only man for me." He remained quiet and Nia was afraid. "Have I lost you?" she asked. "Damon, please say you still want me."

Quietly Damon said the words that would save them. "You haven't lost me, Nia." Damon was so overwhelmed with love for her. He knew how hard it was for Nia to admit her true feelings. "You have no idea how I've longed to hear those words from your lips. I would go anywhere, do anything for you. Don't you know you have my heart? No one can take that away," Damon said, taking her in his arms.

"Oh, Damon," she said, laughing. "I'm not perfect. I come with a lot of baggage."

"And?" he asked. "We all have baggage, but don't worry, because together we can tackle anything. A day hasn't gone by when I haven't been loving you, wanting you. The last week has been absolute torture for me. Do you know how much I've missed you?" He threaded his fingers through her hair and pulled her to him. Their lips met softly at first before turning into a deep, sensuous kiss. "I've missed your voice, your engaging smile, your lips. I love everything about you. When I first laid eyes on you, I knew."

"You knew what?"

"I knew you were my destiny. That I was meant to hold you in my arms. To kiss you. To make mad, passionate love with you." Damon brought her hand to his lips and kissed it. Her flesh burned from his touch. Her body had missed being joined with his.

"Nia, I want to spend forever with you."

"And I want to spend forever with you, too."

"Then let's make it official." Damon jumped off the couch and bent down on one knee.

"What are you doing?" Nia asked, her eyes swimming with tears.

Damon took Nia's left hand in his. "I am asking you to do me the honor of becoming Mrs. Damon Bradley. Will you marry me, Nia Marie Taylor?"

"Oh, my God, yes!" she exclaimed, jumping into his arms. The force of the impact caused them both to tumble to the floor. Damon braced their fall and Nia fell on top of his chest. "Yes, yes, yes, I'll marry you," she said again, kissing him profusely.

"Oh, God, Nia. You don't know how happy you've made me," Damon said. He held her to him and kissed her full on the lips. Her lips parted to allow him entry and he probed inside to fully explore the dark regions of her mouth. Their tongues met and swirled together in an ancient love dance, leaving Nia wanting more.

Damon didn't waste any time reacquainting their bodies. Slowly and leisurely, he made love to her mouth, plunging in and out to taste the very depths of her.

She suppressed a moan when his masculine lips found the sensitive flesh at the nape of her neck and laved it with his tongue. Nia arched her body wantonly against him, wanting to be as close as two people could get. Attacking the buttons on his shirt, she tore it off his chest.

Before she had time to think, Damon divested them of their clothing. He continued to kiss her deeply and thoroughly, stroking her again and again with his tongue.

Then he took each of her fingertips into his mouth and sucked on them voraciously, all the while circling her palms with his thumbs. Her body was on fire for him. She rubbed herself against him, moaning in pleasure when he squeezed her buttocks. Shivers of delight ran through her entire body.

He didn't disappoint; their lovemaking was intense and passionate as ever. Wrapping her legs around him, one climax ebbed and flowed into the next. Damon moaned her name like a mantra, over and over again.

"Oh, Damon, I love you so much," she told him much later as they cuddled underneath the blankets by the brick fireplace. She trembled when she thought how close she had come to losing him. "Promise me that won't ever change."

"I love you, Nia," Damon said, looking into her eyes. "And I promise to treasure you forever."

Dear Reader,

The idea for this book sprang from the notion that in order to open your heart to love, you have to resolve the issues of the past. I wanted to create a heroine that any woman could relate to. Someone beautiful, intelligent, yet flawed. And a strong, caring hero who knew what she needed and gave her all the love her heart could handle. I think Nia and Damon are the embodiment of a real couple and you the reader are given a bird's-eye view to watch their falling in love, from the magic of their very first meeting, to the butterflies of their first kiss, to the passion of their first night of lovemaking.

I hope you enjoyed reading their memorable story just as much as I enjoyed writing about these fun, flirty and incredibly romantic characters. It was indeed a labor of love writing *One Magic Moment,* as it is my very first novel. I intend to follow-up on several characters introduced in this novel and I anticipate you will equally take pleasure in reading their stories in the books to come.

Best wishes,
Yahrah St. John

## ABOUT THE AUTHOR

Yahrah St. John lives in Orlando, but was born in the Windy City, Chicago. A graduate of Hyde Park Career Academy, she earned a bachelor of arts degree in English from Northwestern University. Presently, she is working as an assistant property manager for a commercial real estate company.

An avid reader of romance, Yahrah is a member of Romance Writers of America as well as the Nubian Circle Book Club. Yahrah enjoys cooking, traveling and adventure sports, but her true passion remains writing. Currently, she is hard at work on her second novel.

## ARABESQUE 10th ANNIVERSARY GREAT ROMANCE CONTEST WINNER

### Denise Hayes DeLapp

### Avid Arabesque Reader and North Carolina Native!

Denise Hayes DeLapp, a school teacher, avid Arabesque romance novel reader, and native of North Carolina, is the winner of the 2004 Great Romance contest.

An only child, DeLapp currently cares for her ailing mother, two very active children, and her husband Reuben at their home outside of Raleigh, North Carolina. DeLapp says that reading Arabesque romance novels is "my addictive leisure-time pleasure." She adds that "with an active family life, I often find myself reading into the early hours of the morning."

DeLapp's own life reads like the pages of an Arabesque novel. She met her husband while visiting friends on a trip to Winston-Salem, North Carolina, and they grew close over a two-year, long-distance relationship. Overcoming obstacles and life's challenges together, they recently celebrated their sixteenth wedding anniversary.

A graduate of Broughton Senior High School and North Carolina Central University, DeLapp has always loved the written word and reads approximately 40 Arabesque novels a year. "It's like a latte that you just *have* to have. Especially my favorite author Rochelle Alers," says DeLapp. "I get consumed with the intense passion that her characters experience!"

Denise Hayes DeLapp will donate the Arabesque books she receives as part of her Grand Prize package to a transitional home for women and Shaw University's tutorial program. "I've enjoyed reading Arabesque novels, and it's a wonderful blessing that I get to pass these uplifting novels along to others in my community," concludes DeLapp.

**Arabesque was proud to conduct this nationwide Great Romance contest honoring the avid readers of the Arabesque imprint now celebrating a decade of soulful romance. For a complete list of contest winners, please visit us online at www.BET.com.**

# Arabesque Romances
# by *Roberta Gayle*

**__Moonrise** **$4.99US/$5.99CAN**
0-7860-0268-9

**__Sunshine and Shadows** **$4.99US/$5.99CAN**
0-7860-0136-4

**__Something Old, Something New** **$4.99US/$6.50CAN**
1-58314-018-2

**__Mad About You** **$5.99US/$7.99CAN**
1-58314-108-1

**__Nothing But the Truth** **$5.99US/$7.99CAN**
1-58314-209-6

**__Coming Home** **$6.99US/$9.99CAN**
1-58314-282-7

**__The Holiday Wife** **$6.99US/$9.99CAN**
1-58314-425-0

***Available Wherever Books Are Sold!***

Visit our website at **www.BET.com.**